The Seer and the Scholar

Rosanne L. Higgins

Book layout by www.ebooklaunch.com

To Mom and Dad with love and gratitude for everything you have done or will do.

To Gina –

Happy Holidays!

Rosanne L [illegible]

Part One

Chapter One

November, 2014

Maude Travers sat back and stared at the empty screen of her laptop hoping that words would appear by sheer force of her will to put the story to paper (so to speak). She had been trying for months to write a novel based on the diary of Ciara Nolan, the first Keeper of the Buffalo Orphan Asylum and former inmate of the Erie County Poorhouse. Even seated at her Kittinger desk, surrounded by the Victorian wall sconces and parlor lamps of her antique lamp shop, Maude just couldn't bring nineteenth century Buffalo to life. She was an anthropologist by training, not a novelist. She had published many scholarly articles and book chapters focusing on her poorhouse research, so why was it so hard to write a fictional account using the same data for inspiration?

Because data demanded to be analyzed, that's why. The poorhouse records she had examined for the past two decades offered plenty of quantifiable variables, categories of information such as age, sex, and country of birth that could be scrutinized and organized to create a report of what life was like for poorhouse inmates. The real story of the poorhouse inmates was told by those data, facts that were there for anyone to verify. For example, the vast majority of individuals who sought relief at the Erie County Poorhouse were foreign born, mostly from Ireland and Germany. Thousands of people had traveled to America in search of a better life, only to have their dreams thwarted along the way by some tragedy which left them destitute upon arrival. Most individuals, called inmates, stayed only a few days or a few weeks, just long enough to get back on their feet, or find another source of help. Those who did stay for months, or years, were likely very old, very sick, or both.

In addition to the ledgers that had provided so much detail about the poorhouse experience, Maude had read the journal of Ciara Nolan. That was qualitative data: detailed accounts of daily life at the Buffalo

Orphan Asylum that could not be categorized, counted or massaged by statistics, but were important nonetheless. These were the real life experiences of the Keeper in her daily struggle to keep the orphanage viable. Maude had read about how children had learned to knit their own socks, a strategy employed to keep idle young minds occupied. The pride with which the Keeper recorded yet another healthy year in which no children were lost to the diseases that ravaged other parts of the city was tangible in her report. There was a story to be told, Maude was certain of it, but it would take some getting used to, this concept of fiction.

From her office in the back of the shop she owned with her husband Don, Maude heard the phone ring. For once she was happy that the old building had but one phone jack in the front of the shop as she gave the blank screen a final defiant look meant to convince herself that she wasn't giving up, but she did have to walk away to answer the phone.

"Good morning. This is the Antique Lamp Company. How may I help you?"

"Hi, Maude. It's Christine. Got a minute?"

"Sure. What's up?"

"I just wanted to thank you and Don again for coming last night and to let you know that you won something in the silent auction."

"Oh, we are always happy to support pediatric cancer research," Maude assured her friend. "What did I win?"

"Your family tree."

"My what?" Maude was trying to recall all of the silent bids she submitted at the fundraiser the previous evening. "Oh, right, the genealogical research certificate. How does that work?"

"Well, the researcher is a member of the Western New York Genealogical Society. Her contact info is on the gift certificate. I'm sure she will give you all of the details. Let me know how it goes. I would love to do something like that for my mom."

"Are you going to be in today? I could run next door and grab the gift certificate before I leave for the day." Christine was a graduate student in history and worked at the antique shop next to Maude's. Both women shared an interest in local history and often popped in on each other for a quick cup of coffee and a chat when business was slow.

"I'm not working today, but I'm in the neighborhood now, so I can drop it by if you like."

Maude looked at the clock, noting she had only fifteen minutes until she was officially open for business, and then thought about the blank screen waiting in her office. "Sure, come on over."

The morning was busy, which was not unusual for that time of year when people were out shopping for the holidays. The windows of their shop on Chippewa Street stopped pedestrian traffic on a regular day, with the sparkling crystals and hand-painted glass of nineteenth century lamps and chandeliers. During the winter holidays the shop looked nothing short of spectacular to passersby. Frosted windows were bedazzled with white twinkle lights, drawing shoppers into Christmas past. Featured among the luminary treasures stood a real scotch pine, decked out in Victorian splendor. Maude and Don had learned years ago that by adding other unique items like vintage jewelry, accessories and antique housewares to the already breathtaking collection of period lamps and lighting fixtures, they could increase traffic through their store. Now they were a "must stop" for many downtown shoppers. It was after lunch by the time Maude was able to take a look at the gift certificate she had won the night before.

"Abigail Stevens," she read out loud from the business card that had been clipped to the envelope. "Let's give you a ring and find out exactly what I have won." After a quick look at the certificate inside, she pulled out her cell phone and gently tapped the numbers on the screen.

"Hello," said the voice on the other end.

"Hello. My name is Maude Travers. I am looking for Abigail Stevens."

"This is Abby. How can I help you?"

"I am the proud winner of a certificate for genealogical research. I won it at a silent auction last night."

"Oh, right, the children's cancer event. That was last night? I had actually intended to go too, but I must have got my dates mixed up. I thought it was next week. How did they do?"

"Well, I think. So how exactly does this work?" Maude asked.

"The gift certificate entitles you to eight hours of genealogical research. Are you interested in building your family tree, or do you have a particular ancestor you would like to know more about?"

"Hmm, that's a good question. I know mom's family came from Ireland. I'm not sure about my dad's side."

"Well, let's start with some names. Why don't you send me an e-mail with the names of your parents, and grandparents on each side? Include any details you know, like their place or date of birth, and we'll see what we come up with from that. I will let you know what I find and if you want to continue beyond the value of the gift certificate, we can discuss my pricing."

"That sounds good. Would you mind texting your e-mail address to my phone? If I write it down on a piece of paper, I will likely lose it!"

"No problem. I look forward to hearing from you."

Maude pushed the end button on her cell phone and made a mental note to call her mother to see if she could learn any details about the family that might be helpful to Abby. She felt the phone vibrate as it dropped back into her purse. Remembering she had turned the ringer off to minimize distractions while working on her novel earlier that morning, Maude turned it back on in case Don or the kids needed to contact her. She ignored the phone and prepared for the late afternoon shoppers, assuming the ringtone she heard as it was slipped back into her purse signaled the genealogist passing along her e-mail address. Heading back out toward the front of the shop, the familiar sound of the first few chords of the Rolling Stones song 'Time is on My Side' was coming from the office once again indicating another text had been received. That particular song was the ringtone for incoming texts from persons unknown or persons not special enough to have their own ringtone. Since the text was not from Don or the boys, she ignored it again, deciding whoever it was could wait until she was ready to leave for the day.

Before Maude reached the display in the front window, the land line was ringing. With a sigh of exasperation, Maude turned from the window and reached for the cordless hand set she had left on the front counter. "This is the Antique Lamp Company. How may I help you?"

"Maudie, it's me."

Maude looked at the caller ID and recognized her husband's cell phone number. "Don, why are you calling this phone?"

"I assumed that since you haven't called me already that your phone must be in your purse."

"What are you talking about?"

"Take a look at your cell phone and tell me if you got a text recently. I just received one from our landlord and I am guessing you did, too."

"Hang on." Maude put down the receiver and returned to her office to retrieve the cell phone. As she walked back to the land line she scrolled past the first text, which was indeed from Abby Stevens, to the message she received just before her husband called. Picking the receiver back up she read aloud.

'Hi Maude and Don, it's me, Phil. What time do you guys close? I'd like to stop by and have a word some night this week before you leave for the day.'

"Phil never comes by the shop," Don remarked. "I wonder what he wants."

"Our lease is up at the end of the year," Maude reminded him. "He probably wants to re-negotiate. I hope he is not planning on raising the rent too much."

"I thought we had another full year left. How much did it go up last time?"

"It went up by $150 the last time we renewed. If he jacks it up another $150 per month this time, we should still be okay."

"I suppose. Can you shoot him a text and tell him we will both be in the shop Thursday afternoon if he wants to stop by?" Don asked.

"Sure thing." Maude hung up the shop phone. She hastily typed her reply and then saved Phil's number into her contacts. With a smirk, she assigned him Darth Vader's theme song for a ringtone and was surprised when she heard the thundering brass notes not a moment later as Phil responded to her text.

'Thursday afternoon sounds great. That will give me a few days to sort out some details.'

"What on earth does that mean?" Maude asked out loud. She decided against texting back that very question. Whatever he meant, she didn't want to be discussing it via text. Their meeting was just two days away. They would find out soon enough.

* * *

On the way to work Thursday morning, Maude felt the familiar anxiety she always experienced when she was waiting for important information. Her mentor and colleague from the Anthropology department, Jean McMahon, was meeting with the university administration regarding the fate of the Erie County Poorhouse Cemetery Collection. It had been an unusual situation to say the least, excavating a portion of the poorhouse cemetery on the university's south campus last year. The property had once been the location of the poorhouse, insane asylum and hospital, and was sold shortly after the turn of the twentieth century. Anthropologists had been given a year to learn what they could from the skeletons that had been carefully excavated before the individuals had to be respectfully reinterred.

Maude had no voice in the issues that would be discussed and the decisions that would be made and that was just fine with her. It was a complicated decision best left to the administrators who had more knowledge of the university's needs and long term plans than she. That did not mean that Maude didn't have an opinion on where burials should be laid, finally, to rest. The research team had not been able to provide individual identities to any of the skeletons they studied, but they got to know them nonetheless. Through meticulous measurements and cataloging of various traumatic or infectious lesions, they were able to begin piecing together some of the life experience of those people who had the misfortune to die while at the poorhouse, hospital or insane asylum. These people were an important part of Buffalo's past and deserved a final resting place where they would not be disturbed again.

The historic records for the institutions provided Maude with some of the names of the people and circumstances under which they went to the poorhouse for help. Sadly, there was no way of knowing for sure if any of those names belonged to individuals they had excavated. There was only one person who was buried with a bible that was inscribed with a name. Other researchers on the team would argue that while the bible belonged originally to Frederika Kaiser, that did not prove that the skeleton found at burial location number 116 was actually her, but Maude knew better.

She would never tell anyone else but her husband of the unusual visions she got when cleaning burial number 116, revealing that the poor woman had been beaten brutally by her husband. At first Maude thought she was losing her mind. Every time her bare hand touched an injury on the skeleton she was instantly transported back in time and somehow, through the eyes of Mrs. Kaiser herself, Maude was able to see how the poor woman had been hurt. It became evident that all of the fractures she had identified in those poor old bones had occurred at the hands of the woman's abusive husband.

It was only by chance that Maude had learned that Frederika Kaiser was a widow who had been brought from the poorhouse to help take care of the children at the orphan asylum when Christine had given her the diary of Ciara Nolan. The diary, which was found among the boxes obtained from a clean-out on Delavan Avenue, chronicled one year in Mrs. Nolan's life while she was Keeper of the orphan asylum. It was a rare treasure, forgotten until the sale of the old house in which it sat prompted a call by the new owners to the local antique shop. They sold the contents of the attic to Christine's boss for a flat fee, assuming the boxes of leather bound ledgers and journals held nothing of substantial value. From the pages of that journal Maude had uncovered a scheme of the poorhouse Keeper to sell and profit from the bodies of the unclaimed dead to a medical school to be used for dissection. Mrs. Kaiser narrowly escaped that fate upon her passing only through the efforts of Dr. Michael Nolan and his brother-in-law, Rolland Thomas, who buried her in a secret location in the dark of night. Between the journal and the visions Maude got while cleaning the skeleton, it was revealed to her that burial number 116 was Frederika Kaiser.

It was important to Maude that Frederika and the other individuals who had been excavated remain close by for reasons that she really could not explain. One of the options up for discussion was that the skeletons be reinterred in a mausoleum on campus close to the original location of the poorhouse complex, not so they could be used for further research, rather so they could be part of a memorial honoring an important part of the city's history that had been largely forgotten. That was the outcome for which Maude, Jean, and Brian Jameson, the project archaeologist, all hoped.

At the red light just before her shop, Maude heard the familiar theme song to the '80's sitcom Murphy Brown coming from her purse. She pulled into the alley behind her shop and immediately reached for the cell phone. Grabbing the keys, she hit redial and reached to unlock the back door. Jean picked up after one ring.

"Did I catch you on the road?" her mentor asked. "I thought you might be on your way into work."

"Yes, but I'm here now. So, what's the verdict?"

"I'm pleased to tell you the committee agreed that a mausoleum and a small memorial museum was a great idea," Jean said, obviously pleased as well with the decision.

"Wow, a museum! That is more than I dared hope for. When will all this get underway?" Maude asked.

"Sooner than you think," was Jean's reply. "There are a few outbuildings on campus that would be more than suitable with a bit of sprucing up. I think they just need to decide on which one and get to work. I'll know more after our next meeting." Jean hesitated before continuing. "Maude, they want our department to be very involved in developing the museum."

"That's great. We have an impressive start with all the research we did for the symposium last spring."

"I'm glad you said 'we', because I would like you to be involved in this."

Maude paused before she asked, "How involved?"

"Very involved. The few artifacts found during the excavation will be reinterred with the individuals they were found with, and rightfully so. However, that doesn't leave much in the way of display material, even for a one room museum."

"So, what are we talking about, an adjunct position?" Maude knew that with an adjunct appointment she would be given a university ID card, which would give her access to the libraries, and a parking pass, but no salary. That would be preferable to a paid position. Maude liked being a volunteer because she could enjoy doing the research on her own time. Between running a business and raising two teenage boys, there was little time left for faculty meetings and office hours, the necessary evils of a tenure track position.

"That's what I was thinking. Dust off your CV when you get a chance and I'll take care of the rest."

"Well, hold on here. You know I would love to help, but I need to know the timeline on this and what is expected before I can really commit to anything." This was a busy time of year for the Antique Lamp Company and Maude would have little time for anything not work related until after the holidays. It would also mean she would have less time to devote to writing her novel.

"There's another meeting the second week in January, before classes resume. Any chance you could attend?"

"I don't see why not. We slow way down after the holidays. Send me an e-mail with the details and I'll put it on my calendar."

"Sounds good, I'll talk to you soon."

"Thanks, Jean. I'm really glad to hear that the university supports some way of honoring these people and preserving the memory of the poorhouse."

"Me, too. Talk to you soon."

Maude ended the call and walked toward the front of the store to unlock the door for the day. There were three young women waiting to come in as soon as she opened the door, not the typical Antique Lamp Company shoppers. They had seen the recent post on Facebook and had come together to check out the vintage jewelry and one of a kind handbags referenced in the post. Maude silently congratulated herself for the brilliant use of social media as she tallied the sum of the items each of the ladies had placed on the counter. Thirty minutes later they left the shop, thrilled with their purchases, some of which had been wrapped as gifts and others they were obviously keeping for themselves. Maude hoped they would tweet about their purchases while they were enjoying lunch in the city.

The rest of the afternoon went by with a blur of tassels and fringe as the under-thirty crowd cleaned her out of nearly all of the fashion accessories she had. Fortunately the artisans and craftsmen Maude did business with were local, so it wouldn't be a problem to re-stock the shelves in the next day or two. She was about to go back into the office to retrieve her phone book when the front door opened and Don came in. "Why are you using the front door?" she asked.

"Phil's car is behind yours in the alley so I had to park on the street. I thought he was already in here."

"No, not yet. Come to think of it, I did hear voices upstairs. Maybe he stopped there first to talk to John." John rented the apartment above the shop. Whatever her landlord was coming to discuss appeared to include the upstairs tenant as well. Maude became concerned. "I wonder what this is all about?"

Looking up at the sound of footsteps descending the stairs, her husband replied, "We are about to find out."

Although Phil had keys to the building and could have let himself in through the back door, he came around to the front and the familiar jingle of the bell above the door announced his entry. "Oh good, I'm glad you are both here. I know you are anxious to close up and go home, so I won't take too much of your time."

"It's no problem, Phil. Do you want a cup of coffee or something?" Maude offered.

"Thanks, but no. I'm in a bit of a hurry to get home myself. My wife and I have dinner reservations. Listen, I just wanted to let you know that I am selling the building. My sister-in-law wants to get into the antique business and she and my brother have offered to buy the place. Barb and I have decided that this is our last winter in Buffalo, so I think this will work out well for us, too."

"So you're retiring. That's great! Congratulations," Don moved forward to shake his hand.

Maude smiled, but hung back while the men exchanged handshakes and shoulder slaps. She thought for a moment then asked, "You say your sister-in-law is interested in the antique business. So does that mean she would be converting the upstairs apartment to retail space?"

She knew the answer to that question and was not surprised when Phil suddenly looked abashed. "Well, that is why I came here in person. They will likely keep John as a tenant, but they'll want the retail space on the ground floor." To his credit he made eye contact with both Maude and Don when he gave them the news.

"You mean our space? The space we have rented from you for the past twelve years, the space in which we have built our business?" Don could not believe what he was hearing.

"Look, I know what this looks like." Phil was not able to continue his remarks before Don interrupted.

"It looks like your sister-in-law is going to evict us and then start a new business with the clients we've built relationships with over the past decade. You know it will be next to impossible for us to find other space in the area."

Maude just stood there dumbfounded as Phil attempted to explain himself. "Look, here is my problem. I'm already in enough trouble with my family because I had to fire my brother. If I don't sell them the building, it will just make things worse."

"Forgive me for not seeing that it will be worse for you when you retire and move to Florida if your brother in Buffalo is mad at you!" Don snapped.

"I know it's not much consolation to you, but I'm losing a lot of money on this too. I certainly can't sell the building to my brother at fair market value."

Don was about to fire back another unsympathetic remark when Maude put her hand on his shoulder and gave him a look that meant she had an idea. Wisely, he stayed silent and allowed his wife to speak instead. "What if we buy the building?"

It seemed evident by the identical looks of shock on their faces that neither of the men had expected her to say that. "What if we offered you a fair price for the building? Would you consider selling to us?" Maude looked at Don and he gave her a nod that indicated that he was willing to hear her out, so she continued. "You want to sell off your assets here and move to Florida, right? If you had a fair market offer that your brother could not match, your family couldn't reasonably expect you to sell to him."

Phil rubbed his face vigorously with both hands in an attempt to clear his head. He had only intended to come here to deliver the news and then leave. He had expected them not to be happy about it and even anticipated a few strong words from Don, but he had not seen this coming. "Listen, I really do have to get going. Let me talk it over with Barb tonight. Why don't you two have a discussion as well? Let's get together in two weeks and revisit this thing. That will give you guys a chance to go through your finances and put together an offer. Does that seem fair?"

"None of this seems fair…" Maude cut off her husband's remarks in an effort to end the conversation on a positive note.

"Yes, that seems fair," she smiled and extended her hand to Phil. "We'll give you a call when we are ready to meet." Phil nodded and shook her hand.

Maude was glad they had driven separate cars because she was able to use the time alone on the drive home to think about what she was proposing. They had some money saved, enough for a down payment, she thought. There would be no vacation in the upcoming year and they would have to skimp on their monthly contribution to the boys' college funds for the next few months. On the other hand, this was the worst time of year to have to free up some cash. In addition to the holidays, December meant sales tax was due, not to mention the other taxes and insurances associated with owning a small business in New York State. No, this was not the time to pay for a title search and a building inspector. Would they need a real estate agent? They would definitely need their lawyer.

After dinner, Maude and Don retreated to their home office, leaving the dishes for their sons Billy and Glen to handle. "I gotta tell ya, Maudie, I did not see this coming. The nerve of that woman to think she could just kick us out and take over our business, without even a thought about the fact that we would be completely screwed."

"I didn't either, but I can't say I'm surprised at her. From the bits I have heard over the years, it's pretty obvious that Phil supports his baby brother and his gold digging sister-in-law. I am, however, surprised that Phil would just hang us out to dry like that. He had to know that if she evicted us we would lose our business. I mean, where did he expect us to relocate?"

"He seemed surprised when you offered to buy the building, so it seems to me that he didn't come over here to try and discuss other options. He just planned to drop the bomb and then go join his wife for dinner at the Saturn Club, the lousy bastard!"

"Do you think he will seriously consider any offer that we make?" Maude asked.

"I think he will. One thing I do know is that Phil is not a liar. If he had no intention of considering any offer we might make, he would not have agreed to meet with us in two weeks. Phil didn't get to where he is today by making poor decisions. If he had to fire his own brother, I can't believe he expects the man to be able to run a business, or his sister-in-law for that matter. My guess is that Phil would hold the mortgage and when the business ultimately failed he would get the building back and be stuck looking for another tenant."

"So, this was his way of getting out of town with the least amount of grief from the rest of his family?" Maude asked, clearly as outraged as her husband. "Hand them the building and just continue supporting them from afar? If he expects them to fail, we can hardly hope to motivate Phil to sell to us by offering to pay a fair price."

"He might if he is looking to free up some cash before he leaves. For what it's worth, though, I think he is looking at the whole situation as penance for firing his brother. Somehow we need to convince him to grow a pair and just say no to the entitled prince for a change," Don stated.

"How on earth are we going to do that?"

"I don't know. To be on the safe side, keep your eyes open for any retail space available in the area."

"Will do. It might also be a good idea to spell out in writing just how long it took us to build our business and how much competition is in the area. Assuming we would relocate and that most of our customers would follow us, they would have to put together a pretty unique business plan to be competitive in this area," Maude suggested.

"You know, that may just be the key! They probably think they will just be able to swoop right in and pick up where we left off. If we can get Phil to make them understand just how unlikely that scenario would be, they may lose interest."

"Okay, you are out and about so you are more likely to see what might be available in the neighborhood than I would be." Maude was feeling a little better about the situation now that they were forming a plan. "I will start drafting a letter to Phil that explains details about the antique business in general and our business specifically. I will also make an appointment for us at the bank this week. Are you available most days around lunchtime?"

"Tomorrow I have to go to Hamilton, but any other day will work. We should get a realtor, too. I'll call around and see if anyone can recommend somebody on the commercial end." He reached over and pulled Maude into his arms. "This is going to be ok," he said and then kissed the top of her head.

"I know." She knew they were both just saying what the other needed to hear, but that was reassuring in itself. There was now a plan and each of them had tasks that would keep their thoughts moving towards their goal, and that was important, too.

Chapter Two

Maude looked up as the jingling bell above the door signaled the arrival of her first patron of the day. A woman entered, carrying a heavy olive canvas shoulder satchel, with two spiral notebooks and a laptop peeking out the top. She made eye contact with Maude and smiled as she moved toward the counter.

"You must be Abby Stevens," Maude declared, fairly sure the woman wasn't one of those people who came door to door promising to save you hundreds of dollars on your gas bill each year if you switched to the company they represented. She didn't look like one of those people, but she wasn't lugging a broken parlor lamp behind her either.

"How did you know?"

She laughed, and pointed to the satchel, "Your bag - it screams researcher!"

Abby laughed, "Well then, you must be Maude. I hope you don't mind me dropping in unannounced, but I had a few questions and your shop sounded so interesting. I wanted to come and see it for myself." Abby made it a point to Google all of her clients, and she had been more intrigued with the Antique Lamp Company than she was with Maude's former career as an anthropologist. "This is wonderful," she said, gesturing toward the Christmas tree. "The pictures on your website don't do it justice. Do you own the building?"

On any other day, Maude would not have found that question odd, but given all that was going on recently it took her by surprise. Don had not been able to find any other space in the area that would have been suitable for relocation. They had been to the bank and found that they could make an offer on the low end of fair, but it would be a tighter squeeze on their finances than they had expected. Her reply came out unintentionally defensive. "No, we rent. Why do you ask?"

"Oh, I just love these old buildings. If you were interested, I could have thrown in a bit of history on the place," she said looking around. "This looks to be early to mid-nineteenth century. I'm guessing the apartment upstairs was originally the living quarters for the business owners."

"Yes, I think you might be right. There is a separate entrance from the outside that was added later, but there is also an entrance here, in the back. I have a key so I can feed the cat when the upstairs tenant is away," Maude told her.

"Does the apartment have any of the original features?"

"The rooms still have the original floors, but the trim and moldings have been painted over many times and the kitchen and bathroom are stuck in the 1970s. The tenant has lived there for years and would love to do some restoration, but the current landlord won't pay for it."

"Current landlord…Is the building for sale?" Abby asked.

"Why do you ask?" Again, the suspicion was unintended. All this talk about the building was making her nervous. "I'm sorry, sore subject. You said you had some questions."

"I'm sorry. I didn't mean to pry. I just have this thing - it's silly, really, but I think every one of these old buildings has a story and I love it when the owner is interested in finding out what it is."

Maude was embarrassed by her own behavior. She had been so worried about the possible sale of the building and had totally forgotten to answer Abby's e-mail earlier in the week. Now the woman had taken the time to come in person to obtain the information she needed and Maude was treating her like she was a spy. "Well, I can tell you that the owner of this building is not interested in its story."

"Too bad. This is a great place." Abby continued speaking as she reached in and pulled a notebook from her bag. "Now you mentioned on the phone that your mother's family came from Ireland. Were you able to find out any more information about them or about your father's side of the family?

"Oh, right. I'm sorry I didn't get back to you. It's been on my list to call my mom all week. I've been caught up in things here at the shop and I haven't had much room on my plate for much else lately."

"It's not a problem at all." Sliding the notebook back into her bag, she suggested, "Would you like to put the family tree on the back burner until after the holidays? You're not giving it as a gift or anything, right?"

"No, I hadn't even thought of that. Actually, if it's not a problem for you, I would love to revisit this after the first of the year." Maude was relieved at the suggestion. Until things were settled one way or the other with the sale of the building she would not be able to focus her attention on anything else.

"Okay, sounds good. I'll be in touch after the new year."

* * *

"Explain to me again why a genealogist is so interested in the history of our shop?" Don asked as he poured a healthy dram of whiskey for the both of them and came to join his wife on the couch.

"I have no idea. I suppose she's just interested in history in general. It is a pretty cool old building." Maude took the tumbler and propped her feet up on the coffee table. She and Don had gotten into the habit of having a drink before dinner and catching each other up on the events of their day. "It just caught me off guard, that's all. This whole thing with the building has me edgy and I can't stand all of this waiting around."

"Maude, I've been thinking that it won't be the end of the world if we have to close the shop. We can run the business off the internet. I can sell any lamp we currently have on eBay. Without the overhead of a physical location, we wouldn't need to sell all of the accessories and jewelry."

"That's all well and good for you, but what would I do?"

"Well, you could continue your project at the university. You told me Jean wanted you to help with the memorial museum. You also mentioned something about writing a book. You would have more time for all of that, and for the boys, if you weren't chained to the shop every day."

"Don, I don't feel chained to the shop, and the boys are hardly in need of more attention from me. In case you haven't noticed, they're teenagers and want as little to do with me as possible."

"You know I didn't mean it like that."

"I know, and I appreciate that you want me to have more time to do the things I enjoy, but can we really afford for me not to contribute any income?"

"I ran some numbers and if we are careful we could pull it off," Don argued.

"I can accept that as a worst case scenario, but I really love our shop and I don't want to give it up. Right now I have the best of all possible worlds. We make a comfortable living and we're able to give our sons everything they need. My schedule allows me to fit in my research, and maybe some writing, if I can ever figure out what to say. I'm not going to let Phil's freeloading family take that away from me without a fight."

Don leaned forward and clinked his glass with hers. "Me neither, Maudie, but I need a plan in the back of my mind just in case this doesn't work out in our favor. Have you written your letter to Phil?"

"I am almost done. I want to make sure it is very clear to Phil that they will not simply be able to pick up where we left off."

Don was silent while he sipped his whiskey.

"What?" she asked when the silence stretched on for longer than was necessary to appreciate the spirit as it trickled down the back of his throat.

"Well, it really doesn't matter what we say in the letter if Phil is looking for an easy way out. I mean, if he's doing all of this so he can leave town with a clear conscience, do you think it will matter how much it's going to cost him? The guy is loaded. He will listen to what we have to say, but in the end it may not matter." Don drained his glass. Turning to look at her, he said, "Maude, we need to be prepared for the very real possibility that none of this will matter and we will lose the building and the business as we currently run it."

Maude blew out a deep breath and handed over her empty glass. "Make it a double," she said. She waited for him to return to the couch and took a long drink before speaking again. "Don't be so sure. Maybe when Phil sees just how much this could cost him long term he'll reconsider."

"Well, even if that happens, have you really thought about what it will cost us? We may just be slightly better off if we run the business online than if we buy the building." He turned so that he was completely facing her, readjusting his legs across the edge of the coffee table. "We've both looked at the numbers and we can just about afford to do this. Two mortgages on top of private school tuition for the boys and the obscene amount of money we pay for health insurance doesn't leave a whole lot left over at the end of each month."

"What if we sold the house and moved into the apartment above the shop? John is on the road most of the time anyway; it wouldn't be difficult for him to find another place."

"What?"

"You heard me. I wouldn't have considered it either a few years ago, but the boys are past the point where they need the basketball hoop in the back yard. Between sports and after school clubs, they only come home to eat and sleep these days. Think about it, only one mortgage, and no worries about college when the time comes."

"Well, the place is certainly big enough. The boys could have the entire third floor," Don mused. "That apartment would be beautiful once we restored the woodwork and updated the kitchen and bathroom." He stopped and shook his head. "Wait, we're getting ahead of ourselves. My original point was that it was unlikely that this thing was going to work out in our favor and now we are talking about selling our house and moving above the shop. We have to be realistic, Maude."

"Agreed, but we also need to be prepared for a different outcome than the one we expect. The truth of the matter is that we are financially unprepared for any other scenario but the one we are currently living, and we know that things are going to change one way or the other soon. All I am saying is that if, by some stroke of good fortune, Phil lets us buy the building, we should seriously consider selling the house and living above the shop."

"And if he doesn't sell to us?"

Maude glanced over at the bottle of Jameson on the bar, "The answer to that might just take another drink, and we both have to work in the morning."

Chapter Three

It was a rare occasion that Maude and Don were in the shop at the same time during the day, but given what had transpired that Friday morning, it was just as well they were together. They had agreed to spend a few hours that morning shoring up their case in preparation for the meeting with Phil later in the afternoon. Maude had sent him the e-mail the day before, but wanted to make sure they were confident in their position in the event that he had not had a chance to read it.

The first interruption was John, the upstairs tenant. He must have been waiting for them to arrive because he appeared in the alley when they pulled up and followed them into the shop. Maude noticed his truck was packed with more than the usual duffle bag he took when he went out on the road.

"Got time for a cup of coffee?" Maude asked as she gestured toward the Keurig on the counter in their back room.

"No thanks, Maude. I've got a lot to do today. I just wanted to let you know that I'm moving."

"What? Why?" Maude looked surprised, but her husband looked pleased. Clearly she was missing something.

Don spoke before John could explain himself. "I don't blame you, man. I wouldn't want them as land-lords either."

"It's not just that, although I agree with you," John explained. "I think what Phil is doing to you guys really stinks and I'm not about to make life easier for his brother by continuing to pay rent. They will have to throw some serious coin into remodeling that place before they will be able to find a decent tenant."

Don smiled again and extended his hand toward the other man. "That's damned decent of you, man."

"Well, don't think too much of the gesture. Jane has been trying for months to get me to move in! We've been together about five years now, so I guess it's time."

Don shook his hand and clapped his friend affectionately on the back. "Well, it's about time. Congratulations, that's really great. Jane is a saint to have put up with you for this long. You be sure and behave yourself when you're on the road!"

"I always do, my friend!"

Seeing this recent turn of events as a sign, Maude interrupted the two men. "Does Phil know about this?" she asked.

"Yeah, I called him last night. I also told him he was a despicable bastard for throwing you guys out," John told her. Before he could finish, Maude gave him a big hug.

"I am going to miss you," she said, and kissed him on the cheek.

John took a step back and smiled at her. "I appreciate everything you have done for me and for Harley. That old cat will miss hanging out in your shop, though I think he'll be much happier with someone around the house at night when I'm on the road."

Don shook John's hand again. "Good luck and don't forget to stop in when you're in town."

They stood at the window and watched their friend drive away with the cat carrier safely strapped into the passenger seat. When he was out of sight, Maude turned toward her husband. "You knew," she accused.

"Not for sure. I might have run into Jane at the Flea Market a few days ago. John had told her what was going on and I mentioned we were trying to get Phil to sell to us." Seeing the accusing look on his wife's face he hastily added, "She was the one who thought the deal with his brother would look less attractive to Phil if the apartment were empty. I merely agreed that it would cost him a fortune to make that place attractive to good tenants." Maude's expression only looked more suspicious, but changed into a smile as he continued his explanation. "She is a smart woman. I'm sure she started a seemingly innocent conversation and, by the end, John thought moving in with her was his idea."

Maude turned and snaked her arms around Don's neck. "You are a sneaky man, Don Travers, and I love you for it," and then she kissed him before he could speak and ruin the moment.

Soon they were in their office and discussing how this latest development might work out in their favor, when the familiar bell on the door announced yet another visitor. Before either of them could reach the front of the shop, a voice called out. "Maude, Don, are you back there, it's Phil." They were not supposed to meet with their landlord until after lunch and his early arrival did not bode well.

Don turned and took Maude in his arms. "Whatever happens, we'll get through it together," he whispered and then kissed her soundly on the mouth. Hand in hand they walked out of the office.

"Oh, there you are. I'm glad you're both here. I know that we were supposed to meet later, but I'd rather just get this over with and get on with my day, if it's all the same to you."

Maude squeezed his hand and Don choked back a scathing reply. Instead he locked eyes with the man and said, "Alright then, let's get it *over with*." His emphasis on the last two words made Phil regret his start to the conversation.

"Look, I'm sorry. I didn't mean it that way. I have left you guys hanging long enough and you deserve to know my decision sooner rather than later."

"Thanks, Phil, we appreciate your consideration." This time Don squeezed her hand as she spoke, not in support, she knew, but in an effort to restrain himself from commenting on Phil's idea of consideration.

"So, what's it gonna be?" Don asked.

"The truth is you are good people and I wouldn't have even considered any of this if there weren't pressure from my family to take care of Lester and his wife. You guys get it, right? I mean there's one in every family, right?"

"Phil, just get to the point, please." Maude tried to keep her voice even because she knew if she lost her temper that Don would too, and that would make moving forward from whatever happened now very difficult.

"You're right. I'm sorry. I'm sorry about all of this. I should never have put you in this position…"

"Phil! Your decision, please," Don interrupted, struggling to keep his voice calm.

"The building is yours, if you still want it." Pulling an envelope out from his jacket pocket, he handed it to Don. "I put together an offer I know Lester can't match. It's reasonable. Take a look and talk it over. I'm willing to negotiate within a reasonable margin, but it would make my life a lot easier if whatever we agree on is out of his reach."

Maude surprised them both by intercepting the envelope and tearing it in half. The two men stood with their mouths hanging open as she walked into the office and returned carrying an envelope of her own. "Look, Phil, excuse my directness but I've had just about enough of this. As we see it, you are looking to sell off your assets here and retire to Florida. Your responsibilities toward your family are making it difficult for you to make smart business decisions. It seems to me that if you accept this envelope, you sell the building outright to us and you can be on your way. If not, you have only two other options. The first is to sell it to your brother as you had intended. That will cost you about $50,000 in set up costs for the business plus an additional $25,000, minimally, to renovate the apartment before it can be rented. As another option, you could put the building up on the market. With no tenants upstairs, or down, and both units in need of work, it will likely stay on the market for a long time." She handed him the envelope. "It's a reasonable offer. Take a look and talk it over with Barb, but know this: if you decide to go with either of your other two options, we are leaving and we are taking the clientele and the inventory we have built up over the last twelve years with us."

Phil looked suitably chastised when he took the envelope. "Alright, I guess I owe you that much. I'll be in touch soon." Without another word, he left the shop.

As soon as the door was closed behind him Maude started up. "The nerve of that son of a bitch! He knows damn well that with John gone it's going to cost him a lot more to buy the forgiveness of his family. I can promise you this, the "fair" price he offered would not have taken into consideration the renovation costs upstairs or the cost of updating the mechanicals. How stupid does he…" Her rant was cut short by Don's kiss.

"What was that for?"

"You're brilliant," he told her and then he was kissing her again. After a while he left her speechless for just a moment while he locked the front door.

Chapter Four

Although Phil did not get back to them until Monday, they were fairly confident throughout the weekend, and so were not surprised when they got a call from their now former landlord that his lawyer would be drawing up the papers. Things proceeded very quickly after that. They wasted no time putting their North Buffalo home on the market and agreed to lease the apartment from Phil until the closing, thinking it would be easier to show the house if they weren't living in it. They had Christmas surrounded by moving boxes, and were settled in the apartment with the bare necessities by the new year.

The floors were refinished before they moved in, so the first project on their list once they were living in the apartment was to have all of the trim and molding stripped to its natural wood finish. On a cold weekend in January, armed with hammers and crow bars, each member of the Travers clan took a room and began to carefully remove the heavy oak trim. With the boys in the back of the apartment blasting "Trophies" by Drake, and Maude and Don working in the front, with the Rolling Stones' "Sympathy for the Devil" to keep them motivated, they worked with little communication among them until Glen came in and turned the volume down. "Mom, Dad, come look what I found in the back bedroom." He handed his mother a newspaper, so yellow with age, it looked as if it could have been published well over a century ago.

"Wow, where did you find this?" Maude asked, carefully taking the folded paper and laying it in the floor.

"I was prying off the trim around the closet and the floor board was loose. I pulled it up and this was underneath," Glen answered.

Billy and Don came closer as Maude carefully unfolded the newspaper. It was a single article that had been clipped from the Buffalo Daily Courier and was dated December 7, 1849. The headline read "Medical Student Gone Missing: Family Distraught." The small article went on to describe the Carrington family's willingness to pay handsomely for any information leading to the whereabouts of their beloved son Sherman, a student in the Medical Department at the University of Buffalo, who had disappeared without a trace in October of 1849. She read the headline out loud and then handed the clipping over to Don. "Was there anything else underneath the floor?" she asked Glen.

"I think so. When I pulled the paper out, I heard a clinking sound, but I couldn't see if anything fell out. Do we have a flashlight?"

"We do," his father confirmed as he handed the article back to Maude. "Let's get it and take a look."

Maude laid the clipping carefully on the counter in the kitchen and followed them into the back bedroom. As she came through the door, she found Billy down on his belly with his legs hanging outside of the closet, reaching underneath the floorboard, while his father crouched behind him with the flashlight. "I've got something," he shouted, as he began to inch backward, pulling his arm out from underneath as he went. "It feels like it could be a ring." He sat up and held out his hand.

"Well, I'll be damned. It is." Don took the ring from his son and wiped it with his t-shirt before holding it up to the light. The band was gold, with a sapphire that looked to be at least two carats and as dark as the night sky. The stone was surrounded by pearls, eight maybe, or nine, the ring was filthy from newspaper ink and dirt that had fallen through the floorboards over the last 165 years, so it was hard to tell.

"Is that real?" Billy asked.

Don spit on the corner of his shirt and tried to wipe some of the grime from the gemstone. "I think so."

"If it is, it could be worth a small fortune," Maude commented as she moved closer to take a look. "What on earth was a ring like that doing wrapped in a newspaper underneath the floorboards?"

"…wrapped in an article about a missing rich guy," Billy added.

"Well, there is a story here, no doubt, but we aren't going to get any answers today," Don remarked. "I expect this is older than the stuff we usually see. Maude, why don't you shoot Christine a text and see if she'll be in tomorrow? She knows more about antique jewelry than we do. If anyone can give us more information about this ring, she can."

"Good idea," Maude agreed. "Alright, back to work everyone."

For the rest of the afternoon Maude remained preoccupied with the newspaper clipping and the ring. Was there a link between them? She found that she was making up reasons to go into the kitchen in order to look at the article again or examine the ring. The man had disappeared just at the end of the cholera epidemic in 1849. Maude knew quite a bit about cholera during the nineteenth century from the research she had done with Jean while still in graduate school. The '49 pandemic had come to New York City from France. Some German immigrants had become ill on board the ship and had carried the disease into the city. The disease made its way down the Erie Canal, hitting Buffalo and Rochester particularly hard. Could Sherman Carrington have died during the epidemic? Doubtful. By the fall of 1849 the disease had just about run its course. During the summer months there were so many deaths each day throughout the city it would have been easy for a few names to get lost in the shuffle. Surely if a medical student from a wealthy family had died that late in the epidemic, someone would have known about it. What about that gorgeous ring? Where did that fit into the mystery?

"Maude, did you hear me?" Don came into the kitchen and interrupted her thoughts. "Are you about ready to call it a day? The boys are starving and if you call for a pizza now, I'll have the back hall trim off by the time it's delivered."

Maude put the ring back on the counter. "Yeah, sure. Wings, too?"

"Yes, order them hot, please. I'll go unlock the back door."

They were all exhausted after the day's labor and, with no interest in the playoffs; Maude left Don and the boys to watch their football game and went to bed. She continued to ponder the cholera epidemic in Buffalo and the fate of Sherman Carrington as she drifted off to sleep.

* * *

June 5, 1849

Martha Sloane had a hand on the forehead of wee Gretchen Kebler, supporting the poor child as she emptied the contents of her stomach into the tin basin. A thin layer of sweat formed between the medical student's hand and the orphan's head as the child heaved and coughed up the evening's boiled oats. Martha had heard stories of cholera many times in her young life since coming to Buffalo, New York, from Ireland, and knew all too well that without the proper precautions, the dreaded disease would have its way in the Buffalo Orphan Asylum. Gretchen had arrived recently from Cherry Street, bringing the disease with her. She was the first child to fall ill and Martha prayed she would be the last.

"There now, lass, it will pass soon enough," Martha crooned as she gently rubbed the child's back, knowing it would not ease the dry heaves that had followed the explosion of porridge, but hoping it might provide some measure of comfort.

Having lost both of her parents to cholera not two days ago, poor wee Gretchen had become an orphan just as Martha had all those years ago. In 1835, at the age of four, Martha, the second youngest of four girls, boarded a ship in Ireland with the rest of her family headed for America. The young child had no idea that, when they reached their destination, the Sloane family would be reduced from six members to three. Ian and Mary Sloane and their youngest child, Katie, were all taken by ship fever on the voyage. Martha and her two older sisters, Ciara and Patricia, were left to face the challenges of their new life in Buffalo alone. The city was still living in the shadows of the cholera epidemic of 1832, which had taken the lives of hundreds of its citizens. Pauline Sloane, the wife of their cousin - their only kin in America - refused to take the girls in for fear they would carry the ship fever into her home. With no other family to turn to for help, the girls were sent to the Erie County Poorhouse, where seventeen-year-old Ciara was put in charge of the children's ward. The three sisters lived at the almshouse for nearly a year, each of them doing what they could to help the orphaned children there.

So much had happened since those months spent at the almshouse fourteen years earlier. The Sloane women went from being homeless waifs to respectable women, each making an important contribution to the well-being of the growing population of the city's poorest children. Ciara had become the first Keeper of the Buffalo Orphan Asylum. Patricia and her husband, Rolland, were teachers in the asylum and provided the children with an education sufficient to allow them to attain employment as they got older. Martha had always been interested in medicine and helped her brother-in-law, Dr. Michael Nolan, to the extent that any child could when the young orphans became sick. Today she was attending the orphan asylum as a medical student, still under the supervision of her brother-in-law, but not as an errand girl to fetch this or that. This time she was training to be the first female physician to graduate from the University of Buffalo Medical Department.

"And how's our wee lass?" Michael asked as he entered the small chamber they had converted into a sick room.

"There's no change, I'm afraid." Martha settled the child back into bed before motioning Dr. Nolan out into the hall way. "Are ye sure it was safe to bring her here?" Martha asked, being careful to keep her voice low so as not to be overheard by any of the children or staff.

"Martha, we've been over this more than once now. The growing consensus is that the disease is not contagious. If it was, the both of us would be long dead, for all we've been workin' day and night tendin' to those who have fallen ill."

"You've said that, I know, and I believe ye. It's just that I worry about the other children. The truth is that we don't know how the cholera is spreadin'."

"'Tis true enough, but can ye imagine what would have happened to the poor lass if I had let them take her to the hospital, with nobody to spare her a kind word?" The hospital was in fact an abandoned tavern on a plot of land overlooking Lake Erie owned by Dr. Johnson, the former mayor of Buffalo. It had been, once again, transformed into a pesthouse, more specifically a cholera hospital, in an attempt to isolate the growing number of patients from the rest of the city. "The other children are safe enough as long as wee Gretchen stays here and we follow the protocol established by Dr. Coventry. We must…"

"I know, we must maintain the highest standards of cleanliness about the sick room, the patient, and ourselves if we are to achieve a favorable result."

Martha interrupted, repeating the mantra that had been drilled into her head not only by Dr. Nolan, but by her other professors as well.

"Good. The other children are well and I've told the staff to fetch me immediately should any of them become lethargic or begin to lose their appetites. Dr. Coventry says that…"

"If we can treat the disease at its earliest stage, the chances of achieving a favorable result increase dramatically," Martha recited.

"You'll make a fine doctor one day, Martha Sloane. Now let us be off. We've more patients to see before our supper."

Martha looked in the direction of the chamber door. Like most patients, Gretchen had passed through the initial phase of cholera unnoticed. Loss of appetite and debility were not conditions for which most people sought medical treatment. In the poorer neighborhoods, like the one where she lived, most ailments and injuries were treated in the home with remedies passed along among family and friends. A person had to be seriously ill before seeking professional treatment. Gretchen was well into the second stage of the disease where violent vomiting and frequent diarrhea made it nearly impossible to keep anything in the way of food or drink down. Martha and Michael both knew that children seldom recovered from the disease at this stage. With her parents gone, Michael sent eight-year-old Gretchen to the orphanage rather than the cholera hospital so the poor child might have a bit of comfort before she passed.

Seeing Martha's apprehension as she turned away from the door, Michael said, "Stay with the lass. She'll have a rough night to be sure and it wouldn't be right to place an additional burden on the staff here."

"But what about the hospital? Surely the others there are needin' a break by now." Martha was aware of the scrutiny she came under from some of her colleagues and professors. In addition to being the first female medical student, Martha also carried the burden of having Michael on the faculty as the professor of Physiology. She felt she had to work longer and harder than the men in order to dispel the misguided notion that her connections allowed her special treatment. In truth, Martha was smarter than most of her classmates and did not need any favors from her brother-in-law.

Still, she knew if she were allowed to stay at the orphan asylum caring for a single child while the others toiled at the hospital, she would hear about it eventually.

"Before this is over there will be too many of them and too few of us. Scores of people will die alone, while their caretakers are wiping the brow or holding the bucket for someone else. Right now we can allow ourselves the luxury of providing that poor child with comfort of knowing that, without her parents, someone who cares will be by her side in this strange place."

"But surely the other students will have somethin' to say…"

"Never ye mind the other students," he interrupted. "I'll tell Mrs. McClaverly that ye're stayin' here on my way out." Before she could say another word, Michael was heading down the back staircase to the Keeper's office.

Mrs. McClaverly was a widow who had worked as a night nurse at the orphanage when Ciara Nolan had been the Keeper. Ciara continued on in her position after the birth of her first son, Ian (named for her father), leaving him in the care of her best friend and housekeeper Karin Edwards. However, her second pregnancy, a year and a half later, was a difficult one and she was confined to her bed for six months. Michael insisted she not return to work after Daniel - named for Michael's father -was born, and Ciara reluctantly agreed. She resigned her position as Keeper and did her best to convince Mrs. Farrell and the other members of the Board of Directresses to recommend Mrs. McClaverly for the job.

Sarah McClaverly was a kind woman in her early forties who had done an admirable job on behalf of the children for the past seven years. Ciara remained on the Board of Directresses and met with Mrs. McClaverly each month, just as Colleen Farrell had met with her when she was Keeper. "Come in, Doctor Nolan," the Keeper answered to the knock on her open door.

"I'll be off to the hospital, but Martha will likely stay the night. Can ye have one of the kitchen lasses bring her some supper?"

"Of course, Doctor. Will the child last the night?"

"I can't say for sure. If she keeps on as she has, she'll be gone before days' end tomorrow," Michael said with a heavy heart. "Thank ye, Sarah, for allowing the child in." He had come to know the Keeper well over the years, yet still only rarely addressed her by her first name. He had tremendous admiration and respect for this woman, who, like his wife, often considered the needs of the children above her own.

"'Tis not me ye should be thankin', Doctor. 'Twas Mrs. Schneider who gave up her chamber so the child could be kept away from the others." Mrs. McClaverly granted Michael's request to admit Gretchen to the orphanage without question. It was because of him, after all, that not a single child had died there in over three years. She knew he would not have asked if the other children would be placed at risk. They agreed that it would not do for Gretchen to be in the sick ward along with other children who were being treated for minor ailments or injuries. Both the Keeper and the Doctor knew the child would die and did not want to expose the other children to the violent progression of symptoms that would lead to her passing. Mrs. Schneider, one of the night nurses, graciously gave up her chamber so that Gretchen could be treated in isolation.

Michael passed by his medical practice on Niagara Street as he drove his carriage on toward the cholera hospital. He hadn't seen the inside walls of his own clinic in almost a week, since the first patient was found nearly dead at the American Hotel. It was just luck that Michael happened to have been there. He rarely indulged in an afternoon pint, like so many of Buffalo's professional men did. However, on that day he had agreed to meet the father of one of his less ambitious students. He had not even sat down in the pub when the hotel manager tried desperately to get his attention from the doorway while at the same time trying not to look like he was desperate. A man had come from New York City by way of the canal just the day before, the manager told Dr. Nolan. The chamber maid could hear him retching from the hallway as she worked. The entire city was on high alert, knowing cholera was working its way along the Erie Canal from New York, and would find its way to Buffalo before the month was out. She wasted no time alerting her supervisor, who immediately came down to the main floor in search of any one of the many physicians who frequented the pub in the afternoon. No need to panic the other patrons, the manager assured Michael, but he would be ever so grateful if the good doctor would check on Mr. Schumacher on the second floor.

Seeing the thin, watery diarrhea stained sheets of Mr. Schumacher's bed was indication enough that he was already entering the second, more dangerous stage of the disease. The man's feeble pulse and cold extremities confirmed the diagnosis. It took some convincing, and not just from Dr. Nolan, to allow Mr. Schumacher to stay in his room. All four physicians serving on the recently established Board of Health were required to convince Augustus Umberide, the manager of the American Hotel, that Mr. Schumacher, a jeweler from Long Island, posed no threat to the other patrons of the hotel. However, moving him would certainly unnecessarily alarm the other guests. Sadly, the jeweler died the next day.

Michael arrived at the hospital still with thoughts of Mr. Schumacher on his mind. They could not yet send word to his family, who would undoubtedly be concerned by now that he had not returned home. The cholera epidemic of 1832 was still in the collective conscious of the older residents of the city and they knew well how fast the disease would spread. One confirmed case was all that was needed to bring travel in and out of Buffalo to an abrupt halt in the hopes of keeping the dreaded disease at bay. Michael wondered how many husbands, wives, mothers and fathers would hear the same news that Mrs. Schumacher would eventually be told: that their loved one had been taken by the brutal disease that was cholera. Leaving the carriage with a stable lad, who would see the doctor's dependable mare fed and comfortable for the night, Michael took a deep breath to steel his nerves for what he knew would be a long shift and walked toward the door.

* * *

Maude woke up disoriented, still half in the nineteenth century. She wasn't yet used to waking up in her new room, and, in the dark, the sparse furnishing, fireplace, and bare wood floor did nothing to ease her confusion. It had been a dream, she knew, but the details were so real. She had gone to sleep thinking about the past, and had ended up dreaming about Martha Sloane and her family. Looking over, Don was not there. She could smell the coffee and guessed he was already dressed and puttering downstairs in his work room. Maude looked at the clock on her nightstand. It was only 6:30 and the boys wouldn't be up for another half an hour, so she crawled out of bed and padded out to the kitchen.

Still in her robe, Maude made her way downstairs to find Don. It was a strangely perverse feeling, walking down to the shop in her robe and pajamas, like she was getting away with something. Don must have heard her coming down, because he did not look up as she entered the room. "One of these mornings, you are going to forget to change and end up greeting the morning clients in your PJ's," he teased.

"Well, I'll have to buy some respectable jammies, just in case! What are you up to so early?"

"I've got to go to Corning today and these two lamps have been waiting since well before Christmas to be rewired. Between getting the house up on the market and working upstairs, I've been letting things here slide. I'll feel better if I can get these done before I leave."

"Okay, I'll leave you to it. Christine is coming around nine to take a look at the ring. Will you still be here?"

"No. I'm almost done here and I'll leave in about an hour."

"Okay, stop back upstairs and get something to eat before you leave." She kissed him on the cheek and went back upstairs to shower and get breakfast for the boys.

Maude was not surprised when Christine called at 8:45 to say that she was just outside. "I couldn't sleep after I got your text last night," she told Maude as she unpacked a few tools from her bag. "How exciting, finding a ring under the floorboards. I wonder how it got there."

Knowing Christine's taste for intrigue and inability to keep a secret, Maude had not mentioned that the ring had been accompanied by a newspaper clipping that told of the mysterious disappearance of the son of a wealthy family in 1849. With Christine, it was better to have all of the facts before you told her anything that interesting. "I have no idea. Do you have any idea how old it is?"

Christine picked up the ring. Using a soft tooth-brush, a bit of Dawn dishwashing liquid and some de-ionized water, she gently cleaned the sapphire and pearls, careful in case any of the facets were loose. Once it was cleaned, she picked up her lens and examined the ring for what seemed like an eternity. "Well, it's old, that much I know. The flat cut stone could be Georgian or Early Victorian and the design is simpler than what became fashionable during the later part of the nineteenth century. It's stunning."

"Any idea how much it's worth?" Maude asked, taking the clean ring to examine it again.

"Well, jewelry is like anything else in the antique business. Just because it's old doesn't make it worth thousands of dollars. That sapphire looks impressive, though. You would have to have it appraised by someone in the business to get an actual dollar value." She continued talking as she packed up her tools. "Are you planning on selling it?"

Maude had not even considered the idea of selling the ring and said so. "At this point I am more interested in how it got hidden under my floorboards."

"Well, what I can tell you is I doubt very much the earlier occupants of this place could have afforded a ring like this. Sapphires and pearls were most likely beyond the reach of the average shop owner in the mid-nineteenth century," Christine told her as she zipped up her bag. "Fancy jewelry was worn by very wealthy people, not generally by the average well-to-do merchant."

"Hmm…The plot thickens, I guess." Maude regretted her choice of words as soon as they had left her mouth.

"Why? What are you not telling me?"

A few years ago, being on the receiving end of one of Christine's interrogations would have given her heart palpitations, but she had mastered the art of redirecting the woman's inquisitive mind. "You're telling me that this ring of questionable value today would have been beyond the reach of the average shopowner in 1850. So, I am wondering when the ring was hidden underneath the floor. How many owners do you think this building has had?"

"Do you have your title? That would tell you who owned the building before you."

"Great idea, I'll check at lunch." Maude got up, hoping that would signal that their meeting was over. Christine had given her some interesting details to ponder and she wanted to do so without any probing questions. "I've got some work to catch up on while it's quiet here, but I'll let you know if I find out anything interesting."

Christine gave her friend a long, questioning look, debating whether or not to inquire further, but ultimately decided against it. Maude would give her the details when she was ready and not before. "Sounds good. I know a few people who deal exclusively in antique jewelry, so let me know if you want to have the ring appraised."

As soon as Christine was out of the shop, Maude went to her office in search of her cell phone. "Hi, Abby. It's Maude Travers. Would you be able to meet with me sometime this week?"

Chapter Five

June 6, 1849

It was still dark by the time Michael returned home. The house stood silent as those within slumbered peacefully unaware of the battle being fought just a few miles away at Dr. Johnson's old tavern on the beach. Poor wee Gretchen Kebler had passed during the night in her sleep, thank the good Lord. Instead of returning home for some much needed rest, Martha went to the cholera hospital to give some of her colleagues a break, refusing even to leave when Michael had decided to return home. "Ye'll be of no help here if ye collapse from exhaustion," he told her. The man smiled to himself as he quietly opened the back door. Martha was as stubborn as her oldest sister and determined to prove herself a capable physician among her male colleagues. He knew one or two of them would succumb to fatigue before she did.

Removing his boots at the back door, he padded across the smooth oak floor in the direction of his study rather than to the stairs that would lead to his chamber. The occupants of the stable had given him a hearty welcome when he arrived, hoping to receive their breakfast early. He did not want to disturb the household any more, as its residents still had a few more hours before they had to leave their beds. On the occasions when he returned home in the dead of night, Michael made himself comfortable on a few quilts stored in the study, rather than wake the others climbing the creaky staircase to his bed.

Although the room was dark, he knew Ciara was there waiting for him as he opened the door. She did this sometimes, when the demands of his calling had taken him away from her for long periods of time. She knew he craved her touch as much as she craved his. He undressed quietly and slid down next to her, knowing she was awake. Wrapping his arms around her, he snuggled in, allowing the sleep-warmed softness of her body to permeate his own. "I hoped ye'd be here," he whispered. She seemed to melt into him, drawing all of the stress of the day out of him with a lingering kiss. He was suddenly so relaxed he could feel the pull of sleep, but the fullness of her lips tugged at other parts of him that longed to stay awake.

A while later, just before the first hint of dawn, Ciara gently disentangled herself from the slumbering man laying naked beside her. To her surprise, her escape was thwarted and she found herself held captive in arms she thought hadn't the strength left to move, let alone hold her with such determination. "And just where are ye sneakin' off to?" mumbled her captor.

"I'm off to start the breakfast, or have ye forgotten ye have two strong lads who'll be out of their beds by first light," she told him trying with little enthusiasm to extract herself from his firm embrace. "Besides, ye'll be needin' yer sleep, for all ye've had none these last few days."

"I need ye more than I need…" Michael's arms re-laxed and his head nestled into her shoulder as he settled back into sleep. Ciara lay there for just a few more minutes, watching his chest rise and fall until she was sure he would not wake again before she quietly slid out from beneath the quilt and reached for her shift. She pulled it on with her back to the lump of quilts on the floor so as not to be tempted to slip beneath them for just a wee while longer. They had so little time together. With the worst of the epidemic ahead, she knew not when they might be together like this again. With a wistful look over her shoulder she continued dressing quietly.

Ciara noticed Martha sprawled on the settee in the parlor across the hall as she gently closed the door to Michael's study. She had heard her sister come home not an hour ago, and God bless Charlie for going to fetch her. The poor lass must have been too exhausted to make it up to her own chamber, or perhaps reluctant to wake the rest of the house so close to dawn. Glancing up the stairs Ciara estimated the boys would not be up for about another half hour, but would make enough noise to wake the dead when they came down. The kitchen was at the opposite end of the house and the lads would be off to school after their breakfast, so it would be quiet again soon enough and her doctors could get a few hours sleep until they were called away again.

Wondering, as she entered the kitchen, just how much longer the boys' school would be opened, Ciara began the breakfast preparations. The city was in a general state of panic over the cholera epidemic, and the schools in the first ward and the German ward had already been closed in an attempt to keep the disease from spreading throughout the city. Her thoughts were interrupted as young Ellie came in through the back door.

"Mama saw Martha come in and sent me to fetch the lads." Ellie had been one of the many infants born at the poorhouse to mothers who had not survived their birth. She had found a place in the heart of her caretaker, Karin Friedlander, a widow with her own infant son, who had helped in those days to care for the infants and children who found their way to the Erie County Poorhouse. Their lives changed dramatically for the better in 1836 when Ciara married Michael. Karin left the poorhouse with her son, Bruns, and Ellie to keep house for the Nolans when Ciara accepted the position of Keeper of the new Buffalo Orphan Asylum.

They were a peculiar family, those who lived at the Nolan farm on North Street, or so thought those who only knew of them, but really did not know them. From the time they were married, Ciara and Michael's extended family included five children and three other adults. In addition to her two sisters, Ciara took on the care of young Johnny Quinn, a lad just eight years old at the time, who had been severely injured while bound out as a laborer on a nearby farm. The clan also included Karin and her two children, just infants in 1836, as well as Charlie Edwards and Alex Handley. Those men, also formerly inmates of the poorhouse, had protected Ciara and the children from the more dangerous inmates. After a long and complicated courtship, Charlie and Karin married and continued to live on the Nolan farm, she keeping the house and he the property and live stock. Old Alex, who'd helped Charlie manage the farm, had passed away just this past winter from the putrid sore throat.

At the age of thirteen, Ellie was much like Ciara's middle sister Patricia had been at that age. She was wise beyond her years and had a way with the younger children. Raised by a German mother and an Irish father, young Ellie spoke without the use of contractions, like her mother, but with a mix of both German and Irish broken English. She had been sent to fetch Ian and Daniel to the Edwards' cabin to eat their breakfast so that Martha and Michael would not be disturbed. "I will bring them, yes?"

"Aye, that would be grand. Thank ye, lass. I'll bring their lunch pails down straightaway."

"Mama has already wrapped some cheese and bread. I will just need their pails, if ye please."

"Away ye, up to fetch the lads, and tell them to be quiet about it. I'll have their pails for ye straight away." Ciara smiled at Karin's uncanny ability to understand exactly what she needed before she even knew for herself. The two women had lived like sisters for the past fourteen years, helping to raise each other's children and keep each other's home. Each had needed the other's help to steer them into the arms of the men who would become their husbands. Ciara did not know what she would have done all these years without her sensible German friend.

It wasn't long before Ellie had the boys dressed and tiptoeing down the stairs. She could barely contain her mirth as wee Daniel made a show of just how quiet he could creep down, carefully avoiding the spot on each tread that tended to creak, all the while shushing his older brother, who wasn't making any noise to begin with.

"Enough with ye shushing me!" Ian scolded in the loudest voice he could muster that could still be considered a whisper as they entered the kitchen with Ellie smirking behind them. "Ma, will ye tell him enough, already?"

"Ian, there's a good lad, off ye go now and have somethin' to eat with yer auntie Karin before ye're off to school." She cut off further complaints over the abrupt change in their morning routine with a quick kiss on the top of his head and a pat on the bottom to send him on his way.

Still whispering, wee Daniel asked the same important question he asked every day before he set out for school. "What 'ave we got for our lunches today, ma?" At seven years old, food was the most important part of Daniel's world, and although he could hardly be considered a fussy child, he always felt better knowing what was to be expected at meal time.

His round chubby face was at odds with the seriousness in his eyes and Ciara had to suppress a smile. "Knowin' yer auntie Karin, it'll be something ye'll well enjoy. Now off with ye!" As she opened the back door to let Ellie and the boys out another familiar face was walking up the path.

"Ah, it seems Karin and I are of like mind," Patricia said as she approached the house.

"'Twas that kind of ye, sister, but Ellie's got the lads well in hand, so come in and have a cup of tea before ye go," Ciara replied, holding the door wider to allow her sister, who was just into the last trimester of her pregnancy, to enter.

As the door closed, she noticed Rolland, Patricia's husband, making his way from their cabin toward the barn that the three houses shared. He had made it a habit since Alex's passing to help with the morning chores before setting out for the day. Charlie and Alex had managed the running of the Nolan farm together. Both men were hostlers, Charlie for the livery on Miller Street and Alex in the stables of a private home, before their circumstances changed for the worse and they were forced to seek refuge in the county almshouse. Charlie's leg had been broken and had not healed properly. As a result he was not as quick and efficient as other men and was unable to find work. Alex had been let go from the stable where he had worked most of his life. It was his age and the aches and pains associated with a long life of hard work that had left him with the same deficits and the same problem. Together at the Nolan farm they had worked to keep the livestock and the property maintained, each having strength where the other was lacking. Charlie would never have asked for Rolland's help, but was grateful for it nonetheless. "He's a good man, is Rolland," Ciara said as she turned to put the kettle on the stove.

"That he is," Patricia agreed. "No man works harder, to be sure. I don't know where he's found the time between teachin' at the school and at the orphan asylum to add two rooms to our wee house." Rolland and Patricia had been married five years and lived in a cabin on the farm with the rest of Patricia's large extended family. The couple was cautiously expecting their first child. Patricia had been with child three times before, but had been unable to carry the babes to term. She stubbornly refused to confine herself to her bed this time or any of the others, maintaining that if it was God's will for her to have a child, she would. There were plenty of children at the orphan asylum in desperate need. Some say God had forgotten those children, but Patricia knew otherwise. She was certain that God had called on her to watch over and protect them, and she would do that no matter what the cost or what others thought. "He'll be needin' some help to finish the job, though, if we're to have the rooms done before the babe arrives."

"Aye, well, there'll be no help from Michael now, to be sure. He tells me the cholera will get worse before it gets better."

"God bless and protect him," Patricia remarked, "and wee Martha as well. I saw the both of them come in lookin' the worse for wear. Will they be off again as soon as they're able?"

"Aye, I'm just hopin' they can get another hour's sleep, but the sun's up now and your Rolland will be pullin' up the wagon to take Ellie and the lads to school. They'll wake soon enough, I think."

"Did I hear last week that Johnny's back in town?" Patricia asked. "He and Bruns could give Rolland a hand in the afternoons, don't ye think? I'll stop by to see Gran and have a word this mornin'." Michael's parents, Katherine and Daniel, who considered Ciara's sisters as well as the others their grandchildren, owned Nolan's Dry Goods Emporium on Main Street. Johnny had taken an interest in the store from an early age and often helped Daniel after school, doing everything from sweeping floors to building displays for new merchandise. As soon as Johnny had completed school, he moved in with his adopted grandparents to help with the store full time. With Johnny to mind the store, Daniel was able to expand his business to meet the needs of a growing upper class in Buffalo. Now it was Johnny who traveled all over the east coast and Canada bringing back fine fabrics, wall coverings and bone china, helping to secure the store's reputation among the wealthier class as the place to find all of the finest goods and most modern conveniences.

"Can ye no sit still and give the poor babe ye're carryin' a wee rest?" Ciara scolded. "I've a meeting with Mrs. McClaverly later this mornin'. I'm happy to stop by the store and speak a word with Johnny."

"This from the woman who worked right up to the time her pains began," Patricia reminded Ciara of her first pregnancy. "Do ye not recall 'twas yer own husband, the good doctor, who pronounced both the babe and myself right as rain?" She did not give her sister a chance to respond before continuing. "The others slipped early on. This one will come into the world a fine healthy lass, and sooner than Michael expects, I should think. Just ye wait and see."

"Lass? Do ye mean to tell me our Martha's finally told ye? I suppose that's as good a sign as any the babe will be born," Ciara speculated. The family had long ago accepted the fact that Martha had the second sight. She had known of each doomed pregnancy before Patricia was aware herself and was reluctant to offer any insight about the child her sister was currently carrying until she was certain it would come into the world healthy. Ciara accepted that her youngest sister, like her husband, also had knowledge that she did not possess about the workings of the human body, but she didn't understand it or have faith in it the way Patricia did, and took more comfort in Martha's prediction that the Lord would bless their middle sister with a child.

"Aye, she's kept my heart whole these last years with the promise of a healthy babe one day. I don't remember much of ma, but I do recall her sayin' a time or two that things happen as they should. I'm happy to accept whatever the Lord has planned for me. I believe he has Mary KarinThomas planned for me, and no mistake," Patricia told her with a smile.

Tears welled up in Ciara's eyes at the mention of their mother Mary Sloane, who had not lived to see how well their lives had turned out, and also at the realization that Patricia had become so much like her. Transported for a moment to another time, Ciara wondered how their lives might have been different if the entire family had survived the trip from Ireland. What would have become of those poor wee souls on the third floor of the almshouse if the Sloane sisters had never come to live there? Their lives were forever linked to that place as a result of their parent's death, for now that they had seen the suffering of so many of God's children, they could never look away.

Chapter Six

June 20, 1849

Michael dismounted his dependable chestnut mare and walked toward Dr. Ryan's clinic still feeling groggy from the few hours of sleep he had managed. 'It was worth it,' he thought, with a self-satisfied smile on his face. He likely wouldn't see his wife or their bed for a few days, thanks to the state of affairs at the poorhouse, and he would need something pleasant to recall so that he could endure more unpleasant days ahead.

Careful to rearrange his features and stow thoughts of Ciara away for a more suitable moment, he took his seat among the three other physicians who made up the city's hastily put together Board of Health. They had serious business to discuss, not the least of which was the high mortality rate at the poorhouse compared to the city, which Michael attributed to mismanagement by the Superintendent, Mr. Morris. All of the physicians, who gave generously of their time in the sick ward, had expressed concern over the meager portions and overall poor quality of the food provided to the inmates there. The rooms were poorly ventilated and Michael had lost count of the number of times Morris had failed to tell him or one of the other physicians about a man or woman up in the dormitories who was in need of care until it was too late.

The only good thing to come of this deadly cholera outbreak was a platform to be finally heard. Michael had been asked by Dr. Ryan, the city Health Officer, to serve on the Board of Health. The Board was tasked with coordinating treatment and recordkeeping throughout the city, mapping the course of the disease as it spread and establishing quarantines where needed in the hopes of containing it. There would be no problem enforcing a quarantine at the Erie County Poorhouse, as most folks were reluctant to go there in the first place. Still, the high mortality, all from cholera, needed to be addressed. This gave Michael and his colleagues once again an opportunity to expose the incompetence of Russell Morris, the Superintendent of the Poor. With a full scale epidemic looming over the city, perhaps they could finally get someone on the County Board of Supervisors to listen.

"Gentleman, if we could bring the meeting to order." Dr. Ryan, unshaven and pale, looked and sounded as tired as Michael felt. Ryan had spent his evening among the tenements on Mortimer Street attending the eight cholera patients dispersed there. "Our job is far from over, so let us complete our business here with haste so that we can return to the wretched souls in desperate need of our care. Dr. Grant, do you have the most recent mortality statistics?"

"Six more dead as of this morning at the hospital and three at the poorhouse," Andrew Grant reported. "I await the statistics from Black Rock, Suspension Bridge and yours, sir, from the private homes." Grant continued. "The shanties at Suspension Bridge have been hit hard, and no surprise, given the squalor in which they live. I don't think we will have an accurate report until week's end." There would be no rest for Grant, who had labored all night in the tenements on Exchange Street and was still expected for the day shift at the hospital. "I shall go to the village of Black Rock at the conclusion of our meeting, so those statistics will be included in my written report," he promised without complaint.

"Thank you, Dr. Grant. Four of the eight cases on Mortimer Street have been transferred to the hospital; two more will recover, I expect, and can stay in their homes. The others were too weak to be transported. A mother and child. I fear they will not last the day. They may be gone already." Matthew Ryan took off his spectacles with a weary sigh and passed his right hand over his face in an attempt to wipe away the very thought of the beautiful Mrs. Haas, recently widowed, and her young son. Clearing his throat, if not his mind, he continued, "The five patients that I have seen in their homes in the area of Pearl Street are all in the early stages. Given the superior conditions in which they live, I expect each to recover." Dr. Ryan based his expectation on the widely held assumption that a clean and well ventilated sick room combined with adequate nutrition, were the weapons needed to vanquish this deadly foe.

Michael saw his opportunity and took it. "Since we are in a rush to conclude our business gentleman, I hope you will forgive the breach in protocol. I've a matter to discuss that can be put off no more." Not waiting for the approval of the group, he stood up and continued speaking. "Now, as ye say, Dr. Ryan, superior cleanliness and nutrition are critical to recovery, and no mistake. 'Tis high time we addressed the situation at the poor farm. Dr. Ferris reported twelve of the fifty-four adults dead in a day and a half, and most of them from the insane department. Now I'm told there are three more. That is a mortality rate worse than any hospital in Philadelphia or New York. Gentleman, as the Board of Health we cannot ignore this."

Dr. Winston Papineaw, who was the fourth member of the Board, waited for Michael to take his seat again before speaking. "Dr. Nolan, we all know of your concern for the city's poor, but what would you have us do? The inmates do as they please and as a result the building is a shambles. There are simply too many of them for the matron to control. You really should address your concerns to the superintendent himself."

Michael suppressed an exasperated sigh, but the sentiment was still evident in his tone as he spoke. "I have brought my concerns to Mr. Morris too many times to mention, as has every other physician to walk through the doors. It's a working farm and yet the poor souls receive only poorly baked bread and rusty salt pork. Not a vegetable to be seen in winter! We have to beg to get a bit of beef to make broth for the sick ward." Michael held up his hand in an uncharacteristically disrespectful gesture meant to stop the inevitable comments that usually followed the voicing of his concerns. "I know they sell the produce, milk and cheese, to help support the house, but other Keepers have wisely kept a wee bit back to feed the folk who toil to produce the goods they must sell!" Michael had made this argument many times before, only to have it fall on deaf ears. "The mortality rate at the poorhouse is higher than even the German ward. Do we not have an obligation to investigate as we did the tenements on Clinton Street?"

Again Dr. Papineaw stood, placed his hands flat on the table and leaned in toward Michael, speaking only to him, as if there was no reason to state the obvious to the others. "Dr. Nolan, the poor farm is on the edge of the city and surely poses no threat to those who steer clear of it." Turning briefly to make eye contact with the others, he continued. "This dreaded illness will cost the city a small fortune by the time it runs its course.

I'm quite sure the County Board of Supervisors appreciates the frugal tendencies of Mr. Morris in light of the current demands of the county's budget."

Not waiting for Papineaw to sit back down, Michael began speaking as he stood. "Gentlemen, the truth of the matter is that we do not know how this disease is transmitted, although hygiene and nutrition are undoubtedly important in the treatment. There's many at the poor farm there for only a day or two before they move on. If we don't get control of the epidemic there, 'tis likely more than a few folk will fall ill and be forced to stay longer or die, thereby taxing the county's resources even further with the cost of their burial!" Michael was growing ever more frustrated with the idea that dollars and cents were more important than human lives.

Before Dr. Papineaw could argue any further, Dr. Ryan cleared his throat and spoke in an uncharacteristically loud voice, emphasizing his first word. "*Gentlemen,* that is quite enough. I agree with Dr. Nolan. If the situation at the poorhouse threatens the health of the rest of the city, we must investigate. Do we need to put it to a vote?" The last comment was directed at Dr.

Grant, as Ryan was the chairman and therefore did not vote.

"No need for a vote," Grant confirmed. "Beyond the potential threat to the rest of the city, we owe it to the inmates of that dreadful institution to provide what relief we can."

Michael directed a quick nod at Andrew Grant in acknowledgment of his support. He knew the man would agree to his efforts to see that miser Morris called out for his abysmal treatment of the poorhouse inmates. Dr. Ryan's willingness to inspect the poorhouse came as a surprise. Ryan seemed ambivalent when it came to the needs of the poor. It wasn't that he had no compassion for the city's less fortunate citizens; it was just that he had, in his opinion, more important things to consider. Michael hoped that once the Board had actually seen how dreadful conditions were, they might take a more active role in watching over Morris, if not for the benefit of the inmates, perhaps to reduce the spread of disease.

"It's settled, then. I will send an official letter to Mr. Morris by day's end to expect us Wednesday morning, first thing, if that seems satisfactory to everyone." Looking around the table he could see no objections, although Dr. Papineaw did not meet his eyes, looking down instead as if to gather his things together. "Moving on, my own analysis of the areas of the city from which the most fatal cases have come indicates that the streets there are largely unpaved. Nearly two-thirds of the cases occurred on unpaved streets and well over half of the deaths thus far have occurred on the same. Consider Genesee Street: while it is paved, it intersects with many unpaved streets and is so unclean in itself as to do away with the usefulness of the pavement to some degree. The same is true for Seneca, Exchange and South Division streets east of Michigan, where a great many cases have occurred." Looking around the room to make sure that he had everyone's attention, he continued, "The central portion of the city has a pavement far better than most cities can boast, and in the houses of its inhabitants are found as much comfort and abundance as can be found anywhere. The effect of these factors is seen in the record of its low mortality."

Dr. Papineaw spoke up, "I move we recommend to the Board of Supervisors that streets intersecting

Genesee, particularly in the German ward, be paved as the budget permits."

"I second the motion," Michael said.

"All in favor?" Ryan asked, looking at each of them. "Good. Dr. Grant, let the minutes reflect that we will recommend to the Erie County Board of Supervisors that the streets intersecting with Genesee Street in the German ward be paved as soon as funding permits. Have we other business to attend?" Looking around the room, none of the other physicians indicated any other matters needing the Board's attention. "Good. Dr. Hunt will attend our next meeting to present his research on the issue of climactic conditions and the spread of cholera. I move to adjourn so that we might get back to it."

"Seconded," chimed in Dr. Grant.

"All in favor? Good. Thank you gentlemen and Godspeed." Dr. Ryan rose from his chair and exited with Dr. Papineaw just behind him.

"Well, I'd best be off if I'm to get to Black Rock before my shift at the hospital," Dr. Grant commented as he stood and buttoned his coat.

"I'll see ye there," Michael said looking at his watch. He decided as he walked toward his horse that he had some time to stop at the poor farm and have a quick word with Dr. Ferris. His old friend would undoubtedly be there to check on his chronic patients right about now. Ferris would be pleased to hear of the Board's decision to inspect the poorhouse and would appreciate a few days notice to generate his own list of concerns about the institution.

* * *

Dr. Alvin Ferris raised his hand and gingerly tilted the head of his patient toward the window so he could better examine her eyes, the wretching and groans from other patients audible behind the screen that separated this woman from those with the deadly cholera. Lucinda Gefroren had the worst case of chronic ophthalmia he had ever seen, as if the woman didn't have enough problems. The green discharge had nearly glued her eyes shut. Mrs. Gefroren had come to the poorhouse nearly a decade before because she experienced periodic fits and could not work. How she was still alive after all this time, when a similar condition took the lives of three of her own five children, her mother, grandmother, aunt, and three of her nieces, was a mystery to all of the physicians who had treated her over the years. Now forty-seven years old, she had long ago lost track of her two surviving sons, who had been bound out as farm laborers when their mother was sent to the poorhouse. At seventeen and eighteen years old they would have found their own way in the world or have perished by now, she knew not which.

"Mrs. McGowen!" Dr. Ferris looked around for the matron of the sick room, as it was called by the inmates. A kind old widow, Janet McGowen did the best she could to care for those in the hospital wing. But she had arthritis in her hips and knees, the result of a lifetime of work as a laundress. She wasn't terribly efficient with her tasks but did as she was told and was kind and gentle with the patients.

"Yes, Doctor," the old woman answered as she slowly made her way toward the patient.

"Mrs. McGowen, please prepare a collyrium of rose water, zinc sulfate and wine of opium to bathe Mrs. Gefroren's eyes. I shall need them open to examine them fully."

"Yes, Doctor. Doctor Nolan has come to have a word. He's waitin' just outside the sickroom."

"Thank you, Mrs. McGowen. Please see to Mrs. Gefroren's collyrium and I'll be back in a moment."

The hospital wing had its own entrance from the street because it not only served poorhouse inmates, but also those residents of the city who could not afford to be seen in their home by a physician. Ferris saw Michael standing by the bench just inside the main door. "Dr. Nolan, good day to you, sir."

"Good day to ye, Dr. Ferris. I'm that sorry to be interruptin' yer rounds, but I'd like a word if ye have the time."

"It's no interruption at all. Your visit is perfectly timed. You recall Mrs. Gefroren?" Seeing Michael nod in recognition of the name, he continued. "The poor woman has a most dreadful case of chronic ophthalmia and I was wondering what your thoughts were on the treatment suggested by Dr. Parker in The Journal." The journal he was referring to was the Buffalo Medical Journal and Monthly Review of Medical and Surgical Science, edited by their esteemed colleague Dr. Austin

Flint who also attended patients at the poorhouse hospital.

"I've used both the collyrium and the mercuric ointment on two patients recently with success. How is Mrs. Gefroren otherwise? Any fits of late?"

"No, not in more than a fortnight, though she's been in and out of the hospital wing with chronic ophthalmia over the last six weeks. I was hoping Dr. Parker's treatment would clear it up once and for all."

"I've corresponded with him over the past few months and he continues to have success with cases far worse than the ones I've treated," Michael told him.

"Well, I am hopeful it will provide the poor woman some relief. What brings you here? I would have expected you to be at the cholera hospital."

"I'm on my way there now. How do things stand here?"

"We have two more cases here this morning and neither looks as if they'll survive the night," Ferris replied. "I'll need more help. The widow McGowen has but two other women to help her, which is hardly enough considering there are other patients to tend to as well." Michael detected the fatigue in his friend's voice, which he knew reflected both physical exhaustion and also the weariness that stemmed from repeated requests continuously falling on deaf ears. With many of the other doctors putting in long hours at the cholera hospital, Ferris was the only physician at the poorhouse. "This is only the beginning, I'm afraid. I'm told that 23 more people were admitted to the poorhouse today, most of them widows and children." Cholera in the city meant that not only would many lose their lives, but a fair number of those who survived would lose their wages, jobs and even their homes if they were too sick to work. Ferris thought it more than likely that one or more of those left homeless due to the epidemic had brought the disease to the poorhouse with them, although he did not know how. "There appears no means to stop the spread of this disease." The physician slowly shook his head, frustration evident in his voice, "We dare not close our doors to those left destitute from this disease, for where else could they go?"

Michael felt the same frustration. There simply were not enough trained medical people to manage an epidemic of this magnitude. "We have six students who have been working 'round the clock at the hospital. I dare not ask Dr. Ryan if any of them can be spared, for I know well what the answer would be. Have ye spoke to Morris about sending some more women from the kitchens, or perhaps from the asylum? Surely one or two could manage simple tasks like changing the bed clothes?"

"I expect you know the answer to that question as well. Not an able-bodied person can be spared according to Mr. Morris. To be fair, I'm not sure how many able-bodied are counted among the inmates these days. Two or three fall sick every day and nearly as many dying. If this keeps up, we'll lose nearly half the population!"

Michael looked around to be sure they were alone before he spoke again. "Well, that will soon change, I hope. What I've come to tell ye is that the Board of Health has finally agreed to inspect this wretched place. They'll take their report straight to the County Board of Supervisors."

"You'll forgive me, Michael, if I am less enthusiastic than you had expected. Complaints to the Board fall on deaf ears as long as Morris doesn't ask for anything from them. After the likes of William Proctor stealing the unclaimed dead and selling them off for cadavers, Morris seems an upstanding steward of this institution to them. The man is miserly and cruel, but he's never done a dishonest act in all his days, I daresay. It will be hard to get the Board of Supervisors to act."

"Alvin, have ye still not learned the way of it? We've the Board of Directresses on our side. Now, they've had their hands full keepin' the orphan asylum these past few years, but once they understand that the conditions here could easily find their way over there, they'll move heaven and earth to keep the cholera away from the children." Seeing the confused look on his colleague's face, Michael elaborated. "Ye see, some of the women on the Board of Directresses are the wives of men who are on the County Board of Supervisors." Michael was growing frustrated as Ferris still did not appreciate the significance of what he had just been told. "Don't ye see? If the wives start carryin' on and go to the papers as they have in the past when somethin's got them concerned, the Board will have to act."

"Ah, I see your point now. I remember how Mrs. Farrell could rouse the women when the situation at the poor farm was not to her liking, God rest her soul. I daresay the place started to decline just after she passed."

Michael nodded in agreement, remembering Mrs. Farrell's tireless efforts to improve the quality of life for the city's poor. Many things changed for the worse after her death from pneumonia two years ago. Without the power and influence of Colleen Farrell, Ciara had been consumed with keeping the orphan asylum running, particularly after the Board of Supervisors voted to withdraw municipal support a few years ago. It broke her heart to see the poorhouse fall into disrepair. The women's efforts in recent years had been further hampered by religious differences. Although Colleen Farrell was Roman Catholic, she was the wealthy widow of Cain Farrell, one of the city's founding fathers, and she always seemed to garner enough support to keep the poorhouse inmates well fed and warm in the winter. Ciara was also a Catholic, but without Mrs. Farrell to back her up, she was no match for the Protestant ladies who dominated most charitable societies and had little regard for the county poorhouse.

While Michael's wife didn't have the money and power her mentor had possessed, she was not without a few allies of her own. The Board of Directresses for the Buffalo Orphan Asylum recently welcomed among its members Maeve Farrell Malone, daughter of Cain and Colleen and daughter-in-law of esteemed attorney, Charles Malone. Charles Malone was an original member of the Board of Supervisors, and his son, Charles, Jr., currently sat on the Board. Another important and recent addition to the Board of Directresses was Anke Metz Farrell, wife of Sean, who had inherited Farrell Flower and Seed Company and was every bit the man to be reckoned with as his father Cain was.

"So, it's up to the women, then?" Alvin Ferris asked.

"It always is, man, and no mistake." Michael clapped his colleague on the shoulder and turned to leave. He turned back just before he opened the door that lead out and smiled. "They've yet to disappoint!"

Chapter Seven

February 4, 2015

Maude woke as if coming out of hibernation, disoriented and struggling, again, to figure out where she was. It did not take her long to realize that she had been dreaming again. The vivid images that had occupied her mind while she slept were not all together unpleasant. She had dreamt of the poorhouse, and the cholera epidemic that plagued the city in the mid-nineteenth century. In the middle of all that, her mind had conjured the Nolan family again and Maude found it curious that her subconscious had given them prominent roles in the story it was telling. The most confusing part of these dreams was figuring out what was triggering them, which she mentioned to Don later that morning over coffee.

"You should write your dreams down," he suggested. "You've been struggling to start your novel, but maybe if you start recording your dreams, an idea will come to you."

"I suppose, but I wanted my story to be based on Ciara Nolan's journal and the struggle to get the orphan asylum up and running. The 1849 cholera epidemic occurred after that point in history. I have no idea how the poorhouse or the orphanage fared during those times, let alone what Ciara Nolan was up to."

"Spoken like a social scientist, not a novelist, Maudie." Don took a sip of his coffee before continuing. "Maybe this is the story you are supposed to write. You have a peculiar connection with the poorhouse and the people who were there; maybe the dreams are telling you to write this story instead of the one you had intended." Don was a very open minded guy, always willing to listen to what the universe had to tell him.

"Maybe, but right now I'm more interested in what happened to Sherman Carrington. Maybe there's a story there, too. The mysterious disappearance of a wealthy medical student sounds more interesting."

"I would still write down what's going through your head, the dreams, the ring, Sherman Carrington. Maybe you'll connect the dots in the process."

Maude was still thinking about her husband's advice later that afternoon when the bell above the shop announced a visitor. "Abby, thanks for coming. Here let me take that from you."The genealogist handed over her canvas bag, which was filled to overflowing with notebooks and file folders, tapped the excess snow off her boots and followed Maude to the front counter.

"I have to say, your message piqued my curiosity. I was watching the clock all morning, waiting to find out what mystery you stumbled across."

Maude chuckled, "Sorry to be so cryptic, I just didn't want to leave you a long winded message. Come on back and I'll show you what we found."

After a quick inspection of the ring and a more careful perusal of the news clipping, Abby was thoughtful for a moment before she spoke. "Boy, you weren't kidding. There must be some fascinating secrets attached to this story. What can I do to help?"

"Well, I'm wondering if I can use my gift certificate to unravel this mystery instead of building my family tree. There are two areas in which I think you can help. I am interested to know more about this building and who owned it in 1849. I am also wondering about

Sherman Carrington and the circumstances surrounding his disappearance."

"I don't see why not. Let's take Mr. Carrington first. I'll check the city directories and period newspapers and see what I can find out about the family and Sherman's disappearance. I know 1849 is too early for a death certificate, but I can at least check for an obituary. Often the deaths of prominent citizens were mentioned in the newspaper."

"He was a medical student, so maybe the university has some record of him. Do you think their admission records go back that far?"

"I don't know. You might try the History of Medicine Library. They may have the records from the early years of the medical school," Abby offered.

"Good point. I'll take a look. Is it reasonable to meet again in a few weeks?"

"I think so. Thanks for including me in this. I'm really looking forward to learning more."

"Thank you for helping me. This kind of research is a bit outside my scope. It is a huge help to work with someone with more experience. My biggest obstacle is not knowing where to look to find out what I need to know. I really appreciate your help."

"I am happy to do it. What about the ring? Do you know anything about it?"

"I know its approximate age, but I would have to have it appraised in order to find out what it's worth now, and more importantly, what it was worth then," Maude replied. "I have some contacts that specialize in antique jewelry, so I'll make a few calls. Maybe I'll have more to tell you when we meet again."

"Sounds good. I'll be in touch." Abby reached for her bag, the weight of it evident as she slung it over her shoulder.

"What on earth do you have in there?"

"I have about three different projects I am working on right now and I find it easier to have everything with me, rather than having to repack my bag every day."

"If I had thought of that while I was working on my dissertation, I probably would have finished a year earlier! Keep in touch."

"Will do."

In the weeks after the New Year, traffic into the shop usually came to a screeching halt as consumers received startling reminders of their holiday spending with the arrival of their credit card bills. Typically any home renovating/remodeling or spontaneous shopping would pick up in the spring. In recent years, since her involvement with the poorhouse cemetery project, Maude had come to welcome this time, when there were long afternoons she could spend in front of her laptop without interruption. When Abby left, Maude decided it would be a good time to ponder the dreams she'd been having, organize her thoughts, and take another stab at her novel. Once her fingers hit the keyboard words flew out like they were being channeled through a medium, and the past came to life on her screen.

July 10, 1849

Martha stood just outside the back door of the hospital in hopes of catching a breeze. Even before dawn the summer air was hot and heavy with the stench of stomach acid and feces, and she needed just a moment before going back inside. The sound of footsteps approaching from within signaled that her break was over before it had even begun. "Miss Sloane, you are needed inside." The tall man leaned out of the open door, taking full advantage of a few seconds outside the building . "A woman has just come in and Dr. Grant needs your assistance."

Martha was not prepared for what she saw when she returned to the main floor of the hospital. A young woman with barely the strength to keep her eyes open was clutching with all her might the infant - clearly dead - that she held in her arms. Another child, almost skeletal, lay beside her in the small cot. Dr. Grant looked to be trying, without success, to get the mother to part with her stillborn babe. The tall man approached, taking the opportunity while the poor woman was distracted, to gently remove the small girl from the cot. Martha had come up behind him and silently waited for the physician to notice her.

Dr. Grant turned from the patient, and in a low voice, he explained the situation. "Mrs. Suhn was found about an hour ago in a state of collapse. Whether from the cholera or child bed fever, we have yet to ascertain. Either way, I fear there is little to be done for her." He looked back in the direction of the patient and lowered his voice further to be sure he would not be overheard.

"She was holding both the older girl and the stillborn child to her breast when her husband discovered her. He could not get her to relinquish the babe. Miss Sloane, please do what you can to get the infant from her while I see to the husband. He looks to be in the very early stages of the disease himself."

Martha approached the woman, whose face was flushed with fever, eyes open but unfocused. "There's a fine lad ye have there, Mrs. Suhn." The woman pressed the lifeless infant closer to her breast. Martha placed a hand on the patient's forehead, caressing along her face down to her throat and gently probed in search of a carotid pulse. Dr. Grant had been accurate in his prognosis: there was nothing to be done for her. Before she broke contact, Martha had a brief vision of the woman, seated in her own kitchen, the bright sunshine streaming through the window as the babe suckled contentedly from her breast. The older daughter was also there, chubby arms and legs protruding from a crisp white dress, as she jumped into her father's arms. Martha understood that what she was seeing was the peace they would enjoy when their souls rose to heaven. "Now, now, don't ye fret. I'm no' here to take the babe from ye. Just ye sleep now and when ye wake, it will all be better." Mrs. Suhn's eyes began to close, she had not the strength to keep them open, as Martha wiped her brow with a damp cloth. "Rest, Mrs. Suhn."

"Is she gone?" The tall man had returned and was watching Martha as she said a small prayer for the woman and her children.

"Not yet, Mr. Carrington, but soon, I hope, for she goes to a much better place." In response to his nod toward the dead child, she simply said, "I couldn't bear to force the babe from her arms. What of her daughter?"

"She is in the final stages of the cholera, but is fretful since I have taken her away from her mother." Sherman Carrington gestured at the poor child, curled up so tight she was hardly discernable from the pillow on which she rested.The roundness of her one visible eye in search of her mother and the tiniest whimper betrayed the child's anxiety and nearly broke Martha's heart.

"Bring her back here," she directed. "I'll have the time she has left be as peaceful as can be in this place." Her classmate just stared,uncomprehending. Dr. Grant would not approve of all of the fuss over patients for which there was no hope, so it seemed a poor use of his time to move the child. "Mr. Carrington, the poor wee thing has but a few hours left. Would ye have her meet her end with fear in her heart, and ye could do somethin' about it?" Without waiting for an answer, Martha walked over to the child and scooped her up, scrawny limbs hanging lifelessly. "There lass, just ye rest with yer ma and yer wee brother." The girl settled into the cot next to her mother with a sigh and was asleep before Martha could raise the sheet to her shoulders.

Sherman stood there, ashamed to admit that he really hadn't given the girl a second thought. He had only mentioned her because Martha asked. Before she had finished her kind words to the child, he had moved on, eager to redirect his attention to the many other patients in need of care.

Martha moved on as well to the boy who had come in a few days earlier. He was found in a small stable in the First Ward. A man had heard him vomiting when he had come in to feed the pigs. Myron Crim, only twelve years old, was in the second stage of the disease then. He was a large lad; with proper care, he might just live. "Ye've finished yer beef tea, there's a good lad." She placed a hand on his brow; he was sweating - they all were - but he had no fever.

"I'm feeling that much better, ma'am and I'd like to be on my way. My grandparents are expecting me."

The tattered boots beneath his bed indicated that Myron had walked a considerable distance. "Are they in Buffalo?"

"Yes, ma'am. I came all the way from Sandusky, ma'am, that's in Ohio. Do ye know Ohio?"

"I've heard of it, yes. What brings ye all this way?"

"I lost Pa last winter, the feet froze right off him. It was just the two of us and then it was just me. My ma's folks live in Buffalo. I've been making my way here since the spring, workin' when I could for my bed and supper, and livin' off the land when I had to. I was nearly here when I took sick."

A twelve-year-old boy walking across the country to find his kin…it wasn't the most remarkable thing she had ever heard of, but it was rather amazing that he had made it here alive. The lad certainly had not starved along the way, a factor that favored his ultimate recovery. Still, he would need to regain his strength before he could be released from the hospital. "Will ye tell me yer granda's name so that we might let him know ye're here?"

"Well, I'm named for him, ma'am. His name's Myron, same as me: Myron Dowell. He's a blacksmith."

Martha reached for the boy's wrist to take his pulse. Strong and steady, but another few days rest and solid food would protect him against a relapse. "Well, just ye keep to yer cot for another day or so while I find yer granda. 'Tis hard work he does and ye'll need yer strength if ye're to learn the trade."

Myron smiled at the thought of working side by side with his grandfather, learning to be a blacksmith. "I expect ye're right, ma'am, and I thank ye for yer kindness."

Martha smiled and turned to make her way to the next patient when she was stopped by Dr. Grant. "Miss Sloane, there are five beds that need fresh linen. See to it and then go home."

"Yes, Doctor." Although she noticed the male students who had started the shift with her had not been given additional chores before they were sent home, she said nothing. The nurses were as overburdened as the doctors, more so as they were in charge of changing and laundering the soiled bed clothes and keeping the ward clean in addition to helping with the patients. She would not deny them the help they desperately needed, even if it undermined her status as a medical student with the other men.

The old kitchen served as storage for just about everything from linens to tin basins. Martha was surprised to see Sherman and another student, Erik Schuster, exit carrying a stack of clean bed linen. "This will go by faster if we work together," Erik said as he handed her some sheets.

"That's most kind of ye, gentlemen and I thank ye." The three students worked hastily in silence. Every chore had to be done with ruthless efficiency. With ten to fifteen new patients per day, these beds would not stay empty for long. Many of the patients they had seen throughout the evening would pass before they came back for their next shift, including Mrs. Suhn and her daughter.

"I thank ye, again, Mr. Carrington, Mr. Schuster," Martha said as they exited the hospital.

"It hardly seemed fair, us leaving it for you to do when we all started the shift together, isn't that right, Carrington," Erik told her.

Sherman nodded in agreement and smiled, but in truth it would not have occurred to him to stay and help had Mr. Schuster not cajoled him into it.

"Well, ye best get to yer beds, for we must meet back here at sunset," Martha reminded them. There were a total of six medical students still in Buffalo from the currently enrolled class. Along with the attending physicians, the students took twelve hour shifts at the hospital. Martha, Erik and Sherman had worked through the night. Each would get a few hours sleep before helping the physicians working in the tenements and then heading back to the hospital again. Their schedules were full, considering that classes were currently not in session.

"Hello, Martha."

She turned to see a large man with cropped dark hair and a neatly trimmed beard approaching her. "Johnny! When did ye get back?" She wanted to hug him, but resisted, not wanting to have to explain herself to her colleagues, although they were already on their way. It was always awkward introducing Johnny to others. They had grown up together, yet he was not her brother. She had never thought of him in that way. To say he was a friend of the family didn't seem right either. He was more than that. As a girl, she was certain they would be married, but then he finished school and moved in with Michael's parents. His work kept him away from the Nolan farm often during those years. Recently, between his traveling and her studies, she had not seen him in almost a year.

"I've been back about a week and I daresay I won't be leavin' again until this is over," he gestured with his head toward the hospital. "I stopped by the farm to have a word with Rolland. Patricia said yer shift was just about over if I had a mind to see ye home, so here I am."

"I'm glad of it and I imagine Charlie is as well. He's enough work to do without havin' to stop everything to come and pick me up."

"Aye, he's a busy man, is Charlie," Johnny said as he helped her into the carriage.

Martha ran her hand over the smooth leather padding of the seat and took in the fine clothes that Johnny was wearing. He had grown into a man, respected among his peers. He still walked with a slight limp, the only vestige of the compound fracture that had gone septic when he was a child. Had it not been for Ciara and Michael, Johnny might have died at the poorhouse. "'Tis a fine carriage. Is it new?"

"Aye, I picked it up in Albany on my last trip. She's a beauty." He was silently pleased that she had noticed. Johnny had realized long ago that Martha was special, not just because she had the second sight, but because she had a rare gift as a healer. He knew that firsthand. He was eight when he had broken his leg and she was not quite five. It took months to fully recover from the resulting infection, and weeks after that before he could walk. He never would have had the courage to get through it if not for her help and encouragement. Martha had a calling. Johnny had realized it when she was just a girl and, as she grew older, he had not wanted to stand in the way of the work God had put her here to do. Martha would go forward and do great things, but she had noticed that he was doing well for himself too and that made him happy.

They passed the short journey home catching each other up, he telling of all of the interesting places he'd visited, while she relayed her experiences during her first term in medical school. Although they would go long periods of time without seeing each other, they were always able to pick up just where they left off. "So the lads I saw ye with, they're students too?" Johnny wasn't sure why he felt the need to ask. Maybe he just wanted to hear more about her life and the people in it, or maybe he noticed the way one of them was looking at her.

Chapter Eight

July 19, 1849

Dr. Matthew Ryan knew he was in for it the moment he exited the hospital and saw Michael Nolan approaching on horseback. Ryan could be a coward and go back inside; he knew Michael hadn't seen him yet. But he owed his fellow board member an explanation after the inspection of the county poorhouse had been delayed indefinitely. Michael dismounted before the mare even came to a complete stop, having finally spotted the City Health Officer.

"Dr. Ryan, a word if ye please." While his tone was even, the lack of a formal greeting left no doubt as to Michael's mood.

"Dr. Nolan, I know what you're here about and I shouldn't have to remind you that we are in the middle of an epidemic. There simply isn't time to do a formal inspection of the poorhouse. As fast as a bed is empty here, it is occupied again. We are losing this battle, I fear."

"Dr. Ryan, do I need to remind ye that for every person that perishes within these walls, two die at the poor farm."

"No, Michael, you needn't remind me again. I've already spoken with Dr. Ferris, and he and I both paid a call on Mr. Morris at his home. As the City Health Officer, I have given Morris an official warning to clean up the wards, provide more help to the hospital wing and make the additions to the daily diet of the inmates and patients that Dr. Ferris has requested."

"That's not enough and well ye know it," Michael argued.

"At Dr. Ferris' request, the laundry and cooking facilities will be moved up from basement to temporary facilities out of doors. Removing them from the miasma that festers there should reduce the risk of disease for the inmates who work in those areas. Beyond that, temporary quarters for the insane are being built so that the necessary accommodations and repairs to the ward can be undertaken." Dr. Ryan was growing impatient with this conversation and was just too tired to keep his tone neutral. "Does that meet with your approval, Dr. Nolan?"

"And what assurances do ye have that Morris will comply?"

"I've told him to do what must be done or face a full inquiry from the Board of Supervisors, but he's made a fair point that there are few able-bodied inmates to carry out the daily chores, let alone undertake the building that must be done. Hiring laborers for the job will cost the county more money."

Michael groaned in frustration, taking his handkerchief and wiping the back of his neck. "So, what ye're tellin' me is that yer instructions have, once again, fallen on deaf ears."

"Man, have you not heard a word I've said? We are in a battle here that we are losing. Every minute we spend arguing about the poorhouse is a minute we have not spent trying to save the lives of the people right here. I have done all I can and now we need to focus on the people who are right in front of us and leave the poor farm to Dr. Ferris. I'm sorry, Michael."

Michael watched the man climb into his carriage and drive away. Dr. Ryan's body swayed with exhaustion as the carriage continued down the road. He was right. There was no time for a formal inspection of the poorhouse, not with twenty new patients each day arriving here at the hospital in the late stages of the disease. It was time to rally the women. Michael had known it would come to that. He headed into the hospital in search of Martha. Her shift would be up soon and she could carry home a message for Ciara.

* * *

Erik Schuster watched again as Martha proceeded without argument or grudge to collect the pails under each bed and replace them with clean ones. Typically, the emptying and scrubbing of the vomit encrusted pails was a chore for the nurses, but Dr. Ryan had called on Martha. Perhaps the man was too weary to distinguish her among the other women who were usually assigned such chores, or perhaps he was making a statement, as some of the other physicians had. She was, after all, a woman. Should she not help with the women's work? Scanning the room, Schuster could see no sign of Carrington and assumed he had disappeared the minute their shift had ended. With a groan, Erik caught up with Martha and took the pails from her, being careful not to allow their contents to slosh over the edge.

"Let me get these, and you can grab the ones over there," He gestured toward a cluster of cots that contained a group of small children, siblings by the look of them.

"I thank ye, Mr. Schuster, but ye must be weary to the bone. Away wi' ye home. It won't take me but a few minutes to finish this up."

"It will go faster, Miss Sloane, if we work together. I wish you would call me Erik. I would like to think we have become friends."

Martha smiled. "Ye have been most kind to me, and yes, we are friends, Erik, and so ye must call me Martha. I thank ye again for yer help."

Outside they worked silently in the hot morning sun, both too tired to think of anything to say. Finally, Erik asked her, "Why do you not say something when the doctors give you chores they should be asking of the nurses? Surely you have noticed that they do not assign the rest of us such tasks."

Martha rinsed the final bucket and left it in the sun to dry with the others. "What would ye have me say?

The nurses are working as hard as the rest of us and I wouldn't begrudge them a helping hand - and they needed it." Martha wiped her wet hands on her apron not willing to say what she really felt. To speak up in her own defense would only subvert whatever progress she was making in gaining the respect of her superiors and her peers. Erik nodded, understanding both what she said and what she didn't say. The two students walked back toward the hospital to drop the clean buckets by the back door chatting about what they looked forward to most when they were no longer needed at the hospital.

"A good night's sleep first thing," Martha said, "and then I would like to be of more help at home. My sister is with child, so I am needed to help keep her house during her confinement. What about ye?"

"I dare not say after you have expressed such noble intentions," he told her, but after some coaxing, he admitted, "I would like to enjoy my supper. All too often I must choke it down. Worse yet, I have woken with my head in my plate and potatoes stuck to my whiskers!"

That admission made Martha laugh out loud. It might have been the heat, or the fact that she was so weary she could barely walk, but the more she attempted to contain her mirth, the more she sputtered and hiccupped. Soon she was laughing uncontrollably at the thought of Erik Schuster sound asleep in his boiled potatoes. Her amusement was contagious and soon he was chuckling with her.

"Martha, a word if ye please." Seeing Michael standing near the back door of the hospital looking cross brought the moment to an abrupt end. Martha quickly thanked Erik again for his help and hurried over to her brother-in-law.

Erik deposited the clean pails by the door without comment and walked toward his carriage, leaving the two in discussion. Although he tried to look uninterested, adjusting the horse's harness, he was able to hear pieces of their conversation. Dr. Nolan had issued some instructions and Martha had agreed she would set out straightaway. It seemed apparent she would not get the sleep she longed for any time soon. Erik did not have time to register that thought when he heard the doctor call his name.

"Mr. Schuster, would ye be kind enough to see Miss Sloane home?"

Erik looked around. There was always someone there to see Martha safely home. Usually it was Dr. Nolan's stable man, the one with the severe limp. The other day, he noticed that a different man, younger and more prosperous by his look, had come and that Martha had been very glad to see him. Erik had wanted to ask about that man, but feared it would have been inappropriate to do so. Today there was nobody waiting for her. He nodded. "It would be my pleasure, Dr. Nolan."

"I thank ye, sir." Helping Martha into the carriage, he told her, "Be sure and have yer sister go straightaway. There's no time to be wasted."

"Yes, doctor, I will tell her first thing." Martha did not address her brother-in-law by his first name in front of her colleagues. She settled herself in the carriage and waited for Erik to climb in. Soon they were off. Martha did not offer any details of her conversation with Michael and Erik did not ask.

* * *

Ciara made herself comfortable in the sitting room of Anke Farrell while the mistress of the house welcomed her young sister-in-law. When the three women were seated and the tea was poured they got down to business.

"Now, Ciara, what can we do to help you?" Maeve Farrell Malone asked.

"I thank ye, Maeve, for askin'. Since yer ma's death, I am ashamed to say that we have all but abandoned those whom God still considers worthy of his love. Michael tells me that the cholera is a vicious foe at the almshouse, and his concerns continue to be ignored. The poor souls are in need of a clean place to lay their heads and wholesome food to nourish their bodies if they are to survive this dreadful plague."

The other two women listened carefully as Ciara told of the penny-pinching and mismanagement that had left the institution badly equipped to fight the deadly cholera as it made its way through the poorhouse. Maeve spoke first, "Mother would never have let things deteriorate into such a state, sure enough. What can be done?"

"The City Health Officer has issued an official reprimand and has left a list of improvements that must be completed," Ciara reported. "'Tis a start sure enough, but Michael fears naught will come of it."

"I do not understand what we can do to help beyond what has already been done." Anke was a kind and generous woman, but she was nothing like her late mother-in-law. Colleen would have sweet-talked her husband, rallied the other women and demanded the newspapers make public her concerns. As a result of her efforts and those of her allies, mismanagement had not taken root at the poorhouse, until now. Anke was a good wife and would not consider any action that might embarrass her husband, so it would not occur to her to do any of those things. Maeve, however, was her mother's daughter.

Maeve knew that Ciara was asking them to use the influence their names and - more importantly - their husbands, offered. "So we need to make sure that the improvements at the poorhouse are carried out as soon as possible. What would mother have done?"

Ciara smiled, knowing that she had come to the right people. Maeve would not hesitate to speak to her husband and her mother-in-law, who had often been an ally of Colleen's. Anke adored her young sister-in-law, and since Maeve and Ciara presented a compelling case, Anke would take her concerns to Sean to see what could be done. Sean was also no stranger to his mother's tactics when it came to affecting change and he considered Ciara and Michael among his dearest friends. It would not take much to get his support.

Confident that the matter was well in hand, Ciara explained the details to her husband later that night as they readied themselves for bed, a ritual they seldom had the luxury of enjoying these days. "I should think members of the Board of Supervisors would be wise to stay on the good side of Sean Farrell."

"What of the other women on the board?" he asked.

"Oh, Michael, things have changed so since Colleen passed. We manage well enough with the orphan asylum. We're mostly mothers, after all, and share a concern for the children's welfare. The poorhouse is another matter entirely. Now that the orphan asylum is a private charitable institution, the board of directresses has dropped any pretense of concern for what goes on at the poor farm." About eight years ago Kathleen Proctor used her considerable influence to convince the county to pull its support from the Buffalo Orphan Asylum, which was once a municipal entity and managed under the Superintendent of the Poor. She was furious at Ciara for exposing her son's involvement in the stealing and subsequent illegal sale of deceased inmates to Geneva Medical College for dissection. William Proctor, then the Keeper of the Poorhouse, had been caught in the laboratory of the medical school rifling through the pockets of a cadaver in search of money. Kathleen had been determined to seek revenge.

"I daresay Mrs. Proctor did ye a favor, although that was not her intention." Michael took the brush from his wife and continued to speak as he brushed her hair. "The orphan asylum would hardly have been spared the wrath of this dreaded disease were it still located on the poor farm."

Ciara leaned into the brush as the bristles pressed against her scalp. "It hasn't been easy to keep the orphanage going, to be sure, but I agree, we're better off without the support of the county. Before, our needs were the county's lowest priority. Now we are blessed with a number of benefactors who provide for the children. 'Tis remarkable how many children are in need and how many orphan homes have opened their doors since Mrs. Farrell and the Christian Ladies Charitable Society began their work."

"What I find curious is that we are beginning to see new orphan homes established so that the children would be raised in their proper faith. There are places for homeless children to find their God, yet still only one poor farm where God has apparently abandoned those who need him most," Michael remarked.

Ciara turned to face her husband. "Michael, God has not abandoned those people, but we have. I once called that place home and now it seldom enters my thoughts let alone my prayers. I am a poor excuse for a Christian woman, so I am."

Michael tried to continue brushing, but she waved him away. "Ciara, love, ye're only one woman, and have ye not been busy these last years with the raisin' of yer own lads? And still ye have not forgotten all the children ye love so." It was true. In the years since the orphan asylum had moved Ciara's life had been consumed with the raising of her own children and trying to keep the new facility on Pearl Street from falling down around them. In truth, the loss of support of the county meant that they had to seek additional donations over and above those for food, clothing and medicine to maintain the new building. When they were a county institution, able-bodied men and women from the poorhouse helped with everything from caring for the children to keeping the grounds and buildings in repair. Ciara was horrified to realize that she had spared the poor farm and its occupants few thoughts over the years.

"Aye, 'tis true enough, but what would have become of my sisters and me if we hadn't been taken in there? Sure enough, it would have been different for us if not for those months in the poorhouse, all of us." Ciara was not just referring to her sisters, but to the rest of the people who shared their home and were considered family.

"Don't ye fret, love. We've set things in motion and we've help enough to see the job done. Now, come to bed. I've got precious little time left before I'm off again and I don't mean to spend it talkin'."

Chapter Nine

Buffalo Daily Courier

Saturday Morning, July 12, 1849

Office-Main and Lloyd Streets, upstairs

BOARD OF HEALTH
BUFFALO, JULY 11- 11AM

Thirty-nine cases of cholera have been reported by the Board of Health for the last 24 hours-thirteen fatal as follows:

Abigail Smith, Rock St, Cholera Hospital
Samuel Bartell's son, reported on 19th
Mrs. Schoenle, an emigrant
Margaret O'Shea, S. Division St.
Mrs. Anna Suhn, Falsom St., Cholera Hospital
Daughter of A. Suhn, Falsom St. Cholera Hospital
Jacob Suhn, Falsom St., Cholera Hospital
Mrs. Cleary, Eagle St.
Erik, son of D. Schictel, Genesee St.
Greta Scharf, Millicent St.
Mrs. Marianna Meli, Hydraulics
Molly Toole, Batavia St., Cholera Hospital
Julius Welch,State St., Cholera Hospital

F. Hollingsworth, Clerk

Maude stared at her laptop not knowing how to react to what appeared on the screen. Grabbing her empty mug with the assumption that coffee would somehow bring clarity to the situation, she crossed the kitchen to brew a pot. Don had been right. The cholera epidemic demanded a place in the novel. Once she sat down to write, the story became so clear in her mind that the words flowed easily. A quick phone call to Abby revealed that the Board of Health Reports had been printed in the newspaper during the worst of the epidemic. Maude was only looking to add a few authentic details to the tale. She wasn't looking for *them*, and certainly didn't expect to find them, but the Suhn's were real people who had actually lived and died in Buffalo during the cholera epidemic of 1849.

Their story had come so easily and with such vivid details, almost like she had known them, which was ridiculous since they had died over one hundred sixty years ago. The specifics of their experience could not be verified from the report in the newspaper. Maybe that was for the best. It defied explanation how people she had invented for her novel were in fact real. To have confirmation of the details would be freaky.

In truth, the whole situation was freaky. There was the discovery of the ring and the newspaper clipping, then the strange dreams, including Sherman Carrington, and now her apparent ability to write with historic accuracy about people and events that occurred well over a century ago. These recent experiences were not as visceral as were her visions of Frederika Kaiser. The lesson learned from that experience was that she was connected to those people and that link served to bring to light matters that had long been buried. It was unnerving, to say the least, this new connection with the past. It seemed evident that the cholera epidemic in 1849 was somehow linked to the mystery surrounding Sherman Carrington. How it would all play out remained to be seen and she would just have to wait.

"You have to push the button for the machine to work." Maude turned toward the sound of her husband's voice. He was standing in the doorway, dressed with his jacket on. She hadn't even heard him get up. He walked up and gently moved her aside and pushed the button on the coffee machine. "You were lost in your thoughts," he added as he opened the cupboard to get a travel mug for himself.

"Where are you off to?" Maude asked as she went to the fridge in search of cream.

"I'm going to pick up the tile for the bathroom floor. Wake the boys so they can be in and out of there before I get back. I want this project done today so we will have use of the shower by Monday morning." Don handed her a full mug of French roast before pouring his own. "What has you so perplexed that you forgot how to make coffee?"

"How long were you standing there?"

"Long enough to see you had something under serious contemplation."

Maude considered for a moment deflecting the question, but instead decided to share what was on her mind. "Weird things are happening again." Seeing the look of concern cross his face, she hastily added, "Not like before. A few of the characters I am writing about in my book turned out to be real."

"I don't understand. I thought most of the people you were writing about were real?"

"They are, but I made up quite a few, too, you know, to round out particular parts of the story. I was just looking at a report of the cholera deaths during that summer to add some authentic details and I found some characters I developed listed among them." She turned the laptop around so that he could see the newspaper report and pointed to the three members of the Suhn family. "I wrote about a woman, Mrs. Suhn, who was brought in by her husband. He was sick too. She had with her a stillborn baby and a young daughter who was near death. Look, these are the people I was writing about."

Don looked closer at the screen. "I'm guessing that you don't want to hear that it is probably a coincidence."

"What's that supposed to mean?"

"Well, I know you feel connected to these people, but you might be reading too much into this. It makes sense that entire families would die, given that contaminated water was the true source of the disease."

"C'mon Don, I'll admit objectivity is difficult given my past experiences, but I don't think I'm imagining this. I've done some checking. Both Sherman Carrington and Martha Sloane were medical students at the Buffalo Medical College in 1849 and Michael Nolan served on the Board of Health during the epidemic. It was weird enough when parts of my dreams turned out to have really happened, but now apparently my conscious mind is able to conjure up historically accurate details too."

Not convinced, but wise enough not to say so, Don chose his next words carefully. "You have been struggling for a long time to write this story and now you are finally making progress. Do yourself a favor and don't overthink it. Keep writing. The mystery is always revealed in the end." He put the lid on his travel mug and kissed Maude on the cheek. "I'll be back in about an hour."

"Bring back bagels." What else was there to say? Don was right. Overthinking was Maude's specialty. The truth will come out in the end and she would just have to see it through.

"You got it."

Maude closed out the newspaper and clicked open her e-mail. Just as the screen popped open, the phone rang. It was Abby. "Hi, it's me. I need you to check your e-mail right now." She was obviously very excited about something.

"Hi, Abby. Your timing is excellent. I was about to do just that."

"You are not going to believe what I found. I just can't believe it. I wanted to be on the phone with you when you opened my e-mail and saw for yourself."

"Saw what for myself?"

"Open the e-mail. Hurry! I can't stand it!"

"Okay, okay, hang on." Maude put her on speaker phone and clicked open the e-mail. There were two attachments, so she opened the first one. It was a portrait of a woman; or rather it was a photo of the portrait. She was seated with her hands folded in her lap by a grand fireplace, with a Russian Wolfhound laying at her feet. From the clothes and the furnishings, the portrait looked to be from the early nineteenth century. "Who is this?"

"Before I answer that question, open the second attachment." Abby's voice was positively giddy at this point.

There was a brief silence while Maude opened the second file. "Holy crap! She's wearing the ring!" Maude clicked on the photo, a close up of just the woman's hands, to enlarge it. Looking back at the other photo, she noted the ring appeared to be the sole accessory. "Who is this?" she asked again.

"That is Marcia Carrington. The portrait was painted in 1830, the year she married Ashton Carrington. She was Sherman's mother."

"Where on earth did you find this?"

"The Carringtons were a very wealthy family in Albany, old money from England. That portrait hangs in the family's home in the Hudson Valley. It's an Inn now. The portrait was in their online brochure."

"What are the odds? How did you get the close up of the ring?"

"Would you believe I'm here now? I noticed the ring in the brochure. It was too small to really tell if it was your ring from that picture. Bruce and I were due for a weekend away, so I booked a room yesterday and here we are. The portrait is in the main sitting room. I had Bruce stand watch while I snapped the pictures." Her voice dropped to a conspiratorial whisper as she told Maude how she had to remove her boots and stand on the Queen Anne chair to get a good shot. "It gets even better. I bought a book on the Carrington family history in the gift shop."

"I can't believe this! Have you had a chance to read it? Does it mention Sherman's disappearance?"

"No, I haven't. I'm really hoping it will give us some information on what happened to him. I did a search of all of the period newspapers and there was only the article that you had already found."

"Well, you have certainly earned the rest of the weekend off. Go and have a good time with your husband and we can talk when you get back."

"We'll be back late on Monday, so I'll call you first thing Tuesday morning."

Maude hung up the phone and looked at the pictures again. The ring was the most beautiful thing in the portrait. Marcia Carrington could best be described as plain. Not unattractive, but not beautiful. She wore her hair up in a simple bun, like most women did. Her hands were slender and pale against the grey silk dress. It was almost as if the ring was the focal point of the portrait. "The ring belonged to Sherman's mother. How on earth did it get underneath my floorboards?"

Maude took a long sip of coffee and pondered Don's advice. Don't overthink it and keep writing, he said. Let the story play out and all will be revealed in the end. "Well, I guess I should get back to work."

Chapter Ten

August 3, 1849

Johnny sat at the kitchen table with Ciara and the boys, nibbling at his breakfast of cheese and bread. It was way too hot to eat, even for him. Ian and Daniel were excited to be working with the men on the addition to Patricia and Rolland's house instead of in the barn with Charlie cleaning harnesses and mucking stalls. Ciara could not help but smile as she watched her sons hanging on every word as Johnny carefully explained their tasks for the day. She packed a basket of cold chicken and ale for the men to enjoy later, but did not bother packing a lunch for the lads because she knew they would tire of working in the heat and sneak off to the shade of the woods to cool off. When Daniel was hungry, they would return home for lunch.

The sound of a wagon coming up the drive brought their discussion to an abrupt close. "That'll be

Martha," Daniel said as he stood to see out the window. "She's got a wee lass with her."

"Stay here," Johnny and Ciara said to the boys in unison as they got up and headed toward the door. As the wagon approached the house they could see Martha had a small girl who looked to be about four years old asleep in her arms. Johnny reached up and helped them out of the carriage.

Charlie looked at Ciara and said, "I couldn't get her to take the child to the orphan home," by way of an explanation before he directed the horse toward the barn.

Martha took a moment to adjust the dead weight of a sleeping child before she spoke. "I just couldn't take her there, sister."

"Okay, let's get the poor soul out of this heat and ye can tell us." Ciara ushered her sister toward the door.

Johnny held her back, looking at the child suspiciously. "Wait, the lass's not sick, is she?"

"No, she came in with her ma early this morning. Her ma was found collapsed in a tenement on Mortimer Street. She was dead by the time they got her to the hospital. The wee lass is deaf, I think." Martha smiled and gently brushed the damp strands of hair from the child's face. "She took to me straightaway. I couldn't bring her to the orphan home, and her so frightened."

Ciara walked around Johnny and opened the door. "Let's get her settled and then we'll talk." She immediately put her finger to her lips to signal to the boys to be quiet. "Away ye down to Rolland's with Johnny," she whispered. "Tell Patricia I'll be down in a bit. Martha, just ye go put the lass down on the settee and I'll get ye a bit of somethin' to eat."

Martha walked into the parlor and sat down with the child still in her arms. The girl began to fuss as she tried to lay her down. Instead, Martha held her until she settled again. The weight of the sleeping child relaxed her into bonelessness. A cool breeze from the window just behind the settee caressed the back of Martha's neck, and with a sigh she was asleep. Ciara came in and placed the plate on the side table, closing the door on her way out.

* * *

Heading down the small hill to Patricia's house, Ciara noticed the boys had been diverted to the barn. She knocked on the door and then let herself in. It was no surprise to find Patricia, Rolland and Johnny seated at the kitchen table. "So, ye've heard, I expect, about our wee visitor?"

"Tell us, sister, is the lass deaf?"

"I don't know, Patricia. The two of them are sound asleep. All I know is her ma died and Martha thinks she's deaf. I suppose we'll know more after they've had a good rest."

"Her ma, she died of the cholera, Johnny told us. Will the child get sick, then?" Rolland asked.

"Martha says the child is not sick," Johnny answered, "but she's not told us if she could become sick."

"Michael says the cholera is not catching," Ciara reminded them, "But if the child falls ill, he'll know what to do."

"Ye seem to be unconcerned that yer sister has brought home a child who is likely deaf and may become gravely ill."

"There's nothing to be concerned about yet, Rolland," Ciara answered. "Martha saw a child in need and brought her home. I'll hear what she has to say before I settle my own mind on the matter. If we can help the lass, we surely will."

"Ye'll want to see if she has a father or other kin," he continued. Rolland was not convinced that this girl did not pose a danger to Patricia and their unborn child and thought they should determine straight away if there was another, more suitable place to bring her.

"Rolland, ye know well that the women at the orphan asylum could not manage a deaf child, or a child sick with the cholera for that matter," Patricia told him. "Martha would not have brought her here were there any other place she could go."

"Aye, I know that, love, I do. I am only thinking of ye and the babe. I would feel better were ye to stay here, in our house, until we know more."

"I think Rolland is right, sister. Ye must stay here at least until Michael has had a chance to examine the child," Ciara told her. "I must get back. The lass will need a bath and some clean clothes when she wakes. Ye'll keep the lads down here?"

"Aye, we best get to work, for all we have lost any cool the morning had to offer," Johnny said as he rose from the table.

It was late afternoon before the occupants of the parlor woke. Martha shared the plate of food with the young girl before they emerged. The child was a sight to be sure. The hair that had escaped from her braid, now damp with sweat, clung around her chin and neck. The poor waif had wet herself while she slept and the front of her dress was soaked. Martha looked at the wet spot on her own dress and was silently grateful the child had soiled it and not the settee, although Ciara would not have been concerned if she had.

Ciara pulled out the tub from the storage space underneath the stairs and then thought better of it and put the tub back. The child had just lost her mother; a bath could wait. Instead she filled a bucket with water and set it aside with a small cloth and towel. She was just about to peek in the door of the parlor when Martha approached from the hall. "It looks like ye're both needin' a change," Ciara said, detecting the strong smell of urine even before seeing their wet clothes.

"Aye, we're both needin' a good bath as well, but it will have to wait, I think. Are the lads still workin' then?"

"The men are, but the lads were in for a bite before they were off again. I don't expect we'll see them until supper." Ciara reached out for the child. "Away with ye and change yer dress. I'll just get to know the wee lass. Does she have a name?"

"Her ma was found collapsed in her home. She never spoke, so I don't know her name. I'm not sure it matters, though, since she can't hear," Martha said as she handed off her new companion. Although the girl could not hear her, Martha said "Now don't ye fret, I'll be right back." The smile in her eyes seemed to reassure the child and she did not fuss when Martha left the room.

The young girl lifted her hands and placed them one on each side of Ciara's face and stared into her eyes, as if trying to take the measure of the woman. Ciara waited patiently until the girl smiled and dropped her hands. "Now ye must be wantin' out of those wet things," she said and took the child over to where a clean set of clothes was folded neatly next to the bucket and towel. Ciara unfolded afresh pair of pantalets, a small shift and a calico dress that had once belonged to Martha. She offered them to the girl in an attempt to help her understand she could change her clothes. The child nodded in acknowledgement and turned so that Ciara could undo the fastenings of her dress. It was obvious from both the smell and from the girls red bottom that it wasn't the first time she had wet herself. "It's no' so bad. We'll just let ye run about in yer shift for a while."

Ciara took the small towel and dipped it into the cool water and gently wiped the child's face. "Now this surely will help ye to feel better." She continued to speak while wiping behind her ears and neck, as she had for hundreds of children over the years who had come to the orphan asylum in much the same predicament. Many frightened and withdrawn children had found themselves comforted by her soothing voice. Although this child could not hear the words, she was nevertheless calmed by Ciara's warm eyes and gentle touch and stood without protest until she was clean. "Aye, yer hair could use a good washin'... but I expect we can wait a day or so," she continued as she helped the lass into her shift. She presented the child with a comb and loosened the leather tie that held the remains of the braid to indicate that her ablutions were not quite done yet.

* * *

Martha sat in the carriage as it made its way down the drive toward the road, relieved that the child did not fuss when she left for the hospital. She had dreaded leaving her and feared the girl would not understand she was coming back. Ciara had instructed Ian and Daniel to include her in their game of Jackstraws and the little girl watched intently as each brother took turns trying to pick out a strand of straw from the pile without disturbing the rest. She hadn't even noticed when Martha left. The boys would distract her until it was time for bed, and Martha knew Ciara would stay with the child until she fell asleep.

"Have ye thought of what will happen to the lass if she has no kin?" Johnny asked as he guided the bay gelding toward the Cholera Hospital. "I mean are ye hopin' there's someone willin' to take her in or no?"

"Whatever do ye mean by that?" Martha replied, knowing very well what he meant.

"The child is quite fond of ye already, and no mistake. I think ye are smitten as well."

"I have only showed her the love and kindness she deserves. As for her kin, if they're willin' to take her in and show her kindness, I'd be well pleased."

"'Tis not what I asked ye, Martha. We don't even know what her name is, and the child can't tell us. Raising a deaf child is no easy task for any woman, but ye're not just any woman. Ye're a doctor and I suspect ye'll not marry and keep house as other women do. 'Tis much to ask of Karin and yer sisters to raise a child that can't hear."

Several rebuttals fought to escape Martha's mouth and for a moment she sputtered, deciding which part of his remarks angered her most. "Do ye mean to say that I'm not capable of raisin' the child?"

"I'm not sayin' that and well ye know it. Ye have a higher callin' is all. I believe God put ye here to heal the sick, not to keep a house and raise a family."

"Are ye daft, man? Ye're tellin' me that I can't be a proper wife *and* a doctor?"

Johnny was not quite sure how to back out of what he'd said. His remarks had opened the door for a conversation he thought he would never have and one he certainly wasn't prepared to have now. "I just assumed ye didn't want… Would it not be difficult for ye…" Seeing the look on her face, Johnny had the good sense to stop speaking.

"Now I know ye've lost yer mind! Do ye not recall that my own sister, who was the mother to both of us, was the Keeper of the Orphan Asylum?"

"I do, and I also recall that we were a wee bit older and we could hear when we were spoken to! Martha, the child can't hear. Ye were that fashed just tryin' to make the lass understand that ye were leavin' and that ye'd be back come the mornin'."

"Now just ye listen to me, Johnny. I can be a doctor, *and* a wife, *and* a mother should I choose and I'll not hear another word about it!"

The remainder of the journey to the hospital was silent and Martha only glared at him as she exited the carriage. The glare was followed by a snort when Johnny told her he would be back in the morning to pick her up with news of the child's family one way or the other.

The scene outside the hospital left no time to reflect on their conversation. Three wagons pulled up at the same time Martha had arrived, each carrying patients in varying levels of distress. At the same time, a wagon approached the back of the building to carry away the dead. She headed toward the first wagon, which carried an elderly man, a younger man who looked to be his son, and a young woman. The men were groaning in agony, the stench clearly indicating they had lost control of their bowels along the way. The woman was not conscious. Martha immediately felt for the carotid pulse on the woman's neck while directing Erik, Sherman and the two nurses that had exited the hospital behind them to the wagons behind her. The woman was alive, for now, and would have to wait until someone came out to fetch her. "Sir, can ye stand?" she asked the younger man.

"Yes, but my father will need help," the man replied in a stronger voice than Martha anticipated given his pallid complexion.

"Driver, help me with this man," Martha directed.

"My orders are to drive the wagon and that's all, ma'am." Martha blew out a sigh of exasperation and climbed out of the wagon in search of help.

"Let me get him," Sherman said, approaching from behind. "There's a woman with a child back there. The woman can walk on her own, but the girl will need your help."

Martha found an older woman and a girl who looked to be about five. The watery stains on both of their dresses and acrid smell of feces indicated that they were no better off than the rest of the new arrivals. Almost all of the patients in the last few days were in the acute stages of the disease. As fast as the wagons were dropping off sick patients in the front, others were picking up the dead from the back. The old woman was whispering to herself, a prayer maybe, Martha thought as she hoisted the girl out and beckoned the woman to follow.

The misery was palpable. Moaning, retching and other sounds of human suffering could be heard as Martha entered the building and the caustic reek of evacuated bowels filled the main room. Calomel and castor oil were used liberally as purgatives in the early stages of the disease, although with questionable efficacy, she thought. Above the pitiful dirge was the buzz of the flies swarming around overflowing buckets of vomit, shit and blood, the latter resulting from the treatment used in all but the final stage of the disease, bloodletting.

Looking around, Martha realized that not one of the twenty-five beds wedged around the former tavern was empty. "We've cleared floor space in the kitchen, Miss Sloane," nurse Doyle said, her head barely visible over the basket of soiled linen she was carrying. "All new patients will have to go in there. Miss Scofield is already in there; she'll get those two cleaned up," she gestured toward the child in Martha's arms and the old woman staggering behind them.

"I thank ye, Miss Doyle." Martha spoke to the back of the woman's head as the nurse was already on her way to the next task. Millicent Doyle seemed to do the work of a small army all by herself. Efficient though she was, Martha had seen the young woman stop what she was doing on more than one occasion to hold the hand of a dying child so that they would not pass alone.

Looking at the small, narrow kitchen, Martha had no idea how they would fit the twelve new patients in. The oak floors were still damp from scrubbing. The miasma of the main sick room hadn't followed her in and the smell of lye soap was like perfume by comparison. There were no pallets or cots for patients to lie on, just buckets or basins distributed in regular intervals across the room. Nurse Scofield helped settle the woman and child on the floor and began the process of changing them out of their soiled dresses and into smocks made of rough calico. It was critical that both the patient and the sickbed be kept scrupulously clean and the nurses ran themselves ragged to keep up with the washing.

"I forgot to ask them their names," Martha said out loud as she stared at the open ledger on the desk in the main room. The Board of Health insisted that all incoming patients be immediately entered into the book. It was all too easy at times like this, when patients were being admitted in large numbers in the late stages of the disease and requiring immediate medical assistance, to forget about the record-keeping. The Board was meeting several times a week now in an attempt to manage the epidemic. They required the most up-to-date and accurate statistics to determine which part of the city posed the biggest health threat. The cholera deaths were also being reported in the *Buffalo Daily Courier* as well as any other information about the disease that the Board considered important for the general public's awareness.

The men hired to transport people to the hospital were to keep a list of everyone they brought in, although Martha had been in the habit of speaking to the patients directly when they were able to answer for themselves. In the flurry of activity she had forgotten to ask.

"I didn't." Martha turned to see Sherman standing just behind her. "The old woman is Mrs. Rupert. The child is of no relation to her, but her name is Christina. They came with the others from Genesee Street."

"What of the child's parents?" Martha asked as she handed him the pen and stepped aside.

Sherman looked confused. He had been told by his superiors to record the names and places of residence for all incoming patients, which he had done. Beyond that, he had discerned that the child was too weak to walk into the hospital without assistance. There wasn't time for extensive patient interviews about family. "I don't know." It was all he could think of to say.

Dr. Ryan was on his way toward them, and an explanation of why she was concerned about a sick child alone in a strange place would have to wait. "Mr. Carrington, Miss Sloane, have all the incoming patients been settled and entered into the ledger?"

"Yes, Doctor," Martha answered.

"What is your assessment, Mr. Carrington?" Dr. Ryan asked.

Sherman glanced at Martha, who gave him a barely perceptible nod of encouragement, before he cleared his throat and answered. "Nine of them appear to be in the acute stage of the disease. The nurses will administer the standard calomel cathartic. Three are in the late stages of the disease. I will monitor them as usual."

"Well done, Mr. Carrington. Now get to it. Miss Sloane, I would like you to evaluate the six patients I have moved over to the far corner of the room. In each of those cases the cessation of vomiting and purging has been followed by cerebral softening. Dr. Nolan suspects an intolerance to the heavy doses of opiates are to blame for their apparent lack of mental acuity rather than the natural progression of the disease, however I am not so sure. Just the same, I stopped their regular treatment of laudanum this morning. I want you to monitor them for the duration of their convalescence. I'll expect regular reports and want to be made aware immediately should any show improvements in memory or their ability to focus their attention while you speak."

"Yes, doctor." Martha had been concerned that the liberal use of opiates in the treatment of cholera might be contributing largely to the end stages of the disease, whereby the patients slipped into unconsciousness and ultimately death. She had brought her concerns to Michael, who deliberated on the issue for several days before agreeing she could be right. Martha felt strongly that opiates should be discontinued if a patient survived the purgative phase of the disease, but she feared the suggestion from a medical student, let alone the only female one, would not be well received by the attending physicians.

"The Board meets again tomorrow afternoon and I would like to discuss the use of opiates at various stages of treatment at that time. Write up your evening observations for me."

"Yes, Doctor." Martha hurried away.

From the short hall leading to the kitchen, Sherman observed Martha as she went about trying to get the attention of the first of the six patients Dr. Ryan had asked her to observe, relieved that the task had not been assigned to him. How on earth would she be able to tell if the patients' condition was actually a result of the treatment? Martha looked to be making a thorough job of examining each patient, beckoning nurse Doyle to record her results. They were much alike, those two women, and not at all like any of the women he knew from his parent's social circle. They were always asking questions, wanting to know why a particular treatment was used favorably over another. Millicent Doyle was every bit as competent as Martha, and could have attended medical school if she had had the means.

"Sherman, we are needed on the main floor." Erik's voice pulled Carrington out of his thoughts. "There are four beds that need to be emptied so that the nurses can remake them." Four people had lost their battle. By morning there would be more. With a final glance at the young nurse, Sherman followed his colleague.

Chapter Eleven

Johnny made his way back to the Nolan's shop at the corner of Main and Chippewa not sure how he felt about his trip to Mortimer Street. He had knocked on several doors before finding a person at home. The tenements had been hit hard with cholera and many of the units were now empty, having lost their tenants to the disease or because those that had survived could no longer afford the rent. There was an old man on the second floor who had told him that the father of the deaf child, whose name was Felicity Taylor, had died over the winter from the putrid sore throat. He did not know the family well, but suspected the man had a brother in Batavia who was supporting Felicity and her mother.

"Mr. Quinn, come quick." A young lad came running out of the Nolan's Dry Goods Emporium as Johnny's carriage pulled in the back. Peter Moulder had lost both his mother and his baby sister during her birth a few years ago. Mr. Moulder was a blacksmith for the Millers, who owned the biggest livery in the city. Rolland had arranged for the boy to work at the Nolan's store before and after school stocking shelves and sweeping floors, in exchange for his meals and a clean change of clothes each week. "Sir, ye must come. They're sick, both of them."

Johnny jumped from the carriage and flew into the building, not bothering to shut the door behind them. The acrid stench that beckoned as he moved into the living quarters confirmed his worst fears. He turned and ran quickly back outside. "Go now and fetch Dr. Nolan," he told Peter. "Take the carriage and make haste."

He returned and found Daniel at the kitchen table in his shirtsleeves, a bucket at his feet. "Are ye poorly, Granda?" Johnny asked.

"I'm not so bad, but yer Gran's feelin' poorly, to be sure. She's asleep now, poor dear."

"I've sent wee Peter fetch Michael."

"Oh, no need, lad. The man's near to collapse himself for all he's been runnin' between the hospital and the Board of Health. Imagine our Michael, a physician on the Board of Health. Yer Gran's that proud of him…" Daniel's comments were cut short as he grabbed for the bucket just in time to add to its contents. The old man's torso contorted in a violent attempt to rid itself of the toxins within.

"Granda, let me get ye a bit of water to rinse yer mouth."

Daniel looked up, his face was pale and sweaty. "No self respecting Irishman will drink water when there's whiskey to be had. For all we know, 'tis the water causing this whole mess. Be a good lad and grab the bottle from the pantry shelf. That will surely cure what ails me."

Johnny chuckled as he went in search of the bottle and two glasses.

"Ye're wise to have a wee dram yerself just to be safe." Daniel took a sip of the whiskey and then bowed his head as if to make sure it stayed down. "Aye, I hate to worry Michael. Sure enough he's got bigger concerns than Ma and I."

"Ye know well he'd have my hide if I didn't send fer him."

"Aye, he would at that."

It was dark when Michael arrived, and by then Daniel had gone back to his bed. Johnny was up and down the stairs several times during those few hours emptying the buckets and scrubbing them out as Martha had described to him. He was just coming downstairs when Michael came in the back door. "They are both resting now," Johnny said, taking out the handkerchief from his pocket to wipe the back of his neck.

Looking at the full bucket, Michael asked, "Vomiting, both of them?" Johnny nodded and he continued, "Anything from the other end?"

"No, not since I've been here, but I didn't ask about before."

"Alright, I'll go up and have a look. Can ye manage a bit of beef tea? It would be good for them to have a bit to eat."

"Aye, away ye go. I'll see to it straightaway."

Michael came down a short time later and found a large pot of beef broth simmering and the kitchen stifling from the use of the stove. The bottle of whiskey that had been on the table was gone and the backdoor was open. Johnny had escaped to the porch. Michael found him sitting on the rocker, jacket off, sleeves rolled up and a glass of whiskey in his hand.

"I've given them each something to let them sleep for a while," Michael told him as he reached for the bottle and poured himself a healthy dram. "Can ye stay with them?"

"Of course. Will they be needin' any additional medicine?"

"I'll come back tomorrow on my way to the hospital. I'll determine then if they require a cathartic." Michael took a long drink and swallowed slowly, feeling every drop trickle down the back of his throat. "Ye're in for a rough night, I'm afraid. Are ye up for it?"

"There's nothin' I wouldn't do for them, and no mistake," Johnny answered, pouring himself another generous drink. "Have ye met Martha's wee friend?"

"Aye, she's a pretty lass. What did ye find out on Mortimer Street?"

"There may be an uncle in Batavia, but who knows when we'll be able to try and find him or if he'll be alive and willin' to take her in if we do."

"Well, she gets on fine with the lads. I suppose she's better off with us until we can sort it all out."

"Martha will be pleased to hear it. She's quite taken with wee Felicity Taylor. That's her name." Johnny drained the glass, blew out a long sigh, and set it on the table beside him.

"I'm wonderin' what has ye concerned: that the lass will stay with us, or that Martha will be pleased about it?"

"As long as she's not sick and is unlikely to become sick, I've no issue with the child stayin' with ye for a while. But surely ye must see that it will not be easy to raise a deaf child. I'm wonderin' who will be responsible for the lass, is all."

"Has Martha anything to say on the matter?"

Johnny snorted and poured himself another drink. "Aye, she's plenty to say, and who am I to suggest she can't raise that child should she have a mind to."

Michael smiled and took another drink. "Ye know better than to try to tell our Martha she can't do somethin' she's already set her mind to. The same goes for her two sisters and well ye know it." Michael looked at the bottle and decided against another drink. "I must ask ye, Johnny. Have ye an interest in our Martha?"

That question took Johnny by surprise, mostly because he did not know what his intentions were and he said so. "I thought she had no interest in marriage, what with her studies and all."

"Why ever would ye think that? Have ye been gone so long that ye've forgotten all about the home ye were raised in? The Sloane women have all been called by the good Lord to do important things. The older two are happily married, last I checked. What makes ye think Martha wouldn't marry? Has she said as much?"

"No, she hasn't, but do ye not think a husband and family would keep her from the important work God has intended for her?" He picked up his glass, but then put it down again and continued to speak. "'Tis no easy life, bein' a doctor, and well ye know it. She'd be called away at all hours of the day and night. I just don't see how it would work."

"'Tis true, Martha will likely not keep a home the way other wives do. But should she decide to marry, she'll have her sisters and Karin beside her for help. Sure enough, it won't be easy for her or the man she weds. I'm not sure I know a man who would tolerate his wife leavin' their warm bed in the middle of the night, even if it is to tend the sick, do ye?"

Johnny considered Michael's words, unsure if the man expected an answer or if he merely wanted to make a point. "Are ye askin' if I am such a man?"

"I'm askin' ye to know yer own mind before the matter comes up again. Martha is a rare woman and ye understand that she will never be the kind of wife most men would want. It won't be enough just to love her. Ye must accept the person that she is and want the life ye will have with her. Can ye do that?"

"I can accept who she is, but I'm not sure I want the life we would have together. Come to that, she may not want it either. I wouldn't even be here now if it weren't for the quarantine. I'm on the road weeks at a time for nearly half the year. What kind of life would that be for us?"

"Well, ye are here now. It's been more than a year since ye have spent any time with her. Get to know the woman she has become. Talk to her about what it is she wants. If ye both decide that ye want to marry, I would only ask that ye wait until she is done with medical school. The rest will sort itself out."

"Aye, well, I'll do that."

Michael collected the bottle and glasses to return to the kitchen. "I must go now. They'll sleep for a few more hours, I hope. Try and get each of them to take some broth when they wake." Johnny nodded. "Now get some rest, ye've got a long night ahead of ye. I'll be back at dawn."

Johnny stayed outside in the cool night air, knowing he would hear through the open window just above the porch if his patients needed something. The end of his day had taken several unexpected turns and now he found it necessary to consider things he had talked himself out of years ago. Martha had always been special. He had fallen in love with her before he really understood how things were between a man and a woman, so it had always just been there waiting for him to acknowledge. While he had convinced himself that there was no future for them, he hadn't managed to find another woman to share his life with either, although more than a few had expressed an interest. It was a wonderful life, full of exciting places and interesting people. Martha did enjoy hearing all about his adventures, but would that change if they married? Would any woman want a husband who traveled as much as he did? The sound of moaning brought him out of his thoughts and he hurried into the house.

He reached the bedroom to find Katherine trying to sit up. "Gran, can I help ye?"

"Aye, if ye could just help me to the pot, there's a good lad."

The process of getting both of his patients to and from the chamber pot became more difficult over the next few hours as they became weaker. No sooner had he gotten one of them settled back in bed then did the other need to go. Michael had moved Daniel to a separate room earlier, knowing that they would each need their privacy as the disease progressed. That left Johnny running back and forth between the rooms all night and although they were spared the indignity of having to relieve themselves in front of each other, each still suffered the humiliation of having to be cleaned and changed by their grandson when they did not make it to the pot.

A few hours before dawn, Katherine was able to take a bit of beef tea and keep it down. "Oh no, lad, I dare not take a drop and it'll just come up again," Daniel said, refusing even to try the beef tea.

"Won't ye just try a wee sip?" Johnny coaxed.

"Just let me rest a bit, lad. I'll try some come the mornin' to be sure."

By first light each of the Nolans was sleeping and Johnny was hanging a sign on the front door of the shop that said 'Closed due to illness'. Posting the sign was an admission of how serious the situation was. It would not be possible to deal with customers and care for his grandparents, even with wee Peter's help. If the previous night was any indication, it would be a busy day of emptying buckets and changing bed sheets. He was surprised to see Martha, rather than Michael, pulling up in a carriage driven by one of her fellow medical students.

"I thank ye, Sherman," Martha said and climbed out of the carriage, reaching up for the basket he was handing down to her. Ciara had sent along more clean sheets and dressing gowns, knowing they'd soon go through their own things.

No sooner did the basket change hands then the carriage was off again and Johnny was a bit put out that its driver didn't even offer to help Martha to the door, but thought it wise not to say so. Exhaustion and worry took the upper hand and he was unable to keep the irritation from his voice. "What brings ye here?"

Handing him the basket, she replied, "Michael had to meet with the Board of Health and asked me to come and check on Gran and Granda."

"They're both asleep. Gran took some beef tea a bit earlier. So far she's kept it down. Granda's a bit worse off, I'm afraid."

Martha could tell that it was not just fatigue showing on his face. Johnny was terrified. As a young boy he had lost both of his parents to dysentery, a sickness not unlike cholera. Martha saw before her now that same scared young boy she had met at the poorhouse so many years ago and any trace of anger she was feeling over their conversation the previous night vanished. "Ye look tired. Are ye hungry? I could fix something." She followed him into the shop, the whimpers and moans growing louder as they walked into the living quarters. "I'll go and see," she told him, but he followed her up anyway.

A series of grunts followed by a rather loud expletive came from inside Daniels room. The acrid stench in the hall seemed strange in these surroundings. She had never known either one of the senior Nolans to have been sick and now they were fighting for their lives. Entering the room Martha could see that Daniel had soiled the bed sheets…rice water, the thin and watery diarrhea discharge that indicated the old man was well into the critical stage of the disease. "Oh, Granda, let's get ye cleaned up a wee bit."

"Let me do it; he'll not want ye to have to change his drawers, for all he's too weak to argue about it." Martha stepped aside and let Johnny enter the room, the large basket under his arm."There's a cauldron out back for the bed clothes," he told her, "but ye'll have to stoke the fire."

Martha went out to the cauldron that sat in the middle of the small yard. Two sets of sheets hung on the line, drying in the morning sun, evidence that Johnny had been kept busy the previous night. The cauldron was already filled with water in anticipation of the need for more washing. The coals underneath were still hot, so it did not take long to revive the fire.

By the time Johnny came down with the soiled sheets, Martha was preparing some cold meat and cheese for them both to eat. "Is Granda still awake? I'll need to examine him," she told Johnny as she pushed a plate of food in his direction.

"Aye, but just barely. He's refused the broth again. Gran's still asleep."

"I'll just run up and check on him then. Ye need to eat somethin' and then ye should rest a bit yerself."

"What about ye? Ye've been up all night."

"I'm fine. I'll get the washin' sorted when I come down and then I'll take a wee lie down."

Martha climbed the stairs, the effort of lifting each leg becoming more laborious, and found Daniel had fallen back asleep. Reaching for his arm, she felt for the pulse at his wrist. It was weak, yet another sign of the disease progression. The sounds coming from the other room told her that Katherine was awake.

"Let me help ye, Gran," Martha said as Katherine struggled to get out of bed.

"Ach, I'm fine love. I'll just go and check on yer Granda."

"Granda's sound asleep. How are ye feeling this mornin'?" Martha settled the old woman back in bed and brushed her hair aside for a serious look. Her color was good and her pulse was strong, both positive signs. "Now just ye stay here and I'll bring ye a bit of broth."

"Really, love, I'm fine. I'll need to get Johnny his breakfast and the store will open soon."

"Now, don't ye fret, Gran. We've closed the store until ye and Granda are feelin' better and Johnny's already had a bit to eat. Now I'll just run down and fetch yer broth."

Confused, Katherine tried once again to get out of bed. "We've just had a bit of spoiled beef is all. Sure enough yer Granda will not allow the store to close over it. We've never closed, not one day since the first day the doors opened."

"'Tis just for today. Granda will not mind just the one day."

Reluctantly, Katherine gave up the attempt to rise and agreed to stay in bed at least until she had finished her broth, although Martha knew she was too weak to move on her own. The old woman looked drained, but she appeared to be doing much better than her husband. If Katherine was able to keep the broth down, Martha was hopeful for a full recovery. The same might not be true for Daniel, and the reporting of that news to his wife and son would not be easy.

When Martha came back downstairs she found Johnny in the back yard tending a simmering cauldron of bed clothes. "I can finish that. Away ye go and rest for a bit," she insisted, and nudged him back toward the house.

"I'll rest when ye do," he countered, turning around so that they were nose to nose. Looking into her green eyes, he was reminded of the first day he had ever seen her, walking up the drive of the poor farm with her sisters. Johnny had never seen anything like it, three girls who looked to be the same person at different ages. Only Martha had noticed him peeking out from behind the house. She had grown into an exceptional woman and he smiled at the thought of it. Could they really have a life together? At that moment a thought entered his mind and exited through his mouth before he had time to consider it. "What plans have ye for the future, Martha?" He did not regret asking the question and he would know her mind before he would make up his own.

Recalling their conversation the previous evening, Martha looked wary. She was too tired for another argument. "What makes ye ask such a question now?"

"Well, I find I am wonderin' just now how ye'd do it. Ye know, if ye married. For all ye've worked through the night, now ye're here pushin' me away from the washin'and ye'll not rest until ye've fallen over, I expect. How long can ye keep this up?"

Martha took a step back, their proximity and his smile unnerved her and as a result her response sounded peevish. "I don't see how the matter concerns ye, Johnny Quinn. We are in the middle of an epidemic, do ye understand what that means? 'Tis no time to consider if I'll marry, or how it'll be if I do?"

Johnny's smile only grew more mischievous. "There was a time, not too long ago, ye told all those with ears on the sides of their heads that one day ye'd marry me."

His teasing only made her more annoyed. "'Twas a long time ago, when I was but a wee lass."

He reached up and gently caressed her cheek. “Ye’re not a wee lass any more. Ye’ve become a fine woman, Martha.”

He seemed pleased to have caught her off balance, so Martha decided to do the same right back. “Are ye askin’ me to marry ye?”

“I don’t know…maybe.” He wasn’t teasing anymore and his smile softened into something more genuine. “I guess for now I’m askin’ to know what ye want for yerself. For all ye’re able see the future for others, I’m wonderin’ if ye can see yer own. Sure enough I’ve noticed the way yer doctor friends look at ye. Ye’re a rare woman, Martha, and the lads will start to show interest.”

Martha was too exhausted to even begin to process what Johnny was saying, let alone to plot the course of the rest of her life over the laundry cauldron. “Now is not the time to consider such things. Help me finish this up. We both should rest a bit while we can.”

Johnny looked into her eyes, searching for some indication of what she was thinking. The conversation had taken her by surprise, no doubt, but she did not seem frightened or confused and that was enough for now. "Will ye promise me that ye'll consider what I've asked ye and talk to me again when the time is right?"

Martha thought for a moment before she answered. "Johnny, it could go on at the hospital for months like this. Now we've got Gran and Granda, and wee Felicity to worry about." Michael had already told her about Johnny's discovery on Mortimer Street. "I can't say when the time will be right for such a discussion, or even when I'll know my own mind on the matter." She turned her attention back to the cauldron, but then turned back. "To be sure I'll have yer thoughts for the future when the time comes. For all ye're askin' me what I want, I'm thinkin' ye have no idea of what ye want for yerself."

He could hear the annoyance surfacing again in her voice. It had not been his intention to start an argument. "I've no wish to add to the burden ye're already carryin', but I'll need to be on the road again as soon as the travel bans are lifted. If it's as ye say, and that's months ahead yet, we'll both have some time to consider the matter. Can we talk again before I leave?"

Martha sighed and gave the cauldron a quick stir. "Aye, we can, but consider what ye have just said to me. I've been up all night and still there is work to be done before I can rest, but the same is true for ye. How would it be if ye come home after weeks on the road and I'm workin' day and night as I am now? 'Tis not just me who has things to consider, Johnny, for all ye've grown up with Michael away for days at a time when a deadly sickness strikes. Ye must ask yerself if that's what ye want in a wife." She turned so that she was fully facing him now. "Ye're askin' me what I want before ye know yer own mind. I'll have ye to consider this while ye're thinkin'. How would it be if I say I want to marry, and furthermore that I want to marry ye, only to find that ye've decided the opposite?"

That response surprised him, although it shouldn't have. He had never known Martha not to speak her mind when necessary. It did not escape her that he wanted to be sure that she would say yes before he would propose marriage. Ashamed that he had placed such a burden at her feet, he was suddenly bone tired. "Aye, ye're right, and I'm that sorry. 'Twas not fair of me to ask this of ye now, but I did and I can't take it back. I'll promise ye this, though: I'll know my mind soon enough and I'll tell ye so when I do." He took her hand in his before he continued. "Only then will I have yer answer."

"Aye, 'tis fair enough, I suppose, now go and get some rest."

Chapter Twelve

August 5, 1849

Patricia looked out the window at the sound of a carriage coming up the drive. Perhaps it was Johnny with news of Granda. Confined to the house with little to do until her delivery, she was desperate for information and company since Ciara had gone to help care for her in-laws. The children of the Nolan house were under Karin's watchful eye this morning, a formidable task for which she accepted no help. Rolland was busy at the orphan asylum, whose population was increasing daily as children were left either temporarily or permanently parentless as a result of the epidemic. It was frustrating beyond all measure to be confined when her family needed her most.The carriage stopped in front of the house, but it wasn't Johnny. "Father Guth…what is he doing here?" She said out loud and walked outside to greet him. "Good day to ye, Father."

"Ah, good day to you, Mrs. Thomas. I would like a word if you are feeling well enough to receive me for just a few moments. I understand Mrs. Nolan is not at home presently so I would ask that you inform her of my visit."

"Of course, Father. 'Tis a wee bit too hot inside. Would ye care to sit out here? Let me just get us something cool to drink." Eager to be useful and happy for the company, she gestured toward the front porch.

"Do not fuss. I have only time to state my business and then I must be on my way. I've prepared a mass for all those who have passed at the poor farm for this morning. The dead shall go into the ground with the same dignity as any other decent Christian if I have anything to say about it." Father Guth exited the carriage, but continued to speak where he stood. "Michael tells me you have taken in a deaf child."

"Aye, we have. The cholera took her ma and we thought it best not to burden Mrs. McClaverly at the orphan home. She'll stay with us until the travel bans have been lifted. There may be kin in Batavia willin' to take her in."

"That is most kind of you, Mrs. Thomas. I thought it might interest your family to know that Bishop Timon is determined to establish a school for the deaf right here in Buffalo. He has been corresponding with the Sisters of St. Joseph in France. Members of their order have also had success teaching deaf children in St. Louis, Missouri. His Most Reverend has been working to bring the Sisters here to help him to establish a school."

"That's wonderful, Father. The Sisters of St. Joseph, in France, ye say?"

"Yes. I could inquire about a letter of introduction if your husband or Dr. Nolan would like to correspond with the Sisters in St. Louis on the matter, or pass the information on should you find family willing to take the child in."

"I thank ye, Father. Please convey our most respectful thanks to Bishop Timon. Are ye sure I can't offer a wee somethin' to send ye on yer way?"

"No, thank you. I have kept you on your feet too long as it is. Forgive me and God bless you and your child." Father Guth made the sign of the cross over the swell of her belly and then hoisted himself back into the carriage.

Later that afternoon Patricia had managed to convince Karin to let the children come to her for their afternoon meal. She watched as Felicity sat at the table with Ian and Daniel as if she had known them her whole life rather than just a few days. It was rather remarkable that a child who had been through so much, and couldn't hear, could adjust so well to her new surroundings. Patricia had rocked many an orphaned child to sleep at night and knew well that some of them never got over the loss of their parents. Perhaps the child was just distracted by the boys and life on the farm, which was filled with many more interesting animals and places than the tenement on Mortimer Street. Patricia had seen that before, too. When children came to the orphan asylum they were immediately caught up in a routine that included as many as fifty other children. Sometimes it took weeks before the grief took hold. It was usually at night, when things were quiet.

The child seemed distracted by something across the table. The chair where Rolland usually sat was empty, but the lass seemed riveted to the spot. Slowly she smiled, as if she was pleased to see whatever had caught her attention. Patricia looked out the window to see if another visitor was approaching, or if a deer had crossed through the yard, but nothing was there. She looked back towards the table to find the three children were happily nibbling on their biscuits. Whatever had captured the young girl's interest was gone.

* * *

Martha finished up her chores with ruthless efficiency and hastily shuttled the remaining bed clothes out to the laundry. Sherman stood there, a basket of soiled smocks still clutched in his arms, awkwardly attempting conversation with Miss Doyle as she tended the cauldrons. The nurse had stopped working, her smile and the nod of her head encouraging. Martha felt as if she were intruding and announced her presence, although approaching in plain view. "I've one more load for ye, Millicent."

"Here let me take that for you," Sherman offered. Forgetting he still held his own basket, he nearly knocked Millicent over turning to take the other from Martha. He quickly dropped the laundry and apologized profusely. After repeated assurances that the nurse had escaped injury, he took the basket from Martha and placed it next to the other.

"I thank ye." Martha untied her apron and added it to the pile. "I must be off now," she told them both and took her leave.

"I'll just see you to your carriage," Sherman announced, at first eager to escape lest he embarrass himself further. He fell into step with Martha, leaving a rather befuddled nurse to continue her work. Feeling quite the coward, he glanced briefly behind him one last time, considering his actions. Distracted, Sherman did not hear Martha's question.

"Sherman, 'tis not like ye to wonder off in yer thoughts. Is something amiss?

"I believe I have forgotten something. Good day to you, Martha." He turned abruptly and headed with determination back in the direction of the laundry.

Erik Schuster was sitting at the desk near the window entering the names of the recently admitted patients into the ledger when he saw Martha out of the corner of his eye walking toward the front of the hospital. He waited for her to part company with

Carrington and then made his way out the back door to intercept her. “Martha,” he said, jogging a few steps to catch up with her.

“Erik, were ye needin’ somethin’ before I go?”

“No, it’s just, well, I understand the report you delivered to Dr. Ryan about the use of opiates after the purgative phase was well received. I would like to hear about your findings now that our shift has ended.”

“I’m that sorry, but I can’t. I’m needed at home while my sister is away.”

Erik looked disappointed. “Ah, yes, I understand your grandparents are both ill. Has there been any improvement?”

“My Gran’s much better. I thank ye for askin’. Now if ye’ll excuse me, I must be on my way.” Martha said nothing about Daniel, who was growing weaker each day. Truthfully, she did not expect him to last the day, but it would serve no purpose to say such a thing out loud.

“Perhaps I can drive you home and you can tell me of your study along the way?”

“I thank ye, Erik, for the kind offer, but I’ve a ride already. Perhaps another time.”

"Yes, another time, then."

Johnny climbed down from his carriage, watching Martha approach with the young medical student. Under different circumstances he'd be pleased by the look of defeat as the lad continued on to his own carriage, but today he could find no joy in it.

Wary to see that it was Johnny instead of Charlie who had come to pick her up, Martha asked, "Is it Granda?"

"Aye, he's passed, Martha. They're at the store now, Michael and Ciara." He helped her into the carriage and moved to put his arms around her should she need some comforting, but stopped when he saw the look on her face. She appeared to have no reaction to the news. Johnny didn't know if she was stunned, exhausted, or just anesthetized from the death that constantly surrounded her. "Did ye hear me, lass?"

"Aye, I heard ye. Let's go."

* * *

Michael sat in the parlor of the house where he'd grown up, a generous portion of whiskey untouched on the table beside him. A traditional wake and funeral were out of the question under the circumstances. Ciara would understand, but he could not bring himself to tell his mother that it would be days before Father Guth could come and even offer a prayer for Daniel's departed soul. That was just as well because it would be even longer before the undertaker could come and remove the body for burial. The sound of footsteps coming down the hall brought him out of his thoughts.

"I thought I'd give yer ma a bit of time alone with him before the others get here," Ciara told him as she entered the parlor. "I don't suppose there'll be a wake beyond the family comin' 'round this mornin'."

"'Tis not right to ask it of anyone else, I think. They'll be afraid he's catching, but they'll not want to disappoint ma by stayin' away. His death will be listed in the paper with the others. I expect ma will have a steady stream of callers in a week or two."

"Aye, and it's just as well. She needs her rest anyway. What about ye? Can ye stay here for a while?"

"Aye, through the mornin' anyway. I've sent word to Dr. Ryan not to expect me at the hospital today, but I've patients to see elsewhere in the city this afternoon and there are arrangements to be made for Da."

"Will ye try and rest a bit before the others arrive."

"I don't think I could sleep, but will ye sit with me for a minute?"

"I'll stay with ye, but won't ye lie down for just a wee while?" She placed a hand on his shoulder, urging him to recline. Once he was lying down, she maintained contact, rubbing his back like she had done for countless children over the years when fear or sorrow had kept sleep at bay. Her hand traveled up and found the base of his skull. He was in need of a haircut and the excess length gathered in damp ringlets that clung to the back of his neck. She brushed them aside, exposing pale skin to the warm breeze coming in through the window. His breathing slowed and she continued caressing his soft black curls until he was asleep.

Ciara stayed with Michael for a little while knowing he would sleep better with her by his side. Eventually, hushed sounds in the kitchen indicated that some of the family had arrived. She found Karin had wasted no time getting started with a basket of fresh baked bread on the table and the kettle on for tea. "Have ye left Bruns and Ellie at home, then?" Ciara asked walking toward the pantry to retrieve some butter and cheese.

"Yes, I thought Ellie would give Patricia some help with the children and Bruns could help Rolland to finish the barn chores," Karin told her, but in truth Charlie wanted the children away from the city. He had lost both of his parents to cholera during the 1832 epidemic and would take no chances with his children. "Charlie is unloading the wagon. He will be in presently."

Ciara looked out the window to see Charlie and Johnny, who had just arrived with Martha, hoisting a large wooden casket into the barn. "Did he make that?"

"Yesterday, he knew it would be a week or more before the undertaker would be by. He told me his mother and father were wrapped in shrouds for weeks behind the chicken coop waiting to be taken away. He did not want Michael to trouble himself over the matter. Has he gone off to the hospital already?"

"No, he's havin' a wee rest in the parlor."

"Make the tea and have something to eat. I will go up and pay my respects to Katherine."

"Aye, I think I will. Shall I pour for ye as well?"

"No, thank you. We have had our breakfast."

Martha came in as Karin turned to walk up stairs. "How's Gran?" she asked Ciara.

"She's still not feelin' quite right, the poor dear. She's confused as well, keeps askin' Michael why Daniel got so sick and she didn't. 'Tis breakin' the poor man's heart not to have an answer for her."

Charlie and Johnny came in through the back door, and soon the conversation brought Michael from the parlor. Charlie went over to him, extending one hand and clasping Michael on the shoulder with the other. "He was a good man, was Daniel, and no mistake."

"I thank ye, man," Michael replied.

"Karin's gone up to sit with Ma if ye'd like to pay yer respects," Ciara informed.

"Aye, I'll do that in a wee while, but we'd like a word with ye, Michael, if ye please." Charlie nodded in the direction of the parlor and three men went off.

Ciara turned to her sister. "Ye must be starvin'. Sit down and have a bite before ye go up and see yer Gran."

"Aye, I am at that. Thank ye," Martha answered as her sister was already sliding some bread and cheese in her direction.

The two women ate in silence , exhaustion keeping them to their respective thoughts. Finally Martha spoke. "Patricia will not be pleased to be left at home."

"Aye, I expect not. Even if Rolland hadn't insisted they both stay, Charlie wouldn't have let her come. 'Tis only his loyalty to Michael that brought he and Karin to the city now. He knows all too well how this wretched sickness can destroy families."

"I've seen it time and again these past weeks," Martha agreed. "I worry about wee Felicity. What if her uncle won't take her in?"

"There may be another place for her," Both women looked up to find Karin coming down the stairs. "Father Guth was by this morning and spoke with Patricia. There is a school for the deaf run by the Sisters of St. Joseph in St. Louis, Missouri. Father will arrange a correspondence if it pleases you. Perhaps if the child's kin will not take her in something could be arranged."

"But that is so far away," Martha remarked.

"Aye, and how on earth would we get her there?" Ciara asked.

"That could be worked out I am sure, if need be." Karin was not one to be troubled by details if something needed to be done.

"Well, there's time to consider any options we may have for the lass. I'm sure it will be weeks before we can even send a letter to Batavia," Martha said.

"Martha, do not consider taking the child in permanently. Her needs are too great for us to manage." Karin would do whatever was needed to help should the child end up staying on the Nolan farm, but she was not shy about offering her opinion anyway.

"Sister, what have ye to say on the matter?" Martha turned toward Ciara, knowing better than to argue with Karin. It was wiser to see if she and Ciara were in agreement and then discuss the issue with her sister at a later date.

"Well, I can't say I disagree, but we've taken the lass in and I'll not turn her out. Perhaps we should write to the Sisters and learn about their school before we discuss the matter again." Ciara's reply seemed to satisfy both women and the conversation turned to the matter at hand.

"We should get Gran settled in her own bed and then the men can move the body into the barn," Martha suggested.

"Aye, and then ye, for all I can see ye're about to fall over," Ciara told her sister.

"I'll do for a while. Let me have a wee visit with Gran and then I'll get her back in her bed." Ciara nodded as Martha rose from the table and headed up the stairs.

* * *

Michael closed the door to the parlor as the other two men each took a seat. "What's on yer mind?" He asked.

Charlie spoke first. "Under different circumstances, I'd not burden ye with such matters, but as yer ma's alone now, I think we best settle a few things. Johnny has asked me if Bruns could come and help with the runnin' of the store. I'll know your thoughts on the matter before I consider it."

Michael looked at Johnny, who cleared his throat and spoke. "If it pleases ye, I would mentor the lad, take him on a few trips with me and introduce him around as yer Da did with me. When he is able to make the trips on his own, I'll stay here and run things for Gran."

There had been no time to consider what would happen to the store if Daniel died and once again Michael found that he was grateful to his extended family for their forethought and wisdom. "Aye, I think that's a fine plan, if it pleases the both of ye. I only worry that Ma will not be able to work as she used to for some time."

"Perhaps Ellie could come and keep the house for a while, maybe help mind the store with wee Peter in the afternoons," Johnny suggested.

"Aye, I'll speak with Karin. I'm sure she'll agree after things have settled down a bit in the city." Charlie said.

"Of course, I'll not ask ye to send them until the danger has well passed," Michael agreed.

"I can handle what little business there is here until then if Ciara can look after Gran," Johnny assured them.

"I thank ye both, truly I thank ye. I'll feel better leavin' this afternoon knowin' ye are both here to take care of ma and the others." Michael stood as he spoke. "We'll need to move Da before I go."

"Aye, we best get to it then," Charlie agreed, signaling the end to the discussion.

Chapter Thirteen

August 20, 1849

The weeks after Daniel's death passed in a blur for most of the residents of the Nolan farm. Michael and Martha were kept busy at the hospital and Ciara made daily trips into the city to see to the needs of her mother-in-law, who was still recovering from cholera. The care of Felicity and the boys was in the hands of Karin and her daughter Ellie who were also kept busy with the meal preparation, as everyone seemed to return for the evening meal at different times.

Patricia sat idle, waiting for her babe to come into the world, feeling frustrated that she could be of no help to her husband. Rolland spent as much time as he dared at the orphan asylum with his wife's delivery date looming. There had been a few cases of the disease there since the passing of wee Gretchen Keebler, but so far none had been fatal. Patricia insisted on a full report when her husband returned at the end of each day, and when he was finished the recounting, they both said a prayer for the safety and health of all of the children in the city.

The women on the Board of Directresses of the Buffalo Orphan Asylum rallied their mothers, daughters and domestic servants to sew and knit around the clock to make enough clothing and bed linens for the increasing population of children. Ciara was assembling the contributions from the Nolan household to be dropped off on her way into the city when Karin entered the kitchen with the socks she and Ellie had knit. "Ye look tired," Ciara told her.

"The same is true of you. We all do what must be done," Karen replied, handing her the basket of socks.

"Aye, we must. I pray every day that this sickness will pass soon and we can return to our lives as we knew them."

Karin had been in Buffalo during the cholera epidemic of 1832 and knew that their lives would not be the same again, but could not bring herself to say so out loud. "Charlie is ready to leave when you are. Let me help you bring these things outside, yes?" She opened the back door and the children could be seen running toward the house. Felicity, with her tiny legs, lagged behind the boys, although they dutifully looked over their shoulders regularly to see that she was still with them. Without warning the girl stopped, her attention fixed on the drive leading toward the road. She smiled and lifted up her hand to wave before continuing after Ian and Daniel. The women looked after her but could see nobody. "She sees someone, I think." Karin said.

Ciara looked again in the direction of the road and then back again at Karin. "Where? I don't see anyone."

"Neither do I, but I have seen her before stop and talk to the air floating beside her. Patricia has seen this too." Karin met her friend's eye. "There is another kind of sight, I think. Not like Martha, who sometimes knows the future. There was a woman who could see the dead in my village when I was a girl, in Germany. Some thought she was a witch; others considered her mad. But my mother told me that women like her were not to be feared, that it was a gift that God gave to very few."

Ciara had grown up in a remote village in Ireland and had heard similar tales. She had accepted without reservation that Martha had the second sight because other women in her village, going back many generations, had been seers. She also knew well that what was accepted and even respected in small villages was often feared in large cities, especially where women were concerned. If Felicity had a special gift, it would be honored as Martha's was, at least here on the farm. "Aye, well I hope it's her ma or her da that she sees. 'Twould be a comfort to her, I think, knowin' they're about."

Karin nodded and brought the baskets of children's clothes out to be loaded in the wagon.

* * *

Sherman found that sleep eluded him. Mrs. Cornish had been told that he would not be present for the morning meal and that he was not to be disturbed until midday. A glance out the window revealed that it was only late morning. He sat up in his bed and considered his conversation with Martha the night before.

"I've recently had word from my parents," he told her. "They traveled to Laona and have been there since before the outbreak." The small town in Chautauqua county was unfamiliar to her, so he added, "They are free thinkers, you see, and have traveled there to meet with others such as themselves."

"Free thinkers? I don't believe I take yer meaning?"

"They are interested in Spiritualism, or rather, specifically, Mesmerism." When Martha still looked confused, he elaborated. "They are interested in communication with the spirit world," he clarified. "Mesmerism is the art of putting a person under a spell of sorts and then maintaining control over his abilities. The mesmerized person might answer questions or engage in activities, but have no recollection of them when they awaken. My mother is intrigued by it and there is a man in Laona who is quite skilled, or so she has told me."

Martha smiled, unaware that people gathered together to observe such things. She had never thought of her gift as something she would display purely for the interest of others, although she often passed on information she received through it. "Why are ye troubled? Are they sick?"

"No, nothing like that. They've sent word I'm to join them immediately."

"How were they able to send word to ye when there are yet travel bans in and out of the city?"

"They are resourceful." What he really meant was that money had changed hands at the check points…a lot of money. "Mother has been furious since she found out I have been working at the hospital. I was supposed to meet them when the semester ended. They are traveling with the Pollards and their daughter Agnes."

"Should I know them?"

"No, they're friends of ours from Albany. Our families have been together for a long time."

"How lovely they are close by. Ye've made no mention of yer family before. I imagine ye'll be well pleased to see them when the danger here has passed."

Sherman shrugged, "We hardly have time for social discourse." As an afterthought, he added, "I would prefer to stay in Buffalo for the duration of my medical education."

"Aye, to be sure. Do yer parents not understand that ye are needed here?"

"No, I am sure they do not."

When no further explanation was offered, Martha asked, "What will ye do?"

That was a good question, he thought. "Eventually I will have to meet them." It was all he could think of to say. It was not in his nature to ignore a directive from his parents, but life in Buffalo was changing Sherman and he needed time to consider the implications of his metamorphosis. For now he felt grateful just to have a friend.

He was roused out of his thoughts by a knock on the door. "Mr. Carrington, ye've a visitor, sir," Mrs. Cornish called out.

"Yes, just a minute, please." Sherman opened the door and narrowly avoided a knuckle in the nose as Mrs. Cornish had once again thrust her closed fist toward it. "Good morning, Mrs. Cornish. How may I be of help to you?"

"A young lady has come to call, unescorted." Disapproval was evident in the ample woman's voice as she emphasized the last word. "She is waiting in the parlor. Shall I put the tea on for ye?"

"Yes, thank you, Mrs. Cornish." Sherman had no idea who this unexpected and unescorted guest might be as he descended the stairs, carefully keeping his pace in check as the slower matron made her way down ahead. He extended his long arm just in front of her as they reached the parlor door and held it as he spoke. "Thank you, Mrs. Cornish. I will see to my guest if you would be kind enough to bring the tea."

Reluctantly the old woman walked away in the direction of the kitchen. Sherman entered the parlor as soon as the kitchen door swung shut with Mrs. Cornish safely behind it. He stood dumbfounded as the young lady rose to greet him. She looked out of place in a boarding house, dressed in a cream silk gown with embroidered floral sprigs of pink and green. "Agnes, what are you doing in Buffalo? Where are our parents? Surely you haven't traveled here alone."

"Oh, Sherman, thank God you are safe! I came as soon as I heard. I feared for your life, my love." She took his hand and directed him to the chair next to the window, taking the one next to it. "I've received the most dreadful news and I rushed here to make sure that you were safe."

He had last seen her the previous winter just before he came to Buffalo to attend medical school, and couldn't help but notice that she had not outgrown her need for theatrics. "Agnes, slow down. Are you alone? Where are your parents?"

"They are still in Laona. I couldn't wait, you see. The sisters, they told me you are in danger."

"Who? What sisters? Do your parents know you have left Laona?"

"Sherman, I couldn't wait, don't you see? You're in grave danger." Among the least favored of his fiancée's attributes was her ability to work herself into hysterics, particularly at times when she had misbehaved. Often when they were children, Agnes would lure him into some adventure that was sure to get them in trouble. When they were found out, she would reduce herself to tears, gaining the forgiveness of her parents and leaving him to the disciplinary measures of his own.

"Agnes, calm down and start from the beginning. Who are these sisters you are talking about?"

"Why surely you have heard of Maggie and Katie Fox, the Hydesville Rappers? They can speak to the dead, Sherman! We prolonged our stay in Laona to meet them, although their travels were delayed this summer due to that dreaded sickness."

Sherman tried, but failed, to contain a condescending smirk. He never did understand his parent's fascination with all of that nonsense and now Agnes was apparently captivated by it as well. "What did the sisters have to tell you that made you travel unescorted to Buffalo?"

Yet another irritating attribute was her ability to ignore that which she simply didn't want to acknowledge and so Agnes went on to speak with the utmost sincerity despite the annoyance evident in the voice of her betrothed. "Sherman, they told me that if you stay in Buffalo something terrible will happen to you. They told me you should leave at once, that I should insist you travel back with me." Actually, the sisters had advised that Sherman leave Buffalo and Agnes took that to mean that he should travel with both of their families back to Albany.

Now Sherman was truly aggravated and took no measures to hide it. "Agnes, did my parents put you up to this? They are here, aren't they?" Shaking her head to deny the accusation, she moved from her seat and knelt at his feet. Looking up at him with tear-filled eyes, she pleaded. "Sherman, we must heed the sisters' warning and leave immediately. Our parents have decided we will be married at the end of this month. I just don't know what I would do if something were to happen to you before then."

She took his hand and he noticed the ring on her right hand. It was a sapphire surrounded by pearls. He recognized it immediately. Looking down at her hand he asked, "Where did you get that ring?" Sherman asked the question although he already knew the answer. It was his mother's. She had told him one day it would be his to give to his wife on their wedding day as Sherman's father had given it to her.

"Your mother gave it to me."

Although it came as no surprise Sherman was still angry. It was bad enough they had arranged the marriage, his parents and hers, but his mother had actually given Agnes the ring he would have presented to her. "I don't believe this!" Sherman was outraged for the first time in his life and took a moment to gather his wits before rising from his chair to settle Agnes back into her seat. He was certain his parents were somehow behind this cryptic message from the Fox sisters. Now pacing the floor in front of her, he tried to maintain what composure he had left when he spoke. "We decided we would wait until I had completed medical school. I still have another year before I am finished."

"Don't you understand my love? We can't wait. We must leave Buffalo now. You are not safe here. The sisters have communed directly with the spirits and the spirits only speak the truth."

"What is this danger they have spoken of, tell me?" Exasperated, Sherman continued pacing the floor as she answered him.

"They did not offer details. They only told me that you were in grave danger and that, if you did not leave the city at once, something terrible would happen to you."

"Agnes, I want you to go back to my parents at once and tell them that I will return only after my training has been completed." Turning towards the opening parlor door, he called out, "Thank you, Mrs. Cornish, but we won't be having tea. Miss Pollard will be returning to her hotel." His stern expression brooked no argument and the matron returned to the kitchen without comment.

"But Sherman, I don't have a hotel. I traveled through the night and only just arrived in the city."

"You came here unescorted *at night*?" He hadn't noticed before, but her dress was an evening gown. Looking around the room, he did not see any bags or trunks. She must have come with just the clothes on her back. "What were you thinking? Have you any idea of the danger of traveling into the city at night?"

"You were in danger, my love. What would you have me do?"

"Your parents really do not know you are here?" The shake of her head told him they did not. Reaching in his pocket for a handkerchief, he handed it to her. "Wipe your tears, Agnes. I'll get you settled in a hotel and then send word to your parents. I'm sure they will be here in a day or two to fetch you."

"But Sherman, you must leave!"

"I have an obligation to care for the patients at the hospital and to complete my education. I will stay in Buffalo until each has been fulfilled."

Two hours later, Sherman returned to his room at the boarding house. Thankfully Mrs. Cornish was going about her afternoon chores and he was able to avoid an awkward conversation. He would have to explain his morning visitor eventually, but for now it was important to think. Whether or not his parents were behind Agnes' visit, he needed to get her out of town just until he could come up with a plan. Then he would explain himself. During the height of the epidemic there wasn't time to devise a plan. With Agnes in the city, both of their parents were sure to follow. His secrets would be revealed sooner than he'd anticipated.

Sherman had always thought of Agnes as the annoying little sister who always got him in trouble. It was only last year that the couple was informed that their marriage had been arranged from the time they were children. Sherman spent his young life doing what he was told, but he did not want to marry Agnes Pollard. It was pointless to raise the issue. He agreed to go to medical school in the hopes of putting some distance between them, thus providing Agnes the opportunity to lose interest or meet someone else.

Meeting someone himself was not part of the plan. Working long hours at the hospital allowed him to become acquainted with a woman he never would have met otherwise, a woman of whom his parents would not approve. It was bad enough, telling them he did not wish to marry Agnes, but adding that he wished to wed another, they simply would not allow it. Defying his parents would take courage he was not sure he possessed.

Part Two

Chapter Fourteen

September 10, 1849

Johnny sat in the small office in the back of the store, going over the account books. The cholera epidemic had taken a severe toll on most businesses, and the Nolan Dry Goods Emporium was no exception. Still, they had weathered the storm. The disease had just about run its course and only a few cases trickled into the hospital each week. The city was slowly returning to its normal bustle. Although the travel bans had not yet been lifted for commerce or personal ventures, delivery of the mail had resumed. It would be months, maybe a year or more, before the shop would see the business it had before the epidemic. Entire families had been lost to the cholera, even more women without husbands and children without parents. Days, sometimes weeks of work had been missed by those who, by the grace of God, had survived the disease.

That meant lost wages, lost jobs, and possibly the loss of homes if there was no money to pay the rent. Thankfully, Daniel had always been a frugal business man and there was some money saved that would carry them through.

The loops and whorls of the handwritten ledger flowed into what looked like one very long word. Johnny closed his eyes hard and reopened them hoping for both mental and visual clarity. The men had all sat through the night with Rolland while he waited for his firstborn child to enter the world. Just before dawn Mary Karin Thomas, named for her Gran on the Sloane side and also for the woman who delivered her, arrived. Rolland wasted no time returning to his own home to meet his new daughter while Johnny, Charlie and Michael stayed a bit longer in the Nolan parlor to toast the new addition to their extended family. It was nearly light when Johnny left the farm to head back to the city. Ellie had breakfast on the table by the time he arrived, so there was no opportunity to sneak upstairs for a few winks before the day began.

The buzzing of a few shoppers milling around the store blended with the hum of conversation coming from the living quarters making Johnny feel like he was sitting in the middle of a beehive. He was lulled by the steady rhythm of conversation which carried with it the sleep he had been keeping at bay all morning. Startled awake by the sound of Bruns calling, Johnny rubbed his bearded face in an attempt to gain some composure.

"Here's the post. Look! There's a letter from your sister." Bruns knew Johnny was eager for news from his biological sister since the cholera epidemic broke out earlier that summer. Megan Quinn had also been bound out to work on a farm when they were children and was obligated to stay there even when Johnny had returned to the poorhouse after his leg injury. It was not an easy childhood for either of them, but eventually Megan left the farm and married. She and her husband lived in Batavia and Johnny was able to see her when his travels took him in that direction.

"Thank God. Give it here." Johnny tore open the letter and was relieved to discover that Megan, her husband and their four children had all survived the epidemic. He looked up and gave the sign of the cross and mumbled a brief prayer of thanks.

"I'm glad to hear they are all well," Bruns told him, standing over Johnny's shoulder to read the news for himself. "Do you think they will know of the wee girl's kin?"

"Felicity, do ye mean? Aye, I was hopin' Megan might be of some help in the matter. I've told Michael I'd write her as soon as I'd things settled here."

"I should think we have things settled now, no?" Bruns was both pleased and proud to be living and working with the man he called brother. They had grown up together on the Nolan farm and it had been especially hard on Bruns when Johnny left.

"Nearly so, lad, nearly so."

* * *

Martha came down from her bedchamber late to find the house empty. As the number of cholera patients continued to decline, so did the number of hours she was required at the hospital. Still not accustomed to this new schedule, it was becoming a routine to rise and find Ciara and the boys gone. Michael was also adjusting to the change but was still usually at the breakfast table when she came downstairs. Enough was enough, she thought. It was time to be of some help around the house. Felicity and wee Mary Karin were keeping the other women busy and it was time to pitch in. The sound of the door opening took Martha by surprise.

"Ah, ye're up." Ciara came in with Felicity in tow, who immediately catapulted herself into Martha's arms. "I'm just in for some washin' soap. I forgot how many nappies ye go through in the beginning."

"Why don't ye let me do the washin'?" Martha suggested, tickling Felicity until she squealed.

"'Tis no bother, ye might see what's left to harvest in the garden if ye have a mind to."

"Aye, I'll do that straightaway. Shall I take this one with me, then?"

"If ye please. Charlie's got the boys down in the barn doin' chores and Karin is busy scrubbin' floors. I expect Felicity is bored with my company and the fresh air will do her good."

Martha disentangled herself from the boisterous child, who had begun to tickle back. Felicity looked at her, as if to acknowledge some unspoken directive and went to retrieve the garden basket that hung near the back door. "Sometimes I wonder if the lass can hear after all," Martha said.

"She just pays attention more, I think," Ciara offered.

"Perhaps, but I suspect she is paying attention to our thoughts rather than our words. Recall when she first arrived, the child had no fear, even when I left her to go to the hospital. She seemed to know she was safe here." Martha looked at Felicity and then at her sister. "I just think she is able to understand our intentions rather than our words."

"How so?"

Martha again directed her attention toward Felicity until the child nodded and smiled. The shock in her older sister's eyes prompted an explanation of what had just transpired. "I just asked without the use of words for Felicity to nod her head if she understood me, and clearly she did," Martha told her.

Ciara turned toward Felicity thinking about how nice it would be if the child would give her a hug and was rewarded immediately as Felicity leapt into her arms. She laughed and twirled the child around before placing her back on the ground. "I would not have believed it were I not seein' this with my own eyes! Do ye think she can hear our thoughts?"

"Aye, I do. I've suspected it for a long while now. Ye can see how she gets on with the lads, and hardly a word spoken when the three of them are together, yet she seems to understand what they are about. I wonder..." Martha took a moment to organize her thoughts before continuing. "For all I have the second sight, I would think it possible the lass has a similar gift that allows her to hear in the same way that I can see."

"God gives us all what he thinks we need," Ciara offered. "I think he has given wee Felicity more than a way to hear."

"Ye think she sees the dead, don't ye?"

Ciara met her sisters knowing look and nodded. "Aye. 'Twas Karin who told me she has often seen the child talkin' away as if there was a person beside her when there was not another to be seen. Have ye noticed it as well?"

"I have. It would explain why she has had such an easy time of it since her ma passed." Martha was thoughtful for a while before she spoke again. "Should we tell her kin, if we find them? Many folks fear these special gifts, and I wouldn't want to give them a reason not to take her in, for all I've been prayin' Megan will find the child's uncle in Batavia and that he'll want her," Martha admitted.

"Is that so? I suppose we would want to meet them first. If they truly have the child's happiness in mind, I would think they'd be glad to have a way to speak to her." Ciara looked at her sister curiously. "What's changed yer mind on the matter? I thought ye wanted Felicity to stay here?"

"Well, I've been watchin' ye lately: ye, Patricia, Karin and even wee Ellie. 'Tis no easy task keepin' a home. What kind of mother would I be to any child, let alone one who needs a wee bit more attention?"

Ciara sat down at the kitchen table and motioned for Felicity, who had been seated on the floor watching the two women intently, to sit on her lap. "Is that how ye thought it would be? Ye expected to raise the lass as yer own?"

"At first, I just wanted to help the poor soul. She seemed so scared when she came to the hospital and she took a likin' to me immediately. I couldn't bear sending her to the orphan asylum when her ma passed.

After a while, I was thinkin' about when I'm done with my medical training. What kind of wife and mother would I make?"

"Are ye thinkin' about Johnny? Michael told me they spoke on the matter. Has he asked ye to marry him?"

"Not in so many words. He's asked me do I want to marry."

"I'll never forget the day ye announced to all of us that ye'd marry him one day. Ye were still but a wee lass. That was the last time we spoke of marriage, ye and I."

Martha smiled at the thought, but her expression faded as recent concerns filtered back into her mind. "'Tis funny, ye know, these days I am more at ease among the men at the hospital than I am among the women in my own home."

"Whatever makes ye say such a thing, for ye know well how we love ye?"

"Ye make it look so easy, the keepin' of the house and the like. I don't know how I'd do it."

"Sweet Martha," Ciara shifted Felicity, who had drifted off to sleep and reached across the table to put her hand over her sister's. "Ma always said women do what must be done. Having said that, Karin has held this family together, and well ye know it. Recall Michael and I came home to supper on the table and clean clothes in our chest of drawers when I was workin' at the orphan asylum."

"I also know that Michael insisted ye be home for the supper each night, and that he often wasn't if he had a patient in need. Women do what must be done, as ye said, but what man would eat supper alone when his wife was not at home?"

"Well, now that's the question, so it is. Have ye asked Johnny?"

"Aye, I have, but he hasn't answered yet. That's part of what troubles me. What if I decide I want to marry him and he doesn't want to marry me?"

"Sister, the good Lord has a way of sortin' these things out. Know yer own heart. Do ye love him?"

"Aye, of course I love him."

"Ye've grown up together and ye love him as we all do, but do ye love him as a woman loves a man?"

Martha considered the question and realized she wasn't sure how that love would be different. Her thoughts could be read easily on her face, so Ciara explained, "Ye see, when I first met Michael, I could see no other in the room whenever he was in it. When I wasn't with him, I dearly wished I was. When he first kissed me, I knew I would spend the rest of my life with him, and now I can't sleep unless he's in the bed beside me. That, sister, is how a woman loves a man."

Martha looked bewildered. She had spent so much time wondering if she could be a proper wife, she hadn't thought about how she really felt about Johnny. Did she love him that way?

"Ye've much to consider, to be sure, but things will sort themselves out. We know now that Felicity will find a way to get by no matter where she ends up, and that will be a weight off of all of us. As for Johnny, he's here for a while yet and he'll only be gone a short time once he's off again, so ye have time to discover your own heart."

The words were meant to ease her mind, but Martha still felt disconcerted. It was a frustrating gift, the second sight. For all the fate of others was often clear, she had not a clue about the direction her own life would take.

* * *

Agnes Pollard stepped out of the American Hotel and stared in wonder at the city street. She knew not which way to turn, it all looked so exciting. Feeling more confident in her newly made peach silk dress, she was eager to set out. There had been no choice but to purchase a few ready-made dresses when she first arrived, but she explained to Sherman that she would need something more suitable to her taste. Now that Agnes looked more like herself, she would use the time Sherman was away to explore the city.

A few wagons made their way along Main Street, one carrying milk, another barrels of something, beer, maybe, and a third transporting bushels of cabbage. Further down, a few fine carriages could be seen hurrying toward their destinations, each passenger focused on whatever important business needed attending. On foot there were servants popping in and out of the shops, carefully balancing baskets laden with bread or eggs as they accomplished their morning errands. Four grubby boys were running as if they were being chased by someone who could not yet be seen, while other folks seemed to just stroll leisurely by with no particular destination in mind.

On the rare occasions Agnes and her mother were out and about in Albany, Mrs. Pollard would hastily usher her daughter into their carriage, warning that the city streets were no place for a young lady. Agnes' mother was not here now, and Sherman wouldn't be meeting her until just before supper. She started out heading inland, in the direction opposite the fleeing boys. It was warm enough out that no coat was necessary, and the sun warmed her face as she continued along the road. Alternating odors of horse manure and rotting garbage gave way to the pleasant aromas of baking bread and well-oiled leather as the city of Buffalo unfolded before her.

It was difficult to see in the windows of the various shops from the street, so Agnes just used her imagination as she passed by. With thoughts of the printer, the shoemaker, and the barber hard at work, she continued strolling along. Easily seen from the street, however, were the signs on some of the shops that said 'Closed Due To Illness', a dark reminder that the shadow of cholera shrouded the city.

Agnes was happy to see no such sign at the Nolan Dry Goods Emporium. She had heard from the hotel manager that Daniel Nolan's store had a fine selection of lace imported from France, by way of New York City and God rest his soul. Most of the ladies like herself shopped there, he told her. Agnes stood at the edge of the street contemplating the sturdy brick building, wondering what else she might find there of interest. With nobody to tell her differently, the coin in her purse could be spent on whatever she fancied. The Canton Tea Company was just a few doors down, and was also a potential spot of interest, according to the hotel manager. Mr. James Sully, the shop's owner, had a story to tell for each and every fragrant tea he had to offer. A most pleasant way to spend the morning, the hotel manager assured her. "Tea it is!" Agnes said out loud as she proceeded up the walk of the sturdy white-washed building.

Chapter Fifteen

Dr. Michael Nolan
Niagara Street
Buffalo, New York
12 September, 1849

Dear Dr. Nolan,

Having received your correspondence regarding the orphaned child Felicity Taylor, I am pleased to offer you some guidance. As it is the general consensus among educators of the deaf that a satisfactory result cannot be achieved until the twelfth year, it is my recommendation that, when ready, the girl attend common school until such time as she reaches the appropriate age. There, under the guidance of a kind and gentle teacher, she can be educated in the elementary branches of knowledge as well as the fundamental principles of morals. An industrious teacher will soon develop an intuitive sign language with which to impart this critical foundation. Should you be fortunate enough to find the child's family in Batavia, and if they are willing to take her in, kindly inform them that, upon her twelfth year, there will be a place for Felicity here, where her physical, mechanical, intellectual, moral and religious education will continue. Until then may God bless you for your kindness and charity.

Your Most Humble Servant,

Mother Agnes Spencer
St. Joseph School for the Deaf
St. Louis, Missouri

Michael looked up from the letter he was reading as his weary brother-in-law appeared in the doorway. "Rolland, come in and take a seat. Ye look as if a light wind would knock ye over."

"Aye, well, ye did warn me there'd be no sleep to be had once the babe arrived."

"I daresay, we've not slept the night through since the blessed arrival of my firstborn. There's always a sniffle or a bad dream keepin' the lads awake. Daniel only just started to use the pot by himself at night."

"My Da used to say 'Ye can sleep when yer dead!' I expect he'll remind me of that when he meets his wee granddaughter." Rolland took the seat in front of the desk, grateful for the gentle breeze coming through the open window behind him. "Martha said ye wanted a word."

"Aye, I should like yer opinion. I've received word from Mother Spencer at St. Joseph's in Missouri. She tells me that they do not accept children for instruction until the age of twelve."

"Is that so? And what is the child to do until then?" Rolland asked.

"She recommends that Felicity attend common school. It is on that recommendation that I would like yer opinion. Can she learn in a classroom with hearing children?"

Rolland adjusted himself more comfortably in the chair and considered the question. "I recall some years back when I was living in Albany, Mr. Harvey Peet, principal of the New York Institute for the Deaf and Dumb, was touring the state with some of his students so that folks would know about the school and what it offered children who couldn't hear. Anyway, I was interested in the methods they used for instruction of the deaf, so I spoke to Mr. Peet for quite a while. He told me that it was important for parents to develop a way early on of communicating with their young children with the use of gestures and pantomime. Later, they would be taught how to use their hands to fashion signs to help them in their formal instruction."

"How do ye mean?"

Rolland thought for a moment, he hadn't actually learned any of the gestures parents might use, but imagined them to be derived from common sense. He patted his belly and then brought the fingers of his right hand to his lips. "Ye see, I might ask if a child were hungry by doing this." He repeated the gesture.

"I take yer meanin' and surely the lass has developed a means to help us attend her needs at home. Martha has no doubt told ye of Felicity's special gift." Rolland nodded. He had spent enough time in this family not to question Martha's claims. Michael continued, "I find that I'm wonderin' if her ability to hear the thoughts of others would help her in a classroom with hearing children? As a teacher, how do ye think ye'd manage such a situation?"

The room was quiet for a few moments as Rolland organized his thoughts. "Well, as I see it, ye're askin' me two separate questions." Michael nodded in agreement. "On the one hand, ye're wonderin' if a teacher would understand and accept that the lass has a rare gift. On the other, ye want to know how I would design a lesson plan that takes her gift into consideration, am I right?

"Aye, just so."

"Are ye thinkin' the lass will stay with us? For if she does ye need not worry about it. I would see to the child's primary education be it in the classroom among the other students or here on the farm. To answer yer question though, I'm thinkin' that her particular gift would serve her better if she were to work alone with a teacher rather than be part of a larger class." Rolland thought for a moment before he continued. "Still, I've only just learned of her ability and I'd like a chance to observe the lass before I share my final thoughts on the subject."

Michael was pleased to hear it. "We won't turn her away if her kin can't be found, but should her uncle be willin' to take her in, I would like to pass on what we've learned about educating the deaf and provide what counsel I can."

"She's too young yet for school and I think the most important thing to do now is to try and find her kin. Should we be fortunate enough to find them, I'll gladly offer a correspondence with her uncle and provide what assistance I can when she is old enough to attend common school."

"I thank ye, Rolland. Ye're right, of course: there's no sense in worryin' about her education in Batavia until we learn if her uncle is there and willing to take her in."

"The child has come here in need, and ye'll worry for her as if she was yer own until such time as she no longer lives under yer roof, and even after that, I expect." Rolland remarked as he stood to take his leave. "Perhaps this will ease yer mind a bit: there's many of us to see that the lass comes to no harm should she leave our care."

Michael only smiled and said, "Get some rest, man," as his brother-in-law stumbled out the door.

* * *

Erik watched the scene unfolding at the rear of the hospital. Mr. Kroeg, one of two critically ill patients left in the hospital who demanded more care than the others, was attended by Nurse Doyle. She held his forehead in one hand and gently rubbed his back with the other as the old man wretched into the bucket. Martha had approached. "Dr. Grant would like a word," she informed the nurse. They were both fine women, and truthfully, he would be happy for the opportunity to bed either of them. His attempts to gain Martha's affection had failed and he began to think he might have a better chance with Millicent. Erik was unaware that the lust he was feeling showed plainly on his face or that another person now stood next to him.

Sherman had no trouble interpreting his colleague's intentions and was glad nobody else could see Erik leering at the two women. "Those thoughts are best served on Canal Street," he said. "You'd do better to mind your thoughts and your manners around here."

Erik turned, relieved to see that it was only Sherman and not Dr. Grant. "Do you mean to tell me the thought has never crossed your mind?" Erik chuckled, "You are a better man than I, Carrington."

Millicent's reluctance to leave the patient prompted Sherman to join the two women without another word to Erik. "I can assist here, Miss Doyle," he told her. The nurse looked up briefly, but never took her attention from Mr. Kroeg. *The thought* had crossed his mind every time he looked at Millicent Doyle and he only hoped it was not evident as it had been on Erik's face. Her compassion was what first attracted him. He had learned empathy by her example. It wasn't just that: Sherman was different because of her. He had come to medicine as a means of escaping, or at least delaying his parents' plans for him. Now, largely because of Millicent, he could clearly see himself as a doctor. How odd to have been reborn in a place where so much death had occurred.

"I thank ye, Mr. Carrington." Shifting her gaze to address Martha, Miss Doyle continued, "Miss Sloane, please let me know if the patient declines further." Martha nodded in agreement and Nurse Doyle left in search of Dr. Grant and her latest instructions for the remaining patients.

Sherman reached for the bucket while Martha got the old man back in his bed. "Why don't I empty that?"

"I thank ye, Sherman." Martha waited until Mr. Kroeg had settled and then went to retrieve the remaining full buckets from the ward. There was still about an hour before her shift ended and in the dark she could make out Sherman heading back toward the door. "Here, you take this one back inside and I'll scrub those out," he offered.

"I thank ye, Sherman, but truth be told, the night air is pleasing and I wouldn't mind bein' out in it for a wee while longer."

"Then let me help you and we can enjoy a bit of night air together, if you have no objections."

"That's kind of ye." She handed him two of the buckets stacked inside one another and they both walked toward the overgrowth of vegetation behind the hospital to dump the contents into a ditch that had been dug for that purpose. Martha got right to work, too tired to draw her colleague into polite conversation and was surprised to hear him speak first.

"It seems odd, the quiet I mean."

"Aye, well there's only the staff and six patients, thank God."

"Yes, I can't recall the last time the hospital had so few patients." He was quiet for a moment before adding, "We have a great deal to be proud of, I think. The way we all worked together during the epidemic, helping each other even with the most vile of duties." He turned toward her, smiling and continued, "We've become friends, haven't we?"

Martha acknowledged a satisfaction in his voice she had never heard before and smiled at the sound of it. "Aye, we have."

* * *

Had Agnes been standing just a few feet over to the right she would have risked being covered in vomit as the subjects of her stealth observation hurled the contents of their buckets into the ditch. Although at a safe distance, she still felt compelled to leap aside just to be sure. She landed among the soft leaves undetected, still upwind of the vile dumping ground. Camouflaged by darkness and a group of saplings, she remained vigilant, determined to rush to Sherman's aid should the misfortune predicted by the Hydesville Rappers befall him. He had insisted on fulfilling his responsibilities to the hospital despite her urgent warning. She was prepared to follow him day and night to protect him if necessary. She ran her hand over the pocket of her skirt, secure in knowing that the pistol she had taken from her father before she left Laona was there if she needed it. But who was this woman with whom he chatted so companionably? Sherman seemed relaxed and confident around her. Agnes had never known him to be at ease in the company of others. By Sherman's proclamation he and this women had become friends. A respectable woman didn't become friends with a man unless she was interested in marriage. "Well, it appears I have arrived just in time," she whispered, watching as the two made their way back to the hospital.

* * *

The steady tapping of hooves on a cobbled street broke the silence as his carriage made its way through a city that was not yet awake. The percussive rhythm distracted Johnny from his thoughts as the horse headed toward the hospital. Quarantines had been lifted all along the canal to Albany and he would be on the road soon with Bruns to New York City. Things had changed dramatically since the last conversation with Martha and he would know her mind before he left. Johnny would travel before winter and make the proper introductions so that Bruns could take over the following spring. After that, he would remain in Buffalo.

Martha was waiting when he arrived at the hospital, sitting alone on the mounting block by the entrance. There was no train of wagons pulling up in front or leaving from behind and it was odd not to see her surrounded by the chaos of the epidemic. She smiled when he pulled up and walked toward the carriage before it came to a stop. "I hoped it would be ye."

"Aye well, with Bruns gone from the farm, Charlie is kept busier with the mornin' chores," Johnny told her. "Besides, I thought we might talk a bit on the way home." Johnny climbed down from the carriage and assisted Martha up.

As they got on their way, both were silent with their own thoughts. Finally Martha spoke. "Well, if it's a talk ye want, perhaps ye should speak first."

Johnny blew out something between a laugh and a snort. "Aye, I should at that." He was quiet again for a moment to regain his composure and then he began. "When last we spoke I hadn't considered a time when I would be living permanently in Buffalo."

"Aye, and now?" Martha shifted a bit on the bench so that she could face him.

"Well, I'll need to be off soon to New York and beyond to make some purchases and see that Bruns learns the way of it, but come next spring it will be him travellin', and I'll be here runnin' the shop for Gran." He dropped the reins, trusting the horse to walk along without guidance and turned to meet her eye. "We could build a life here, together, if it pleases ye."

"Are ye proposin' marriage, Johnny?"

"Aye, I am. Will ye have me, Martha?"

Since her conversation with Ciara, Martha worried over two things. What if Johnny did not want to marry her and what would she say if he did? She felt the queerest kind of relief in that he had asked, but still did not have an answer. Considering for a moment how to put her thoughts into words, she broke his gaze. Taking his hand, eyes flickering between his and the tree on the other side of the road, she spoke. "Johnny, I want ye to listen to all that I have to say before ye speak again. Do ye promise to do so?"

Looking rather wary, he nodded in agreement.

"We have lived as brother and sister since I came here from the Inis Mor, but I've never thought of ye in that way. We've always been close, ye and I, and I do love ye, but now that we are grown, I am not yet sure if our bond is that of a husband and wife. Before I give ye an answer to yer question, I would ask that we spend some more time together and get to know each other as the people we are now, rather than the people we once were. Can ye understand my need of it?"

"Are ye sayin' ye want me to court ye?"

"Aye, I guess I am. I think we both need to see how it will be with me workin' at the hospital and ye on the road. If we can bear that, surely it would bode well for our marriage when ye come home to stay." Martha turned her attention from the tree and looked into his eyes. "Beyond that, well, I want the chance to fall in love with ye. Does that make sense?"

Johnny smiled, relieved and pleased by her admission. "Aye, I believe it makes great sense and I shall very much enjoy courtin' ye." Johnny raised her hand to his lips and pressed a gentle kiss on the back of it. "I shall do my very best to see that ye fall in love with me, Martha Sloane, for I have loved ye since the day I saw ye walkin' up the long drive of the poor farm. I can't see that changin' as I get to know the fine woman ye have become." Placing her hand in her lap, Johnny took the reins once more, pulling hard to the right to turn the horse around. "Let us begin this courtship by takin' the long way home, shall we?"

Chapter Sixteen

September 26, 1849

Millicent Doyle walked carefully from the clothesline toward the rear of the hospital, the basket of clean linens and smocks piled high enough to spill over if she lost her footing. “Let me get that for you.” Erik Schuster took the basket as he spoke. “The faster we get these cots made up, the faster we all can leave.”

“I thank ye, Mr. Schuster. I daresay this is the first time we’ve let cauldron fires go cold since the start of summer.”

“Yes, the day nurses will be well pleased not to have a pile of soiled sheets awaiting their arrival.”

Sherman looked out the window of the kitchen which had been converted once again to a storage area, a scowl spreading across his face as he watched the two chatting companionably as they approached the door. Millicent was just being friendly, but he had seen how

Erik had looked at her and he knew the man had disreputable intentions. At first he did not hear Martha calling behind him. "Sherman, did ye enter the new patient in the ledger?"

"Yes, just after I gave him a purgative." Sherman answered as the other two came in the door.

His expression softened, just for a second, as his gaze passed to Millicent. Martha noticed as she moved to take a stack of sheets and distribute them to her colleagues. "Let us get this done so we can all go home." Without further discussion, the group dispersed.

Martha and Sherman exited the hospital, heads together as they debated Martha's assertion that the recently admitted patient likely had a case of food poisoning rather than cholera. Sherman looked startled as he heard a familiar voice from across the drive.

"There you are, Sherman, darling. I've been waiting simply forever for you to emerge from that dreadful place." Turning toward Martha, Agnes continued, "I'm sorry. I don't believe we have met."

Both the fullness of her skirt and its delicate fabric marked Agnes as a woman who had never done an honest day's work. Sherman found that he was embarrassed by it. "Agnes, this is Martha Sloane. She is a fellow medical student," he told her.

"How lovely to meet you. I'm Agnes Pollard, Sherman's fiancée."

Martha's browse raised in surprise. "'Tis lovely to meet ye Miss Pollard. Sherman didn't tell me he was engaged to be married. May I offer my congratulations to ye both."

Sherman glanced anxiously over his shoulder toward the hospital as Martha spoke, relieved that nobody else had seen his unexpected escort. "Agnes, what are you doing here?" His question sounded more abrupt than he intended and both women looked startled.

"Why darling, you know how I worry when we're apart."

"Well, your parents would not approve of your coming here and neither do I, so let us be off." With a final peek over his shoulder, he guided Agnes toward his carriage. "Good day to you, Miss Sloane."

Sherman wasted no time hoisting Agnes into his carriage and they were off at a brisk trot down the road, passing Johnny on his way to retrieve Martha. Sherman spared the other man a brief nod but continued in the opposite direction.

Martha couldn't help but smile as Johnny came into view. He picked her up regularly at the end of her shift and they took the long way home.

"Who was that with Carrington? He seemed in a bit of a hurry," Johnny asked.

"Her name's Agnes Pollard. Would ye believe they are to be married?"

"They seem a fine match."

"A few months ago I would have agreed, but lately Sherman seems different. To be sure he was less than pleased to see her here."

"He's an odd fellow, is Carrington, but we shall talk of him no more. I've important news to tell ye. A letter came from Megan in yesterday's post. She's found Felicity's uncle. A brief note from him was included. He and his wife lost their wee daughter to the cholera in June. His wife took ill as well, but by God's grace, she recovered. They're willin' to take the lass in." He turned to face her. "Are ye pleased for it?"

"Aye, I am that," she told him and meant it. "I've been prayin' for this very miracle. When will she leave?"

He was relieved to see her answer was genuine and that she had reconsidered taking the child in. "Well, I imagine as soon as it can be arranged. We should write him straightaway, I think. There's nothin' to be gained by waitin'."

"Aye, I'll do it myself by day's end."

"Ye'll be sad to see her go, I expect."

"I'll miss her, to be sure, but she belongs with her kin. I'm well pleased they're willin' to take her in." Martha paused briefly and asked, "They are decent folk? Did yer sister remark on his character, the uncle?"

"She said they have a house in town. The man's a shoemaker and makes a decent living. Megan found Mr. and Mrs. Taylor to be kind and the house well kept. I expect the lass will have a fine home with them."

"Then I am truly happy for her."

"I'm glad of it."

They continued on in silence for a while. Finally Martha detected the aroma of smoked ham. Her stomach growled in recognition and she looked around for the source of the temptation, not at all shamed by the unladylike noises coming from inside her. "Have ye brought along somethin' to eat?"

"Aye, Ellie packed a wee basket." He patted the package wedged between him and the side of the bench. "We'd best find a place to stop and eat lest that monster inside ye get loose!"

"I'll do for a wee bit longer if ye have a particular place in mind."

His smile betrayed the truth of it and a snap of the reins had them moving a bit faster toward their destination. They traveled down Canal Street, turned down a dirt road and crossed the bridge to Squaw Island. The cool fall breeze kept the bugs at bay and they settled in a spot by the creek near the woods.

"Sun or shade?" Johnny gestured around indicating possible places they might take their ease and enjoy a bite to eat.

"Sun, if ye please." Martha sat down on the grass and immediately began rummaging through the basket, retrieving a biscuit and a napkin.

"Ye must be starved, poor lass. I'd have stopped sooner had ye told me so."

"'Tis no bother. I love Deyowenoguhdoh Island, so it was well worth the wait."

"Ye still use the Seneca name for it?"

"Aye, and ye should as well. 'Tis a beautiful place, and undeserving of such an ugly name as Squaw Island. Do ye recall we used to sneak in here and play in the creek when we were young?"

"Aye, I do. I'd wager we're sneakin' in here now, for all the hydraulic company now owns the island."

"I suppose we are. 'Tis a good thing we are tucked away near the woods." She pushed her thumb into the edge of the biscuit, broke it in half and placed a slice of ham between the two sides. "Shall I make ye one?"

"Ye eat up. I'll get my own." Johnny prepared the remaining biscuits and ham to share and the two ate in silence.

"Better now?"

Martha patted her now full stomach and smiled. "Aye, much better now."

"Are ye tired? Ye must be, havin' worked through the night. I can take ye home if ye like."

"No, I'm not a bit tired." She smiled and moved closer, so that they were facing each other. "I must say, Johnny Quinn, I find myself wonderin,' for all ye've been courtin' me for nearly two weeks now, why on earth have ye not yet kissed me?"

Johnny laughed out loud as she leaned toward him, lips puckered, eyes closed, and barely able to contain her own mirth. "And just how am I supposed to kiss ye now with ye sputterin' and snortin?"

She opened her eyes, lips relaxing into a smile. "Well, if ye don't, I'll just have to be the one kissin' ye!" Leaning forward touching her lips to his brought an end to the discussion. They were seated in the grass at an awkward angle, and so parted after just a few seconds. "Ye call that a kiss?" He rose to his knees, pulling her up and into his arms. "Let me show ye how it's done." Cradling the back of her head in his hand, he drew her in and pressed his lips to hers, lingering there as if there was no rush for anything more. He hadn't realized until right then how long he had been waiting to kiss her, how much he wanted to kiss her. Their lips parted and his tongue gently caressed hers. She responded with a soft sigh that could have led to other things she wasn't ready for if he hadn't exercised extreme self-control and gently pulled away. When they parted, he had lost the ability to speak and so was unable to utter the smug remark he'd intended.

* * *

"What's your hurry, darling?" Agnes reached for the reins to slow the carriage as it continued swiftly in the direction of the American Hotel. "It is a lovely morning. Could we not take a drive in the country?"

"I have been working through the night and I would like to get some sleep. I will meet you for dinner as planned," he told her, shooing her hands away and not bothering to hide the irritation in his voice.

Agnes decided to see what she could learn about Martha Sloane. "A woman in medical school, that surely is odd, don't you agree?"

"Miss Sloane is a fine doctor, better than the rest of us, truth be told."

"Why have you not told her you are to be married? She certainly seemed surprised to hear the news. Perhaps she has enrolled in medical school to find a respectable husband." Agnes was looking directly at him, but Sherman kept his eyes on the road. "You need to make it clear to her that you are spoken for."

"I have already told you. We had time only for the work that needed to be done, and often not even enough time for that."

"Sherman, she is in love with you. I can see it in her eyes. Perhaps the Fox Sisters warned of her interest in you. You must stay far away from her my darling. I fear she will bring you to ruin."

"You are being ridiculous, Agnes. Miss Sloane is a colleague and a friend, nothing more."

"Sherman, men who are to be married should not have women as friends. I must insist that you have nothing more to do with her."

Martha was perhaps the first real friend Sherman had ever known, but he hadn't the nerve to tell Agnes so. He had other less pleasant things that needed to be said eventually, and didn't want to add to the weight of his words by telling Agnes there were women in his life that he cared about more than her. "We work together and do not see each other outside of the hospital," was all he said.

"Well, I shall make sure of that now that I'm in town."

"Agnes, I've sent word to your parents and they will be here any day to collect you back to Albany." In truth, Sherman had waited to contact their parents, using the time to build his resolve to break off their engagement. He had sent a messenger to Laona just yesterday, leaving only a day or two more to work up his nerve. He silently cursed himself for waiting so long to act.

"My darling, you know I can't leave you with the threat of doom hanging over your head. I'll tell mother and father what the Fox sisters foretold and they will stay here with me until you are ready to come home. I just know they will."

Their conversation came to an abrupt end when Sherman pulled up in front of the hotel. "We can discuss this over dinner," he offered as he helped her down and through the entrance.

Back in his own room, Sherman pondered the most recent developments in his predicament. His secret had been revealed, to Martha of all people. It had been his intention to tell only Millicent of his engagement. She deserved to know the truth of the situation and he dearly hoped she would not think him a scoundrel when she found out about Agnes. He felt he was a scoundrel. After all, what kind of man would seek the attention of another woman when he was engaged to be married?

To make matters worse, Agnes was determined to stay in town. It would devastate her to learn that Sherman did not wish to marry her, but delaying that discussion any longer would only make matters worse. Better to tell her now so that she would leave when their parents arrived. He had no intentions of telling her about Millicent. While he did not love Agnes, or even like her much for that matter, she did not deserve to be hurt. He would break off their engagement tonight, but first, there was someone else to see.

* * *

Marcia and Ashton Carrington were just about to go down to tea when Mr. and Mrs. Pollard came to call. Eager to announce her news, Susan Pollard dispensed with the formal greeting and got straight to the point of their unplanned visit. "We've had word from your son that Agnes has run off to Buffalo."

"Oh, thank God she has been found. I know you had feared the worst. We all had." The Pollards were indeed distraught over the sudden disappearance of Agnes, but were more inclined to think their impetuous daughter had run off rather than having been abducted. As soon as the travel bans were lifted they had dispatched a man back to Albany in search of her. Marcia rushed over to embrace her friend. "She is unharmed then?"

"Yes. Sherman has seen to it that Agnes has a suite of rooms at the American Hotel. She will be quite safe until our arrival next week."

"My dear, we certainly understand if you would like to leave for Buffalo immediately. Of course, we would travel with you."

"Mr. Pollard and I have discussed the matter and we feel she is well attended at the hotel while Sherman is engaged at that dreadful hospital and we trust him to look after her when he is able. We see no reason to rush off to Buffalo before we have learned the art of mesmerism. Mr. Pollard feels he will soon be able to perform the act himself. Isn't that exciting?"

"That is remarkable after such a short amount of time. We are privileged to bear witness to his transformation. I agree that Sherman can be relied upon to look after Agnes. Don't you agree, Ashton?" Mr. Carrington nodded, although he needn't have bothered. His wife continued speaking as if she hadn't expected him to respond. "I just wish he would stay clear of that horrible hospital. I can see no reason why he is still needed there now that the illness has run its course. Surely there must be others who can attend the few remaining patients."

"The boy has got to do his part, Marcia." It was only rarely that Ashton disagreed with his wife, but on this topic his opinion could not be altered. Ashton was a well-respected business man and he was determined that Sherman be respected in whatever profession he chose, or rather whatever profession his mother chose for him. Men admired other men who pulled their weight, and both Ashton and Hiram Pollard agreed, much to the dismay of their wives, that Sherman's time at the cholera hospital would eventually serve him well.

"Yes, well, the danger has well passed, and I see no need for him to stay in Buffalo when he is needed with his family. If he had come when we sent for him, dear Agnes would not have run off."

Ignoring his wife, Ashton turned to Mrs. Pollard. "So it is settled, then? We will travel to Buffalo next week as planned?"

"Yes, I believe so."

* * *

Sherman eased his door open just a crack in search of passersby. Finding it empty of prying eyes, he proceeded up to the third floor of Mrs. Cornish's undetected. A gentle knock on the second door to the left was answered without hesitation, its tenant launching herself into his arms as soon as it closed. "I hoped ye'd come," she said between kisses.

"I'm only sorry it has taken me this long, my darling." Sherman held Millicent Doyle in his arms, steeling his nerves to tell her what he should have confessed months ago. Finally he took a deep breath and a step back. "Millicent, please sit for a moment. There is something I have to tell you. I only hope that when I have, you will see that you are, and will always be, my one true love."

Chapter Seventeen

Dinner at the Nolan house was louder than usual. Wee Mary was fussy and one or the other of her parents left the table frequently to walk with her out in the cool night air. The lads were thrilled that Johnny had joined them and took turns trying to impress him with their stories of fishing earlier in the day. Layered over that was the clink of dishes being passed around and the adult conversation, inserted into which was their occasional shushing of Daniel and Ian who had decided if they could not outdo the other in deeds, they would do so in volume. Felicity watched it all, engaged in the chaos, rather than on the outside of it. She seemed to follow the boys' conversation and giggled when they used big gestures to punctuate the important parts of their story. When the plates were empty and the babe had finally settled, Michael instructed the three children to clear the table and ready themselves for bed, pointing to Felicity and stacking the plates around him to emphasize that she was included in the directive.

"Don't forget to help Felicity wash behind her ears," Ciara reminded her sons when they finished their task.

"Yes, Ma," the lads said in unison as they each took their charge by the hand and led her up the stairs.

"And mind the washstand!" The somewhat harsher edict from their father was in reference to an incident the night before when their evening ritual of pushing and shoving to avoid being the first to wash resulted in a chipped handle on the water pitcher.

"That was Ian," Daniel called as they climbed the stairs.

"Was not!"

"Was so!"

"It'll be both yer hides if I hear any sort of a stramash up there!" Michael waited for the children to make it up the stairs before he directed his remarks to those still around the table. "I've had a letter from Mr. Taylor and he thought it would be wise for Martha to travel with Felicity to Batavia and stay for a time, ye know, to help everyone adjust to the situation."

"But what of my work at the hospital?" Martha wasn't surprised to be included in the journey, but had mixed feelings about traveling while there were still cholera patients.

"There's naught but three new patients at present and unlikely to be any more. I'll see to it that ye're given leave," Michael told her.

Martha was still hesitant to agree even for the sake of the child, mostly on the grounds that she did not want to receive any special consideration from her professors.

"Sister, ye worked shifts day and night when the other students had to attend to family matters. Surely no one will think ill of ye for attending to yer own." Ciara was proud of her sister's work ethic, but the young woman needed to be reminded that family came first, and Felicity had become family in the weeks she had spent on the Nolan farm.

"Aye, I suppose ye're right." Turning to Johnny, Martha asked "Have ye room for me to travel with ye?"

"We'll make room. "Tis wise to have ye along to see to the child's needs on the road. We'll drop ye off in

Batavia on our way to New York and collect ye on the way back."

"How shall we tell her?" Patricia asked.

"''Tis no tellin' her about the trip I'd be worried about," Rolland offered. "She'll be fine as long as she sees Martha is goin' along. The bigger question is how will ye get her to understand she's to stay when ye leave?"

"She's met her Da's kin. They were in Buffalo about a year ago, were they not? Do ye think she'll remember them?" Martha asked.

"Let's pray she does," Rolland said. "It'll be easier for everyone if they are familiar to her."

"Once ye arrive, it'll be a month or more before ye'll be leavin' again. Surely if they are kind folk she'll grow comfortable around them," Patricia offered. "Mr. Taylor did say as his wife had a soft spot in her heart for the lass from the time she was born, did he not?"

"Aye, he did," Johnny told her. "Megan said they were well pleased to take the lass in. Rolland has informed them of our correspondences with the Sisters of St. Joseph in Missouri and of Mr. Peet's school in

New York City and they are keen to see Felicity properly educated when the time is right."

"I'll say an extra prayer of thanks the child has found a home, for so many others have not," Ciara added. "There are ten more beds occupied at the orphan asylum. I'm told the other orphans homes are full as well. With winter comin' we'll need to see that there are enough boots and coats for the wee ones. I shall go tomorrow and speak to Mrs. McClaverly before the Board of Directresses meet."

"I dearly wish I could come with ye," Patricia said. "They'll be needin' some help in the nursery with all the new children comin' in."

"Ye'll do no such thing, sister. The babe is much too young to be away from ye for that long, and well ye know ye can't bring her out until she's properly baptized. That won't be for another week yet," Ciara reminded her. Father Guth had not yet finished laying to rest all who had died during the epidemic and it would be a while yet before he could bless this new life.

"I do so wish that Father Guth could come sooner. I'm needed at the orphanage."

Rolland placed a hand on his wife's shoulder, speaking to her as if the others were not there. "Darlin', we've had this discussion before. Right now ye'll have to let Ciara and me do what we can at the orphan asylum, for yer own babe needs ye."

"I am truly grateful to the good Lord for blessin' us with such a healthy babe, but I'm heartbroken for the poor souls who lost their mothers and fathers," Patricia told him. "Well ye know I would never deny wee Mary the comfort of her own mothers' arms, but 'tis no easy for me to deny others the same."

Martha truly felt her middle sister's anguish, knowing she would feel the same way. It was really more a blessing than a curse that both of her sisters had spent the early years of their married lives childless. They both felt conflicted when it came time to think of their own over the many homeless children they had previously loved unconditionally. Michael had grown concerned over the amount of time Ciara had spent at the orphanage when Ian was born, and likely Rolland would have similar discussions with Patricia now that wee Mary had arrived. These men had reached adulthood with both parents still alive and couldn't really understand the obligation their wives felt toward those poor souls who'd lost their families so early in their lives, although they wanted to and thought they did. Would she and Johnny have that same quarrel one day?

As he was leaving later that night Johnny suspected thoughts of her sister's dilemma still sat ill with Martha and asked her about it as they walked to his carriage. "Yer mind is still with Patricia."

"How did ye know?"

"I grew up in the same house ye did. Ciara struggled when young Ian was born and now Patricia feels that same conflict. Ye're wonderin' what will happen should ye be blessed with a babe of yer own."

"I would ask ye that very question: what *will* happen? Will ye be at peace with me leavin' a newborn babe should a child from the orphan asylum take sick?"

"Martha, ye forget I knew a different life than did Michael and Rolland growin' up. I lived for a time in the poorhouse with nobody to look out for me before ye and yer sisters came. I understand the obligation ye feel toward the orphan asylum in a way they can't. That's why we are a good match, don't ye see?"

She turned to face him, wanting to see in his eyes for herself when she asked her next question. "Will ye mean that still when I leave our bed in the middle of the night because one of the orphan babes has got the croup?"

Johnny considered the question, asked with great seriousness, yet could not manage to suppress the mischievous smirk spreading across his face. "Our bed, ye've been thinkin' we'll share a bed?" He pulled her closer, unresisting, and kissed her, offering just a glimpse of what she would be missing should she leave their bed.

"Well, ye're a fine kisser, so I find I've been wonderin' what else ye might be good at." Martha smiled, the truth of it plain on her face. Johnny laughed out loud, not at all bothered that she had made him blush. His reaction pleased her so she continued before he could find speech. "Did ye think I wouldn't know what goes on in the bed chamber, for all I'm studyin' to be a doctor?"

Curious to see where this conversation might lead, he chose his next words carefully. "Aye, and would ye by chance bring to yer wedding night a secret or two only a doctor might know?"

This time it was Martha who snorted in amusement. "Given all the time ye've spent among the Onondowagah, women, I'd think ye'd have a thing or two to show me!"

She had rendered him speechless and took no pains to hide her satisfaction. Feigning shock, he responded. "And just what do ye mean by that, Martha Sloane?"

"Ye know well what I mean. Would ye deny it? Ye shouldn't be afraid to speak the truth," she was enjoying this game, free for a moment of the weight of her earlier thoughts, and laughing as he sputtered an explanation.

This was not the Martha he had grown up with, and Johnny found he quite liked that she wasn't at all shy about this particular topic. Perhaps he could shock her in return. "Ye assume that I have had relations with women in the longhouses but not women in the whorehouses?"

"Aye, well, ye're a man, after all, and a fine one at that. I'm sure ye've caught the eye of both, but I know ye, Johnny Quinn, and ye'd not bed a lass who was forced to lie with men to make a livin'. Ye know well some of those whom others call whores showed us kindness when we lived at the poor farm. The Onondowagah women choose who they will lie with, and I'm guessin' more than one chose ye."

There seemed little point in denying his previous relationships, such as they were, with the Seneca women. As much as he was intrigued by this conversation, though, he wanted to put her original concerns to rest. "Yes, I've enjoyed the company of other women, but ye have always been the love of my life and I want to be clear, Martha. Should we marry and be blessed with a family, I will always respect and honor your commitment to your patients, be they orphaned children or not."

"I believe ye mean that, and I thank ye," and then she kissed him, relief and gratitude changing quickly to something more intense as he pulled her closer. He was a fine kisser indeed.

* * *

Sherman looked out the window at the sun sinking low in the sky. He would have to leave soon and meet

Agnes for dinner, but he could not disentangle himself from Millicent's arms. The couple had fallen asleep, fully clothed and exhausted more from the afternoon's revelations than from the previous night's efforts at the hospital. Millicent had no adverse reaction to his confession. However, she vehemently insisted he not break off his engagement to Agnes this evening.

"Darlin' Sherman, can't ye see? She'll have no shoulder to cry on if ye tell her tonight, nobody to wipe her tears when she lays her head to sleep," Millicent had told him. "Don't be cruel. Ye must wait until she has her family about her so that they may offer the comfort she'll need."

He had not expected those words from her. "You are kind to think of Agnes' feelings."

"I only know how I would feel if I learned we could not be together."

Sherman lay awake, still summoning the courage to tell Millicent that when his parents learned of their love he would most certainly be disinherited. His heart filled with dread at the thought and the tension creeping through his body caused her to stir. "Why do ye fret, my love?" she asked.

"I have another confession that may yet be the end of us." He readjusted himself so that he could look upon her as he spoke. "My parents will be very displeased when they hear of my broken engagement. I fear they will banish me when they learn of my love for you and our plans to marry."

Raising her hands to bring his face closer to hers, she replied, "I'm not worried. I am in love with ye, not yer parents or their fortune. It would please me to be counted as family when we wed, but it will not break my heart if I am not. Will it break yers?"

Would it break his heart? Sherman had dreaded his parent's disapproval since childhood, although why, he did not know. Now it didn't matter why for he knew in his heart that Millicent's love was vital but his parent's approval wasn't. "No, it will not." It was both a joy and a relief to admit and he kissed her with a passion he was only beginning to understand. "We will be together soon, my darling, if I can ask your patience and understanding for just a bit longer."

"We have the rest of our lives together. I am happy to keep our secret for now."

Chapter Eighteen

October 2, 1849

Millicent's words still filled his head as Sherman read the patient log, adding notes to the few cases they had treated during the night. He had spent days working up the courage to break off his engagement with Agnes only to be persuaded to wait until her parents arrived. He had no wish to hurt Agnes, but was also desperate to spare himself the endless lecturing and scolding that would come not only from the Pollards, but from his parents as well, as each tried to shame him into changing his mind. There had to be a way to avoid all of that, but he could not see how.

"Sherman," Martha said a second time, clearing her throat to gain his attention.

"Yes, I beg your pardon. My thoughts wandered for just a moment. How can I be of service, Martha?"

"I was just goin' to tell ye that I've got Mr. Perry settled and I don't think he is in need of a sedative." She turned as if to leave, but thought better of it. "Ye do seem distracted this evening. I hope all is well."

Sherman looked briefly around the room, noting the patients resting comfortably and, most importantly, Dr. Ryan and Erik were out of earshot. Still, he lowered his voice. "Martha, may I impose upon our friendship and confide in you? I find myself in a situation and I am in need of counsel."

Martha's brows rose at such an unusual request. "I'm happy to be of help to ye if I can. What troubles ye?"

"It is of a personal nature and I hope you will not take offense. You have always been very easy for me to talk to and you are a person whose opinion I respect." He paused and the look of anguish on his face compelled her to take a seat beside him, shifting slightly so they were face to face. "I've already told you I am engaged to be married."

"Aye."

"I did not ask for Agnes' hand. Our parents arranged the union when we were just children."

"Oh, dear, and ye don't want to marry Agnes, is that it? Is there someone else?" Martha thought better of asking the second question as soon as it escaped her lips. "Do forgive me, 'tis none of my concern."

"There is nothing to forgive. You are correct: I do not wish to marry her, and, yes, there is someone else." Martha's brows rose again and Sherman struggled to explain. "I had not intended… I certainly wasn't looking…Do you think me a scoundrel?"

Martha did not hesitate to answer him. "No, I don't think ye a scoundrel, but I'm not sure how I can be of help to ye."

Sherman drew in a deep breath and blew it back out again, quickly glancing around the room to confirm their privacy before he continued. "It is my intention to marry another, and so I need to end my engagement with Agnes. I do not love her, but I do not wish to hurt her either. There will be… conflict between me and both of our parents. I am prepared to accept what consequences they feel compelled… however… I wish to minimize any damage this turn of events might cause to my relationships with all parties involved."

Martha leaned back in her chair, considering what she could offer in the way of advice. "Sherman, have ye considered tellin' yer parents ye don't wish to marry Agnes?"

"My wishes on the matter, on any matter, are not a consideration. I have always done what my parents have asked of me and they will expect no different this time. You see, appearances are important to them. They chose Agnes because she comes from a good family. Our parents have been friends since before we were born. We are a good match in their eyes."

"What of Agnes? Does she want to marry ye?"

"I believe so, yes."

"Have ye spoken to her on the matter?" When he looked confused, she elaborated. "Did ye not talk about what yer married life would be like? Shared yer hopes and dreams?"

Sherman had confided his most secret desires to Millicent, a woman he had known only a few months, but not Agnes, whom he had known his entire life. "Never," he told her.

"Sherman, she only knows ye as the lad ye were, not the man ye have become. Talk to her. Help her to understand how ye have grown apart. Make her realize she won't be truly happy if she marries ye."

A glimmer of hope appeared in his eyes. Perhaps he could convince Agnes that she did not want to marry him. Surely her parents would support her if she chose to end their engagement. What could his parents do but go along with it? He could spare Agnes' feelings and spare himself the anger and disappointment of his parents. "Thank you, Martha." He reached for her hand, taking it between his own. "You have been so kind to me and I am truly grateful for your wisdom and your friendship."

Martha smiled, understanding the gesture for what it was. "I'm happy I could help." Rising from the chair beside him, she turned to continue about her business. Midway across the room, she turned and called out, "Don't be forgettin' about Mr. Perry."

Sherman looked puzzled. "Oh, yes, no sedative. I'll make a note."

* * *

Agnes grew frustrated. From her vantage point outside the hospital she could only see the desk by the window, which meant that she could not account for

Sherman's activities unless he was seated there. It was proving to be most difficult to protect him when she couldn't see what he was up to most of the time. She was just about to scout around for a better spot when he appeared in the window. "What do we have here?" she whispered when Martha took a seat next to Sherman a few minutes later. The small desk was situated in the alcove by the window, the two chairs practically touching and two heads bent close in discussion. Agnes gasped out loud when Sherman took Martha's hand. "The nerve of that woman!"

After some thought, Agnes decided she would wait until Sherman was done with his shift at the hospital, rather than sneaking back to the hotel as she had done every night that he worked. She would insist that he cease his activities at the hospital and return to Albany with their families before this woman could cause any more trouble in their lives. She took a seat on the mounting block outside of the front door and waited for Sherman to exit. With her dress smoothed of wrinkles and hair free of twigs, there was no longer evidence of her covert evening activities.

Near the end of his shift, Sherman was again at the desk near the window making last minute notes in the ledger. "Oh no," he groaned, peering out the window.

"What's amiss?" Martha asked, leaning over his shoulder.

"Agnes is here." Steering her away from the window, he lowered his voice, "Martha, may I request a favor that will impose upon our friendship yet again?" Not waiting for her to answer, he continued, "Millicent. She knows about Agnes, but it would be cruel for her to see us together, don't you think?"

"Millicent?" He gave her a quick nod and when she realized what he meant, she returned the same. "Oh, yes, quite right." Martha looked at the nurse who was making up a bed at the back of the room. "Away ye go before Agnes has a mind to come in and I'll just ask Millicent to double check that the cauldron fire is out before I go."

"Thank you, Martha." Sherman glanced back at the nurse. "I dare not take even a moment to wish her good day."

"Just ye go on. I'll tell her ye were called away." Martha shooed him off and made her way towards the back of the hospital.

Agnes ran straight up to her fiancé as the front door closed behind him. "Oh Sherman, darling, do not be cross with me. I simply could not wait another minute to see with my own eyes that you are safe."

"As you can see Agnes, I am quite well. Now let us be off. It has been a long night and I am tired."

"Could we not take a short drive? It is such a lovely morning."

Seeing an opportunity to initiate his plan, he agreed and directed the carriage away from the city. "I rather like Buffalo," he told her. "I think I would like to stay here when I am done with medical school."

"Don't be silly, darling. We will live in Albany after we wed, just as we planned," Agnes reminded him.

"I would like to stay. There are many towns just outside the city in need of doctors."

"Well, mother and I agree we should stay in Albany. I can't see your parents consenting to a move."

More assertive this time, he continued to press his point. "Agnes, we are adults and we can make our own choices. I want to stay in Buffalo. I have made some friends here. You would like them, too, once you got to know them."

"We have all of the companions we need back home."

"When I finish medical school I am staying in Buffalo," Sherman insisted.

"Sherman, darling, can you not see? That woman has filled your head with foolish thoughts. You will come back with me to Albany as soon as our parents arrive in Buffalo."

"What woman? You are speaking nonsense." Sherman was careful to keep his tone even.

"I most certainly am not. I see the way Miss Sloane looks at you. Why just last night she took your hand and…" Agnes immediately stopped talking lest she betray her own secret.

Sherman stopped the carriage and turned to face her. "Agnes, what are you talking about? How long have you been here?" Her expression was all but a confession. "Have you been here all night?"

"Sherman, I fear for your safety. I must protect you. That woman is a danger to you, can you not see?"

Sherman was stunned into silence, continuing to stare at the spectacle of his fiancée ranting, and realizing that his plan would be considerably more difficult to implement than he previously thought. When she finally stopped he took a moment to compose his own thoughts before responding. "Agnes, I can't impress upon you enough the danger in which you place yourself by wandering around the city at night unescorted."

"Darling, what am I to do? You will not take seriously the warning from the Fox Sisters. Someone must protect you if you refuse to guard yourself."

Sherman struggled to keep his temper in check. "I do not believe there is any threat to my safety. Frankly, I am unimpressed with this belief in the supernatural you share with our parents. There is no evidence that those girls spoke the truth."

"Sherman, I am suddenly unwell. Please take me back to my hotel so that I can rest." Agnes had learned as a child that feigning illness was the best way to avoid any unpleasant situation.

"I will do that, but I would like to make something very clear to you first. Under no circumstances are you to leave your hotel after dinner for the remainder of your stay in Buffalo and you are not to come around to the hospital. Do you understand?"

"I will honor your request if you honor mine. Leave your work at the hospital. Surely they have no real need of you now. If Miss Sloane is such a brilliant physician, let her handle the remaining patients. We can travel to Laona before going home. I'm sure if you meet the sisters yourself you will not question their abilities."

"Agnes, you have not heard a word I have said. I am not going home and I am certainly not going to Laona to engage in whatever nonsense currently fascinates our parents."

"Exhaustion has clouded your mind, Sherman. It's no wonder working night after night in that dreadful place. Those people are not your true friends, for if they were, they would encourage you to return to your family where you belong." His blank stare only encouraged her to continue speaking. "You may think what you wish now, but you and I both know that when our parents arrive you will change your mind. They will see to it that you are brought back to your senses."

Sherman took the reins back in his hands, prepared to return her to the hotel in silence, but then words were escaping his lips before he was even aware of what he was saying, almost as if someone else had spoken for him. "They will not change my mind, Agnes. We are not the same people we were as children and I do not think it is a good idea for us to wed. Clearly we want different things and I believe you would not be happy with me as your husband."

Compressing her lips in an effort to remain calm, she merely shook her head to disagree. "You are tired, my darling, I can see it in your eyes. You do not mean what you are saying. Please take me back to the hotel and we will talk again this evening when we are both feeling better."

"Yes, I think that would be best." There was no point in pushing the issue and causing a scandal once they reached the hotel. It was apparent that no amount of convincing would result in Agnes changing her mind about the marriage. Sherman also knew that once their parents arrived in town, matters would become worse for him.

* * *

With the older children suitably exhausted in both mind and body from their lessons and some play time outside for good measure, Rolland made his way home from the orphan asylum on Pearl Street with the intent to spend some time with wee Felicity. After his discussion with Michael, he was keen to evaluate her ability to learn in a classroom of hearing children. As he proceeded down the drive of the Nolan farm, he spotted Ian and Daniel creeping about the barn as if they were looking for something, or someone. "Mind ye don't play hide and seek in the barn. Ye'll frighten the horses," Rolland warned.

Daniel, who was *it*, replied. "We've looked every place and we can't find her."

Rolland took the time to dismount before he asked the boys how long they had been looking for Felicity. Panic started to take root when he learned that they had been searching for nearly an hour. She would not hear if they had been calling for her, but would they have heard if she cried out in need of help? "Were ye here in the yard the whole time?" He asked the boys.

"Aye, ma told us not to go far," Ian told him, pointing to the mounting block by the barn where his brother had stood with his eyes closed, waiting for the other two to hide. "He found me straightaway," he added, disappointment evident in his voice.

"Daniel, how high did ye count before ye went lookin'?"

The boy smiled and proudly announced he had been able to count up to sixty. "I did get a wee bit stuck around 20, though," he admitted.

With a minute to hide, Felicity could not have gotten far. "Ye've checked the barn and around the outbuildings?" The boys nodded and Rolland took a moment to think, wondering if it was necessary to alert Ciara or Karin. He tied the horse up to the fence, loosened her girth, and scanned the yard. After another moment he appeared to have made up his mind and then proceeded in the direction of the mounting block. He closed his eyes, as if deep in thought and then opened them and took a seat. Just then the boys noticed Felicity slowly emerge from behind the barn, a devilish grin spreading across her face.

"Well now, there ye are," He was too relieved that he had been right to be cross with her. Assuming that the child would respect Ciara's directive not to leave the yard, Rolland had wondered if she was just playing a trick on the lads by remaining hidden for so long. It was as good a time as any to test the idea that she could read thoughts, so he focused on what the consequences might be if she had not come out of her hiding place and he had had to enlist the help of the women to find her. Within seconds she emerged, her expression betraying her mischievous intentions.

Through a series of enthusiastic nods and chuckles, the boys managed to convey their appreciation for both the prank and her superior hiding ability. Each of them had looked behind the barn several times and neither had been able to determine her location. Felicity laughed and made as if she was peeking out from behind something, then she crouched down and slowly moved forward as if she was creeping up on someone.

"She was following us the whole time!" Daniel laughed out loud and slapped his brother on the back for good measure.

"Ye're a sneaky lass, to be sure," Ian told her with admiration.

Rolland watched in awe as Felicity basked in the glow of their admiration. The three of them had developed a means of communication all their own which was, Rolland thought, some combination of pantomime and the ability to read each other's thoughts. He had been a school teacher long enough to wonder whether the ability for children to communicate nonverbally was just one of the many gifts of being young and unencumbered by the responsibilities of the grown-up world. He had long suspected that it was that very gift that often stood in the way of his lesson plans in the classroom, when the children got up to all manner of mischief without a single word spoken. In time, the ability would fade for the boys as they grew into men, but for Felicity, perhaps not.

"Who has a mind to play a new game?" He asked all three of them, reaching into his pocket and pulling out a handful of lemon drops.

* * *

The evening meal was particularly boisterous because Rolland had made a request that all the residents of the Nolan farm dine under one roof. He had given Patricia a full report of his afternoon with Felicity and the lads. When the child finally emerged from her hiding place, he had engaged the three of them in a game designed to help him understand how much of Felicity's ability to communicate was based on observation and how much was based her apparent ability to hear the thoughts or intentions of others. They each took turns closing their eyes while the others silently determine among them who would hold the small sack of lemon drops behind their back. If the correct person was identified, the guesser could help him or herself to a piece of the candy. Although Felicity was the only one among them to accurately identify each time which of the three of them held the candy, Ian and Daniel had both given themselves away, the former with a sly smile and the latter other by fidgeting. She also was able to determine when none of them was holding the lemon drops, staring at the three of them before confidently sauntering over to the tree in which Rolland had placed them.

Patricia was intrigued and thought it might be worth a try to observe the child during the chaos of the supper table. With multiple conversations layered over the passing of dishes, and, inevitably, the fussing of wee Mary Karin, she wondered if Felicity would be able to distinguish Rolland's attempts to communicate with her nonverbally over the rest of the commotion. Together they had spoken to the other adults and agreed that during the course of dinner, Michael and Karin would also try to get her attention without the use of speech.

Each household had simply brought individual dinner preparations to Ciara and Michael's table and so it was more crowded than usual with additional dishes as well as people. "Da, would ye pass the ham, please?" Ian requested, although the roasted venison was currently making its way from one direction while the potatoes were coming around from the other side.

"Just ye wait until the rest of us have had a chance, for all we know ye'll clean off the whole platter if it passes ye first," his father teased.

Rolland watched as food circulated the table and conversations ensued. When the boisterous chatter was such that a person would have to shout to be heard above the din, he looked at Felicity, who was beaming with pride as the boys told Charlie of their adventures earlier in the day. Rolland continued to focus on her until the child turned to face him. He smiled and thought about the joy he would feel if she were to wave to him from across the table. His smile grew broader as she raised her small hand in his direction.

As if on cue, Karin tried to divert Felicity's attention from Rolland, who had decided to wave back. She often played a game with the children when they were very young where they would blow her kisses and she would make a big show of catching them and returning the gift. It was something each of them treasured, realizing as they got older that their auntie was not usually given to displays of affection. Karin thought about how she wanted Felicity to blow her a kiss. She continued to stare at the girl, who was preoccupied with her game with Rolland. After a few minutes, with a final wave, she turned and blew Karin a kiss. The woman raised her hands and spread them far apart as if to receive a large gift. "Danke, mein Schatz!" Karin blew a kiss in return.

By this time Felicity was on to the game and turned to face Michael, who had decided to wait a bit longer before trying to distract her again. She stared at him expectantly. "What are ye lookin' at me for?" He asked her, knowing somehow that she would take his meaning even if she could not hear the words. He smiled and waved Felicity away, realizing that she had already demonstrated that she knew he would be the next one to communicate with her. Turning to Rolland, he laughed and said, “Well, I guess we have our answer now, don’t we?”

Chapter Nineteen

February 8, 2015

Maude looked up from the screen, pleased with her morning's effort. There was one more thing she needed to do before she turned off the laptop and opened the shop, but still couldn't quite bring herself to do it. The story was flowing like a lazy river, fast enough to move forward but slow enough to take in the scenery. It wouldn't do to have progress halted over the discovery that Daniel Nolan had actually died of cholera in August of 1849. It would just take a few minutes to check. She had downloaded all of the newspapers for the period encompassing the epidemic, but what if it turned out to be true? Before she could open the file her cell phone rang.

"Do it already," Don said through the speaker.

"Do what?"

"Check the newspapers to see if that guy died."

"You have perfect timing, I was pondering that very thing."

"You've probably been putting it off all morning. Just look and get it over with."

"It's not that simple, Don. If that turns out to be true, think of all of the other details I will have to try and verify. It's weird enough that I'm having all of these vivid dreams about people I have never met, during a time period in which I did not live. To find out that some or all of it is true would be just that much more bizarre, don't you think?" Maude got up to unlock the front door while she spoke. "Besides, I remember you were less than pleased about me trying to find out more when I was having all those strange visions from that almshouse skeleton."

"It's not the same, and you know it, Maude. I was worried you would hurt yourself then. I don't think there is any danger of that now. Besides, I can't help but think that somehow the two situations are linked. You have a very unusual connection to the people who were written about in that journal and I'd be lying if I said I wasn't fascinated by it. But, hey, if you really don't want to know, just let it be and forget I called."

"I know myself, Don, and if I go down this road, I will have to keep digging until I find out what all of this means."

"So go for it. Things are slow at the shop. It's probably just as well you have something to occupy your mind so you're not worrying about money."

It wasn't that simple, but there was no point in trying to explain it. This was all very interesting, if you weren't the one experiencing it. If the situation was reversed, Maude would be encouraging Don to go down the path as well. "Alright, well, we should both get back to work. I'll text you if I find out anything interesting."

"Just do it, Maudie."

Maude pressed the "end" button on her phone noting that she still had twenty minutes before the shop was officially open for the day. "Okay, here goes…" She clicked open the file of newspapers and scrolled down to August of 1849. "Wow," she said out loud, noting the staggering number of reported deaths for the first few days of the month. Twenty-two listed on August first, twenty-four on the second and thirty-four on the fourth. The image of the wagons coming up behind the hospital to pick up the dead that Maude had described in her novel came vividly to mind as she searched the lists for Daniel's name. "Well, I'll be damned!" There was barely enough time to register the name on the page when the bell above the door signaled the first customer of the day.

"Why will you be damned?" The sound of Christine's voice floated in the direction of the office and Maude adjusted the curser to mark Daniel Nolan's name in the *Buffalo Daily Courier* before she went out to greet her friend.

"Hey, long time no see. What brings you here today?" She asked Christine.

"I was wondering if you found out any more information about the mysterious ring."

Maude suddenly felt foolish for having kept the story of the ring a secret from Christine. Who knows - with her inquiring mind on the case, they might actually find out something useful. "Actually, I have quite a bit to tell you if you've got a few minutes."

"As a matter of fact, I do. Coffee first?" Christine nodded toward the back and then went in the office to retrieve two mugs. Maude spent the next twenty minutes bringing her up to date on the Carringtons, careful to leave out that some of the historical details discovered from her dreams were turning out to have actually occurred. It just wouldn't do for Christine to have that information before Maude understood it herself. After having heard the story, Christine still focused her inquiry on Maude's expletive when she first entered the shop. "So, why will you be damned?"

Maude blew out a snort of amusement before she answered the question. "I was looking at the report of cholera deaths printed in the *Buffalo Daily Courier* during the 1849 epidemic and found a name I recognized."

"Really? Who? Wait a minute: why are you looking into cholera?"

"Well, Sherman Carrington was a medical student during the epidemic in Buffalo. I wasn't getting anywhere with my novel and so I thought I might change the focus since I've jumped down this rabbit hole. It's been fascinating and I'm making some serious progress on the book."

"Interesting. Let me know if you need anything. So who was it again that you recognized from the newspaper?"

"Daniel Nolan. He was the father of Michael Nolan, the physician who married Ciara Sloane…you remember, from the poorhouse."

"Oh yeah, I remember you telling me about her. Have you seen any other names from Ciara's journal listed among the deaths?"

"No, but I hadn't thought to look. I've been busy trying to track down some of these other details."

"Details from what? Maude, what are you not telling me?"

Maude reminded herself that Christine's keen, inquiring mind would be an asset on this project. "I'm just trying to see where this cholera epidemic fits in. There are so many little details that I don't have time to track down on my own. I really appreciate your offer of help. I'd like to take you up on it." The offer of mysterious details to ferret out was enough to placate the young historian and two made plans to stay in touch before Christine went on her way.

For once Maude was relieved the morning came and went with no interruptions, allowing her to spend it scrolling through the summer editions of the *Buffalo Daily Courier*. The only other name that was familiar was the keeper of the insane asylum, who thankfully had not appeared in any of her dreams…yet. She scrolled back to find Daniel Nolan's name and stared at the screen, hoping some insight would magically float from the screen into her head. Her eyes wandered across the page and a headline caught her eye: *Outrage Over Care Received at the County Almshouse.* "You've gotta be kidding me!" Maude read quickly through the article only to confirm that the society ladies had indeed saved the day. With their repeated complaints to the Board of Supervisors about conditions at the poor farm ignored, they had gone to the newspaper. Sean Farrell himself would be escorting his sister and his wife to the institution each week to note the progress made on the improvements suggested by the City Health Officer, the article reported. Almost dizzy, Maude picked up the phone and called Don.

"Feel like taking a road trip to Lily Dale?" She asked when he picked up.

"When and why?"

"Have you ever heard of the Hydesville Rappers? Two sisters, Katie and Maggie Fox, claimed to be able to communicate with the spirit world."

"I read something about them in an article on the history of Lily Dale. Do they have something to do with all of this?"

"I don't know yet. At first I thought they appeared in my dream because I read the same article you did. Now I'm not so sure. I think it is worth taking a look to see if they were in Laona during the summer of 1849."

"Do we need to drive to Chautauqua to find that out, or do you hope to explore something else while we're there?" The town of Laona was in Chautauqua County, where the first free thinkers gathered. Later in the nineteenth century, as the movement became popular, the spiritualist community of the Lily Dale Assembly was established on the banks of nearby Cassadaga Lake. Don knew his wife very well and figured she was interested in more than just the whereabouts of the Hydesville Rappers if she wanted to drive all that way in the dead of winter.

Maude smiled at her husband's intuition. "Well, I suppose it should come as no surprise that Daniel Nolan died of cholera right about the time I dreamed he did. What may turn your head is the fact that still more of my dreams have been confirmed as fact." She went on to tell him about her dream in which Ciara Sloane had met with the Farrell women in an attempt to enlist their help to put pressure on the Board of Supervisors to clean up the poorhouse. She was gratified by the silence on the other end of the phone when she continued on about the article in the *Buffalo Daily Courier* in August of 1849. "Don, I am as fascinated by all of this as you are, but I'm pretty anxious about it, too. I'd like to go to Lily Dale and talk to someone about what is going on here."

"Okay. Do you have someone specific in mind?"

Maude considered the question. "Now that you mention it, I have no idea who to talk to. Let me make a few calls and see who's there this time of year and then I'll make a plan."

"Sounds good, just let me know what you decide."

Maude hung up the phone satisfied with her progress. With the help of Abby and Christine some of the more important details of her dreams might be verified. That and a trip to Lily Dale might just reveal the meaning of all these unusual experiences, she hoped.

Thinking of Abby reminded her that the genealogist should be back from her weekend in the Hudson

Valley by now. The clock took its time that afternoon and with nothing else to do, Maude decided to give her new friend a call.

Abby picked up on the first ring. "Hi, Maude, I've been dying to call you, but I didn't want to interrupt you at work."

Maude looked out the window at the desolate street with not even a footprint in the fresh dusting of snow and assured Abby that she would not have disrupted the workday at all. "I've actually been using the time to do research for my book. Speaking of books, I'd love to take a look at the Carrington family history. Can we meet for a cup of coffee soon?"

"That would be the other reason I haven't called you yet. Would you believe I left it in our room at the Inn?"

"Oh no!"

"I'm afraid so. I put it on the bed, next to my bag so that I could read it in the car. Bruce was rushing me out of the room and I left without it. I called and they mailed it out this morning, so it should be here in a day or so. I'm really sorry, Maude."

"No worries. I have plenty to look into here. Did you read any of it?"

"I didn't read much, but the owners of the Inn did. They were fascinated by your story. I hope you don't mind that I told them. They ended up giving us a sort of VIP tour of the entire place. The restoration was meticulous; they did a spectacular job."

"Sounds great, and no, I don't mind you telling them at all. What did you learn?"

"Not much from the book. They knew about Sherman's disappearance. You will be interested to know that the Carrington family fortune was nearly lost by Sherman's parents. It turns out they consulted a psychic medium when their son went missing. Word got out they were willing to pay for information and they became magnets for anyone claiming to have supernatural abilities. The Carringtons became obsessed with the idea that there were clues beyond the grave that would lead to the whereabouts of their son and neglected all of their other concerns. Were it not for the interference of other family members, they would have lost everything. It was almost as if they were more interested in talking to the spirits than in finding Sherman."

"Wow," was all Maude could say.

"It gets even better. The Lafontaines, the couple who owns the Inn, discovered another piece of the story when they were researching previous owners of the house. The Carringtons sold the place in 1880 and lived out the rest of their lives in Lily Dale, of all places!"

"You're kidding!" Maude shook her head in disbelief, stunned by this new information, and made a mental note to add the Carringtons to her list for Lily Dale. Unable to bring herself to share the experiences of the last few weeks with a person so new to her acquaintance, Maude cleared her throat in an effort to regain her composure. "Abby, I can't thank you enough for all you have done so far. I can't wait to read the family's history. Please let me know as soon as it arrives."

"You will have it before I do. I asked the manager of the Inn to send it directly to you, but I hope you will let me borrow it when you are done reading it. I have to admit, I am hooked by this story."

"That's really great. Of course I'll return it to you when I'm done."

"Oh, no. It's a gift."

"Thanks again, Abby. You're the best! Let's keep in touch. I still want to find out more about this building. I looked on the title, but the earliest owner I could find was from 1935."

"That doesn't surprise me; in Erie County a title only has to go back eighty years. I'll have to go into the archives and look at the actual deed."

"I'd love to tag along on that if you don't mind. Can we arrange a time to meet next week?"

Abby put her phone on speaker and opened the calendar app. "Okay. How about Friday, late morning? Can we meet at your shop around 11?"

"Sound great, See you then."

Chapter Twenty

The New York State Thruway is a bleak stretch of road in winter and the trees stood stoic against the wind, their skeletal limbs encrusted with ice. Typical of the season, the weather turned ugly without warning near the end of their journey. Don's truck crawled along cautiously as sleet hit the windshield, bouncing off and swirling just out of reach of the wipers, reducing visibility to about ten feet. He typically wasn't much for conversation when driving through inclement weather, leaving Maude to her own thoughts for the long drive to Lily Dale.

When they pulled off the Thruway into the village of Cassadaga, Maude reached for her cell phone. "I told Charlotte I would send her a text when we were 15 minutes away," she told Don, scrolling through the phone for the number of Charlotte Lambert, a year-round resident of the Lily Dale Assembly. Mrs. Lambert had agreed to meet with Maude and show her around the museum and library, which were usually closed this time of year.

Don flipped on his turn signal and pulled to the side of the road. "I'm afraid it will be a bit more than fifteen minutes. I need to de-ice the wipers before they actually freeze to the windshield."

With sleet settling on his hatless head Don patiently tapped the wipers against the glass. Maude thought it was a good indication of what he might look like twenty years from now when his hair turned silver. Not too many men would drive two hours in the dead of winter to consult a psychic medium about a few weird dreams. She smiled, realizing yet again that she had chosen her life partner well, and how eager she was to experience all of the years between now and the time his hair would turn sleet gray from a different force of nature.

Don hopped back into the truck and continued up Dale Drive. "Are you still planning to check out those antique shops in Fredonia?" Maude asked him, turning up the heat to chase away the chill that had entered the truck with her husband.

"I'm hoping to, but this weather has me worried. I'll make a few calls to see if they're all open. If not, I'll find a diner until you're done."

"I can't imagine my conversation with Charlotte will take more than an hour, but I want at least two hours to see what the museum and library have to reveal about the Carrington's life here."

Don turned into the Lily Dale Assembly, the big blue sign above the gate barely visible through the sleet. "Okay, it's eleven o'clock now. How about if I pick you up in front of the museum at two? That should give you plenty of time and still get us back to Buffalo before the boys come home for dinner." He turned down Library Street, the narrow lane which had not been built to accommodate cars and was reduced even further from the piled snow, and stopped in front of the one room schoolhouse that now served as the Lily Dale Museum. "There's a light on, so it looks like someone is there, but I'll wait until you are inside."

Maude leaned over and kissed her husband. "Thanks, Don, for coming with me."

"It is always my pleasure." He kissed her back, lingering this time, reluctant to let her go.

Tempting though it was to stay in the cozy confines of the truck, Maude pulled away. "I'd better get in there before the windows start to fog up."

"Yeah, that would be tricky to explain, but then again this woman is supposed to be psychic, so she is probably well aware of what we are doing behind steamy windows." He smiled and leaned past her to open the door. "I'll see you in a few hours. Oh and Maudie, don't take it all too seriously."

"I'll try not to."

Maude climbed the stairs of the two story building, imagining the second floor to have been the living quarters for the woman who once taught there. Before she could question how she knew the teacher to be female, the door opened and a silver haired African American woman beckoned her inside. "Come in, Mrs. Travers, you'll catch your death out there staring up at that old ghost."

Maude was not aware that she was staring up towards the second story window until she lowered her head to make eye contact with Mrs. Lambert. "Excuse me?"

Charlotte Lambert, custodian of the museum and the library during the winter months, helped Maude off with her coat and lead her through the entry hall of the school house. “I’m sorry. I thought you were looking at Mrs. Westner. She was the original teacher during the late nineteenth century. Mrs. Westner loves to keep me company during these lonely winter months.”

A shiver ran down Maude’s spine that she attributed to the ghost on the second floor rather than the bitter cold still lingering in the entry hall. “Did she die here?”

“She died here in Lily Dale in 1901, but no, not here in the school house. She died from the flux, a rather unremarkable death, but she did love to teach, so I suppose that’s why she’s still here.” Gesturing toward the stairs Charlotte continued, “Why don’t we have a talk in my office so I can get a better idea of what you are hoping to learn while you are here?”

Maude sat in the comfortable stuffed chair in the museum office on the second floor, a steaming cup of Tulsi tea in her hands, describing her experiences with the Erie County Poorhouse skeletons, the finding of the ring beneath the floorboards, and her recent dreams. Charlotte listened intently, nodding as she absorbed the details, never breaking eye contact. When Maude was finished, the old woman was silent for a moment, considering where to start. "Your journey with these people hasn't ended yet. In fact, this project has become a life's work of sorts for you, hasn't it?"

"Well, I started working with the inmate records nearly twenty years ago, so I guess you're right. I hadn't actually thought of it as my life's work."

"My dear, you have always had a special connection to those people. I think that's why they chose you."

"Chose me for what?" Maude felt the shiver down her back again and reflexively looked behind her for the source of the draft.

"Of all the people who worked on that cemetery project, Mrs. Kaiser chose to tell you her story. She trusted that you would honor her memory and expose the truth." Charlotte spoke, glancing back and forth between Maude and the space directly to her right. "She's here now."

"Who is here now? Mrs. Kaiser?" A shockwave jolted through her as Maude realized she hadn't told

Charlotte the almshouse widow's name. "Huh... uh... how?" It was a foolish question to ask a psychic medium, but the word tripped out of her mouth anyway.

Charlotte didn't answer the question directly, but continued to speak. "It is possible that Mrs. Kaiser knows you better than you think, although she has not communicated so directly. This is a personal journey, Maude, and there are those of us along the way to help steer you in the right direction, but you must discover the reasons why you're on this path by yourself."

"I'm not sure what you're trying to tell me. How would Mrs. Kaiser know me?"

"She may know you from a past life. It could be the life you are writing about, or it could be another. Only you will find out your true connection as you proceed."

Maude was speechless as Charlotte explained briefly the concept of past lives and how the experiences during this life would help her to learn something that she was meant to carry back with her into the spirit world. She thought maybe she could feel the presence of Frederika Kaiser in the room with them. "Is Mrs. Kaiser somehow causing my dreams? Is she trying to help me to understand something about my own past life?"

"It doesn't always work the way you want it to, dear. Today Mrs. Kaiser has found yet another opportunity to connect with you and she merely wanted to thank you for hearing everything she had to tell you the first time. Beyond that, she either cannot or will not reveal her true relationship with you." Mrs. Lambert thought for a moment and then added, "Perhaps if she were to reveal her relationship to you now, you would not continue on the path you are meant to travel."

A past life somehow connected to the Erie County Poorhouse was something Maude had never considered, but, given all she had experienced lately, it made sense, if a person believed in that sort of thing. That was the big question, and she had no idea what the answer was. Still, there had to be a reason Frederika Kaiser was still hanging around. "Maybe she wants me to tell her story. I had intended to write about her life, and that of Ciara Nolan, in my book, but it seems now that I'm writing a different story. I'm not exactly sure why that is." Turning left, she spoke to the empty space beside her, "I'm sorry that yours is not the story I will end up telling."

"Oh, she's gone now dear," Charlotte told her. "I think you are wrong, though. I think she wanted you to remember the details of her life, but not so that you could tell others. She may want you merely to remember her and remember that time. Perhaps it is important to Mrs. Kaiser that the Nolan's story be told. You are telling their story as well, are you not?"

"I suppose I am, but I still don't understand how I am able to conjure up in my mind actual events that happened in the past."

"Mrs. Travers, there is much we don't know about the connection between the mind and the soul, but there are ways of asking if you are interested."

Maude was wary and it showed on her face. For all she thought she had an open mind, and, more importantly, an open heart, the idea of pursuing answers to some of her questions was frightening. "How would I do that?"

"There are a few alternatives. You could undergo past life regression. If you knew Mrs. Kaiser in another life, it might be revealed that way. There is also a meditation during which you can ask your spirit guide."

"My spirit guide? Who or what is my spirit guide?"

"Another term might be guardian angel. Your spirit guide watches over you in this world from the spirit world. They often send you signals of one kind or another when you are veering away from your true purpose on Earth. Many people are too preoccupied to understand when Spirit sends them a message."

"So you are saying that I can ask him or her… or it why all of this is happening?"

"Yes, but not in the way you are thinking. Spirit is not there to have a long and complicated discussion with you, but you can ask some yes and no questions. You may not get direct answers, but Spirit will provide clarity when it is needed if you are listening."

Maude was both intrigued and terrified, but ultimately curiosity won out. "How do I go about asking Spirit for guidance?"

"Find a place that is quiet, where you are relaxed and at peace. Visualize that you are walking down a hall with many doors. Stop at the door you know is for you. Think about why you know that is your door. What about the door revealed that it was for you? After you have entered through the door, you can invite your spirit guide to join you there. The answers can be found not only behind your door, but also in the understanding of why that was the door you were meant to pass through."

Maude had no idea what to make of what Mrs. Lambert had just told her. So many questions filled her mind, and they all seemed to tumble out at once. "How will I know which door is mine? How does it differ from the others? Are the other doors all the same and only mine will stand out? How many doors are there? How long is the hallway?"

She only stopped to take a breath, but it was long enough for the medium to interrupt. "I can't answer these questions for you. From what you have told me, you are making great progress on your novel, so it sounds like you are honoring the journey. Go through the meditation and we can talk about it after. If I can answer your questions, I will." Charlotte turned and spoke as if someone was standing by her side. "Oh, Mrs. Westner, do leave us alone." She went on to explain that Mrs. Westner always popped in to check out new people, and was particularly excited over Maude's visit. "She's carrying on so, I don't know what has gotten into her. It has been a long winter and of course the museum is closed to the public this time of year, so she is bored, I suppose." Charlotte spoke of Mrs. Westner as if she was a living person, and Maude smiled as the old woman chastised the ghost and sent her away.

When they finished their tea, the two women went back downstairs to the museum. Maude's eye wandered among the photos and artifacts of the early Spiritualists of Lily Dale. The organization had first been called Cassadaga Lake Free Association, and was no more than a summer camp where like-minded people gathered in its formative years. The community grew, adding cottages for year-round residents, a school, a library, sewers and other infrastructure before becoming the Lily Dale Assembly in 1906. There was an entire display dedicated to Susan B. Anthony and the suffrage movement, which found a home in Lily Dale during the late nineteenth century. Peering through a glass, Maude was pleased to see another exhibit about the Fox sisters and directed her attention to it. "What can you tell me about the girls?" she asked Charlotte, gesturing toward the replica of the cottage the family had rented during the mid-nineteenth century.

"The family lived in Hydesville, about 230 miles east of here. The two younger sisters, Katie and Maggie, claimed to be able to communicate with the spirit of a murdered peddler, who responded to their questions with a series of rappings. That's how they came to be called the Hydesville Rappers."

"What year was that?" Maude asked.

"They moved into the house in 1847. The noises began almost immediately, however, the girls did not confront the spirit causing the disturbance until the spring of 1848. Shortly thereafter, the local interest became so intense that the girls left. They took to traveling around to demonstrate their unique abilities and were eventually joined by their older sister, Leah. The Fox sisters are widely credited with starting the Modern Spiritualist movement," Charlotte told her.

"Would there be any way of finding out if they were in Laona in the summer of 1849?"

"Young Maggie kept a journal," Charlotte pointed to the glass case displaying a small leather bound volume, open somewhere in the middle. The yellowed pages offered short handwritten paragraphs chronicling the girls' adventures from April of 1849 through October of 1851. "We have the original on display here, but the scanned images can be found in the library. I can take you over when we are done here."

"That would be helpful. There are some other people I was wondering about. Does the name Carrington sound familiar?"

Charlotte scowled and turned again as if someone had just approached her from the side. "Oh, for heaven sake, Mrs. Westner, do go away! I'm sorry, Maude. Our school teacher is rather a pest today. Carrington…no, I can't say the name rings a bell, but I'm not the official town historian. I only provide special access to scholars like you during the off season. How would I know them?"

"Well, they were Spiritualists, or they wanted to be. They moved here from Albany in 1880, I think."

"Well, the library would have a record of them if they were members of the association. Shall we take a drive over there now?"

Maude's phone began to vibrate in her pocket. She took a quick look and saw that it was Don. "Excuse me, Mrs. Lambert, but I'd better take this."

"Take your time dear. I'll just get our coats."

After a very brief discussion with her husband, Maude informed Charlotte that she needn't bother with escorting her to the library. "I'm sorry, but I'm afraid I have to leave. My husband thinks we should be on our way now while there is a break in the storm. The weather is unlikely to change for the better and he is concerned that the Thruway might close in the next few hours."

"Oh, well, you'd best be off then." She quickly scrawled an e-mail address on a post-it note and handed it to Maude. "Why don't you send me an e-mail and I'll send you a file of the digital scans from Maggie's journal for the dates you are interested in. I will also look up the Carringtons for you in the registry."

"Oh, that would be wonderful. I can't thank you enough for meeting me here on such a miserable day and for all of your advice."

"It was truly my pleasure, dear. Truth be known, I grow a bit restless myself during these months. It's important to leave the house every once in a while, so your project will give me just enough to do to keep me from sitting idle all winter."

The sound of the horn told her that Don was parked outside and she rose to put on her own coat. "I really appreciate all of your help, Mrs. Lambert. Oh, and thank you for the tea." "It was no trouble, dear. Now you best get going, but come back during the summer season and let me know what you have been up to."

"I will. Thanks again."

"Safe travels, dear."

Maude pulled up her hood before making a mad dash to the truck as the wind whistled its farewell behind her. "Wow, I didn't realize it was getting worse again. I'm glad Mrs. Lambert doesn't have far to go."

"What about the other lady?"

"What other lady? As far as I know it was just the two of us."

Don pointed up to the window on the second floor. "There was a lady waving from the second story window, the same one who saw you come in. You must have seen her. You were staring up at her before you entered the building?"

Maude felt the now familiar shiver down the back of her neck. "Oh, you must mean Mrs. Westner. She is the ghost of the first school teacher at Lily Dale," Maude said matter-of-factly. "I think she liked me."

Don's eyes widened in surprise. It was one thing to call yourself open-minded, but it was quite another to see a ghost in the window, twice. He was amazed that Maude handled the knowledge so casually. He didn't believe that for a second, but was determined to do the same. "Well, that doesn't surprise me. You seem to be popular in the afterlife." Don pulled back on to East Street and made his way carefully through the narrow streets toward the gate. "Well, aren't you going to tell me what you have learned? It will take us an additional hour to get home, I expect, so don't leave out any details!"

Maude drew in a deep breath, oddly thankful that the severe weather would give her a few hours of uninterrupted time to talk things over with Don. She blew out the breath and told him everything. "It's just so hard to know what to make of it all," she said. "I have lived a few decades now as an adult and, while I am not particularly religious, I'd say that I have developed a personal belief system that helps me get from day to day. I'm just not sure where the concept of past lives fits into that system."

Don was silent for a while, more in an effort to keep the truck moving forward on the icy highway than in consideration of Maude's remarks. When he did finally speak his words were unexpected. "So, what would you rather have been told?" Her look of surprise was anticipated and he elaborated. "Maude, you came here more for answers about your own connection to all of this than you did for information concerning the people you have been dreaming and writing about. This is Lily Dale, not the State Fair. You went to consult a person who believes wholeheartedly in what she told you. There's no gimmick here; nobody is trying to profit by your belief in past lives. I'm asking you what explanation of your experiences would have made you feel differently than you do now."

"I suppose there is no explanation that wouldn't have unnerved me, unless Mrs. Lambert truly believed that all of this was just bizarre coincidence."

"That is the point I am trying to make. You went to Lily Dale rather than consulting a book or a website because you knew that the people there truly believe in Spiritualism. Just a quick look around the place tells you that Lily Dale is for them, to honor their belief system. They welcome in the public, but the place is by no means a tourist trap. You knew you would get real answers to your questions. I don't think it really occurred to you that you'd then have to reconcile them into your belief system." As an afterthought he added, "I expect it will be less difficult than you think."

"How so?"

"You don't have to do anything differently, just accept what you have been told and continue on the journey. If you just do that, the meditations or past life regressions that you are not comfortable with become unnecessary."

"How will I really know if I just blindly accept what I have been told?"

"Spoken like a scientist, Maudie. You are looking for proof that what Mrs. Lambert told you is true. If it were me, the bones, the visions, the ring and the dreams would be evidence enough. Even in science, conclusions are never definitive, and they are often revised as new information or technology comes to light. What we believed to be true years ago has been altered by our present reality." She still looked uncertain so he continued trying to convince her that there was no harm in just accepting what she had been told. "Look, nobody is trying to sell you swampland in Lily Dale. If you're struggling with all of this, set it aside and just keep working on the book. This is fiction, so none of the details have to be verified."

"Don, did you miss the part about Frederika Kaiser showing up? That's got to mean something."

"I'm sure it does, but it seems to me that you're not yet ready to understand all of what is happening to you. All I'm saying is don't get caught up trying to find a box in which all of this will neatly fit. Mrs. Lambert seems to think you are proceeding along in the direction that will ultimately give you the answers you're looking for. I'm just advising you to go with the flow for a while.

"Alright, I'll just keep writing."

Chapter Twenty-One

October 2, 1849

Sherman waited until Agnes was securely in her rooms before he ventured over to the front desk of the hotel and asked if he might have some paper and a pen. After quickly jotting a few lines to cancel their dinner plans, he read the note over to be sure it contained nothing that might encourage Agnes to rush to his side for fear her prophecy had finally come true. There was truth in what he wrote, though: he was exhausted. Tomorrow would come soon enough and he would accept the consequences for his actions with a solid night's sleep behind him. He folded the paper and handed it to the man at the desk. "Could you please deliver this to Miss Pollard later this afternoon?" There was no hurry for her to receive this news. The last thing he wanted was for her to be rushing down the street after him, or worse yet showing up at the boarding house.

Agnes lay in bed waiting for sleep to overtake her. The heavy drapes kept out the ever penetrating morning sun, leaving the room dark enough for her to pretend it was still night. Her body had grown accustom to these hours, and she was comforted in the knowledge that Sherman would also sleep the day away. It was thrilling to keep her own schedule, sneaking off into the night, the guardian of her betrothed, and just in time, apparently. It was clear that Martha Sloane was at the root of Sherman's doubts. That would change soon enough. Agnes drifted off, not at all bothered by their earlier conversation, confident in her ability to remove all threats to their happiness.

Hours later a cool breeze blew through the drapes bringing the afternoon in along with it. The chill in the air woke Agnes and she rose to close the window, but a knock on the door diverted her from the task. "Just a moment," she called out and hurried into her dressing gown.

"A gentleman left this at the front desk for you," the young man told her. Agnes thanked him and returned to the window, where the light was better for reading.

My Dear Agnes,

Regretfully I am unable to join you for dinner this evening. I confess that my work at the hospital has left me exhausted and I find I am much in need of sleep. I have arranged to have dinner sent up to your rooms so you will not have to suffer the evening dining alone.

My deepest apologies,
Sherman

Agnes pulled the drapes aside to allow in the remainder of the day. "Just what am I to do this evening?" she asked out loud as she peered out the open window. There was still plenty of daylight left and she had no intention of wasting it in the confines of her bedchamber. Inspiration struck and she rang the front desk to make arrangements for a carriage and driver.

* * *

Ciara looked out the kitchen window, attracted by the sound of the children thundering down the drive. "Are ye expecting anyone?" she asked Martha, watching while the carriage was intercepted by the three little people as it turned into the yard.

"No. Can ye see who it is?"

"Aye, but I don't know them." Ciara smoothed her dress as she stood up from the table where she had been peeling apples. Both women moved closer to the window for a better look.

The driver looked to be about the same age as Bruns, that is to say, he was barely a man at all. He laughed as the children ran alongside while he made his way toward the house. The young woman seemed annoyed by their game. Martha recognized her immediately. "Miss Pollard," she said under her breath.

"Do ye know her?" Ciara asked puzzled by the look of disbelief on her sister's face.

"Aye, we've met. She's engaged to Sherman Carrington. I wonder why she has come."

"I don't know," Ciara answered, "But I expect we'll find out soon enough."

Both women exited the house as the carriage came to a stop by the front door. Martha smiled and greeted her unexpected guest. "Good day to ye, Miss Pollard.

The young man helped her down from the carriage before Agnes spoke. "Good day to you, Miss Sloane. Please forgive my unannounced visit. I was hoping I might have a word with you, if it is not too much of an imposition."

"'Tis no trouble at all. Allow me to present my sister, Mrs. Nolan. Ciara, this is Miss Pollard from Albany."

"I'm pleased to meet ye. Please come in and have a cup of tea."

"Thank you, Mrs. Nolan. That is most kind of you," Agnes replied as she followed the women toward the house.

Felicity and the lads had lingered to investigate the new visitors. Ian and Daniel soon became friendly with the driver of the carriage and offered to escort him down to the barn where he could wait for his mistress to complete her business. Felicity approached Agnes from behind and gently pulled on the woman's skirt until she turned to face the child. Felicity just stared at her and Agnes smiled uncomfortably until Ciara shooed the lass in the direction of the barn. "Don't mind wee Felicity, Miss Pollard. I expect she's not seen a dress as fine as yers." Opening the door, Ciara said to Martha, "Won't ye see Miss Pollard to the parlor?"

Felicity made it halfway to the barn when she turned around and watched the women pass through the door. She stared at the house for a moment, the very air around it seemed to change as that woman and her ill intentions entered. Felicity ran back toward the house.

Martha gestured toward the high-backed chair by the fireplace. "Won't ye take a seat?" After Agnes was settled, Martha took the chair opposite her and smiled.

Agnes looked around the scrupulously clean room, noting the preference for the practicality of the old country rather than the over-cluttered look that was currently the fashion. "This is your home?" She could not think of anything more favorable to say.

"'Tis my sister's home, but I do live here as well." Agnes only nodded smugly, as if she had expected as much. After another moment of awkward silence, Martha asked, "How may I be of help to ye?"

"It is very rude of me to intrude upon you and your family, especially so late in the afternoon, but Sherman speaks well of you and I have never before met a woman attending medical college." Agnes' eyes grew wider, and she smiled, hoping to convey sincerity.

"In truth, I was simply seeking a companion to pass the afternoon with while Sherman is resting. I hope you do not mind."

The door to the parlor opened before Martha could comment and Felicity peeked in. Martha smiled and beckoned the child over. "This is wee Felicity. She's been a guest in our home for some weeks now. Do ye mind if she stays for a bit? She seems quite taken with ye."

Agnes' smile stiffened and she moved back further in her chair. "Of course not, she seems a charming child." Felicity took a seat on the floor by Martha's feet, which Agnes found very odd. The child continued to watch her, expressionless. Agnes was unnerved by the attention and was relieved when Ciara came in with the tea. The awkwardness was hardly noticeable while Ciara was busy pouring out and the other two women fussed about, each preparing their cup just so. However, when Ciara left the room, each woman sat with her tea in hand and Felicity continued watching.

Martha took a sip from her cup and placed it carefully back on the table before speaking. A number of questions entered her mind, like why had Agnes decided to journey into the country in search of companionship? Where were her parents? Had she traveled to Buffalo alone, and, if so, why? However none of those questions was appropriate to ask, no matter how interested Martha was in the answers, so she took a different tack. "Have ye been to Buffalo before?"

"No."

"'Tis a grand city. Are ye enjoyin' yer stay?"

One of the more liberating things about being without supervision was that, for the first time in her life, Agnes could say or do what she wanted without being constantly corrected by her mother, who would have been horrified both at her unannounced visit to the Nolan farm and at how she answered Martha's question. "In truth, no, Sherman spends far too much time at that hospital. Just this evening he cancelled our dinner plans so that he might rest a bit longer." The last sentence Agnes sputtered in such disbelief and Martha's eyes widened as the woman made no effort to hide her irritation.

There were a few things Martha might have said had she known Agnes better, but instead she just nodded, "The life of a doctor is not an easy one. We are often called away at all hours of the day and night when our patients are in need."

"Yes, well, Sherman will not practice medicine once we have wed. Mother Carrington and I have already decided that," Agnes told her, still sounding peevish.

Martha was surprised to hear that. Although medicine might not be a calling for Sherman as it was for her, she had watched him over the past few months and thought it had become more important to him. "'Tis a shame. Sherman will be a fine doctor one day." Martha knew it was not proper to voice her opinion, but she felt a strong urge to defend her friend.

Agnes stiffened just a bit to hear Martha refer to her fiancé by his first name as she took a sip from her cup, "He does not need to work, after all, and we would hardly be able to travel if he were to open a clinic in Albany. It was a folly to attend medical college in the first place."

Martha smiled, searching for some way to direct the conversation onto a more pleasant topic. "Ye intend to travel; how lovely. Where do ye think ye'll go?"

"The Fox Sisters say I will travel the country and meet free thinkers like myself. I know not where we will begin our journey."

"I'm afraid I do not know the Fox sisters. Are they from Albany?"

Agnes was still under Felicity's scrutiny and found it hard to concentrate on the conversation. Instead of answering Martha's question, she gestured toward the child. "Perhaps she would be happier outside with the others."

Martha agreed, not wanting her guest to feel uncomfortable. "Aye, she could do with some fresh air." She helped Felicity up from the floor and guided her to the door. "Away ye go and find the lads." The girl was reluctant to leave and appealed to Martha with pleading eyes, willing her to understand that she did not trust this woman. Martha only turned her once again toward the open door, patted her bottom to shoo her out of the room. Frustrated, Felicity stamped her foot and let out a strangled cry, turning a cold stare in the direction of their guest.

Having heard the ruckus, Ciara came and carried the still struggling child from the room. Turning to

Agnes, she said, "Please forgive her rudeness. Felicity is deaf and sometimes unable to understand what we ask of her."

"Certainly," Agnes said, just able to maintain her composure as she took another sip of her tea.

Martha sat back down. "I am sorry. Felicity lost her mother during the epidemic. Her Da had passed during the winter, so she had no one. She really is a sweet lass."

"Could she not have been sent to an orphan home?"

Martha could hardly be offended at the question. Anyone else would have sent her away. "I thought it would be difficult for her there because she is deaf. I brought her home the day her ma died. I couldn't help myself, the poor wee thing just looked so scared."

"How very kind of you." It occurred to Agnes that Martha's interest in Sherman likely had to do with finding a father figure for the orphaned girl. Her eyes narrowed just a bit as she spoke. "Will you raise her as your own?" Not giving Martha a chance to answer, she continued speaking, "It will be difficult enough for you to attract a husband if you continue your studies, but surely you could not hope to find a decent man who would welcome a deaf child." With a knowing look, she added, "Certainly any man of my Sherman's character would not consider such a match."

Martha smiled, betraying no offense, but chose her next words carefully. "The child was in need. I will do as I must to help her."

That was the confirmation Agnes needed, certain that Martha was the danger the Fox sisters had foretold. Surely Sherman would heed her warning now. The deaf child was proof of Martha's deception. That was all she really needed to know. Agnes brought her arm up in a sweeping gesture and placed the back of her hand on her forehead. "Miss Sloane, do forgive me, but I am suddenly unwell. I fear the country air does not sit well with me and I must return to my rooms."

Confused, but relieved at the sudden turn of events, Martha watched a few minutes later as the carriage rolled away, only returning inside when it had reached the main road. Felicity came running into the hall and propelled herself into Martha's arms, patting her about the head and shoulders as if to ensure that she was alright. "And what's got ye in such a state?" Martha asked her, although she expected no answer.

Ciara came into the hall to find the child still clinging to her sister, "Has Miss Pollard left already?"

"She was feeling poorly," Martha told her, trying to extract the legs that were wrapped like a python around her hips. "She said the country air did not agree with her."

"Aye, the same must be true for our wee lass here. I've never seen her in such a state," Ciara told her. "She was fretful in the kitchen trying to get back into the parlor with ye."

"Aye, she was a bit out of sorts. At first I thought maybe she took a fancy to Miss Pollard's fine dress, as ye said, for all she wouldn't take her eyes off of the woman, but then I got the feeling Felicity didn't like her. I've never seen her become so stubborn as when I tried to send her away."

"Aye, well, perhaps she just doesn't like to be away from ye. She'll be leavin' soon and I suspect we'll see more of the same from the poor wee lass as it gets closer to the time she goes." Martha nodded and they both seemed satisfied with that as an explanation for

Felicity's uncharacteristic noncompliance. Ciara was about to turn and go back to the kitchen, but her curiosity got the better of her. "What brought Miss Pollard all the way out to see ye today?"

"She's lonely, I think." Martha didn't offer any more in the way of an explanation nor did she divulge the details of their very unusual visit.

"I expect she won't be for long. Michael says the sickness has all but run its course. I should think Mr. Carrington will be returning to Albany soon enough."

Martha only nodded knowing her sister would not approve of the information she might share about Mr. Carrington's current situation.

It wasn't long after Agnes' departure that Johnny arrived. He was in the habit of joining the family for supper most evenings these days and although Martha enjoyed his company, she and Ciara were concerned about leaving Katherine with only Ellie for company in the evenings. Not wanting to give up a single minute of time with Martha before they left town, he had come to collect her back to the city for their evening meal, thereby providing their Gran with some company and enjoying some privacy with Martha on the journey each way.

Johnny's carriage moved along at a leisurely pace back to the Nolan Dry Goods Emporium. Martha held an apple pie on her lap, still warm from the oven, and the delicious aroma of cinnamon and sugar held the promise of a fine evening. "We'll be off the day after tomorrow," Johnny mentioned causally.

"Aye, I'll be ready. I must do my last shift at the hospital tomorrow night, but I'll be ready to leave by late mornin' if it suits."

"We're only goin' to Batavia, so it'll do no harm to get a later start if ye'd like to rest a bit before we go."

"I expect wee Felicity will sleep somewhere along the way. I'll just curl up next to her in the wagon and be well rested by the time we arrive at yer sister's door." Martha smiled, unable to hide her enthusiasm. She hadn't left Buffalo since she came over from Ireland and was excited to be sharing one of Johnny's adventures, even if it was only for a small part of the trip.

Just before they turned from North onto Main Street, Johnny stopped the carriage under a large Maple tree whose leaves were changing to a brilliant shade of vermillion. He dropped the reins and turned toward Martha, removing the warm apple pie to the floor beside her feet. Cupping her face in both of his hands, he kissed her long and deep. Martha found that since that first kiss on Dedyowenaguhdoh Island she thought often about when and where more opportunities for kissing Johnny would present themselves. They seldom had more than a few moments of privacy now that she was home more and he was busy running the store. There would be even fewer opportunities once they left for Batavia with Bruns and Felicity traveling with them. She leaned forward, arms reaching inside the warm folds of his coat, wanting to be closer. They might have continued on like that, tucked away under the maple tree wrapped in each other's arms, until the sun set, but Johnny pulled away. The intensity of the moment had left them both slightly unhinged and it took a while for him to regain enough composure to speak. "I wonder," he asked, gently passing a finger over her swollen lips, "if ye've had enough time to get to know me."

Martha smiled, shifting back just far enough to see his bearded face, but not removing her arms from inside his coat. "Aye, I have." She maintained eye contact, still smiling, but said no more.

"And?"

"Ach, ye're a fine man, Johnny Quinn." She knew what he was asking, but couldn't resist teasing him just a bit.

"Are ye goin' to make me ask ye again?" Understanding the game, he climbed down from the carriage pulling her with him, smugly satisfied at the look of disappointment on Martha's face when she no longer had the folds of his coat to warm her. He made a show of standing her next to the carriage and dramatically swooped to one knee. Taking her hand in both of his, he spoke loudly and formally. "Martha Sloane, will ye do me the honor of becoming my wife?"

Martha laughed trying without success to pull the man to his feet. "Oh get up, ye silly fool."

He only smiled. "I'll have an answer, if ye please," he told her, rising and pulling her into his arms, "for I've been able to think of nothing but our wedding night since ye spoke of yer interest in what I might have to teach ye in that regard." He kissed her gently on the lips, and then again. "Marry me, Martha, for ye know as I do that we were meant to be together."

"Aye, I do know that, for I have fallen in love with ye, Johnny, and I'd be proud to be yer wife."

Johnny let out a whoop that might have been heard in Canada. He picked Martha up and twirled her around until both of them were dizzy and nearly fell to the ground.

Part Three

Chapter Twenty-Two

February 7, 2015

Maude followed Abby through the main floor of the Buffalo History Museum to its research library in search of the atlases containing the property maps for the early nineteenth century. They were hopeful that the map would allow them to identify the earliest owners of the building on Chippewa the Antique Lamp Company currently occupied. She was impressed that Abby had already identified the atlas they would need to examine and had called ahead to request it. "I did some research for a client about a year ago and found out that the earliest Deed Atlas for Erie County available is from 1830," Abby told her.

The early nineteenth-century property maps were contained in large atlases and were organized by parcel number. They often identified the structures that had been built on the parcel, its use and the owner/builder (who, in those days, was likely the same person). Seated at the large oak table in the center of the room, Abby expertly flipped to the appropriate page on the 1830 property map. "Okay, here is the corner of Main and Chippewa. I believe your building sits on lot seventeen. See, there was a building on the property in 1830." Turning the atlas toward Maude, she pointed to the parcel.

Maude noted with interest that the old Dutch name of Van Staphorst Avenue was also listed on the street that was called Main Street in 1830 and that the plots there were larger, extending north past Chippewa. Lot number seventeen was three times the size of the lots across the street from it on both Main and Chippewa. She assumed that at some point the parcel was subdivided because currently there were buildings next door and behind her in very close proximity. "It doesn't tell us what the structure was or who built it," Maude remarked.

"That is the unfortunate part of this kind of research. You don't always find the information you're looking for. At least this shows us that there was a building here in 1830. Now that we have a year and a lot number, we can check the deed index. Those are kept in the basement of County Hall. Do you have time for a quick ride? It's just over on Franklin."

Maude looked at her watch and nodded. "Yeah, I don't see why I couldn't open the shop an hour later today." Abby carefully closed the fragile atlas and left the oversized volume on the table, where it would be re-shelved by one of the experienced staff.

Ten minutes later Maude waited in her car for Abby to arrive. Given how difficult it was to find street parking downtown in the winter, she hovered between two spots on Franklin Street, ready to move over when her friend arrived. No sooner did she look at her watch than did the honk of a horn behind her indicate that Abby had pulled up. Maude moved her car forward and got out.

"Thanks," Abby said. "How lucky for you to have found a parking place so close to the building."

"I know, and your timing was perfect. I didn't have to take up two spots for more than a few minutes."

"I should warn you that although the record didn't specify the type of building built on your parcel, most buildings in Buffalo during the early decades of the nineteenth century were made from timber," Abby mentioned as they made their way to the basement of the large Victorian Romanesque building that held the deed index ledgers. "Given the frequency of fires during the rapid development of that area back then, there is a possibility that the building represented on the map is not the one you currently occupy."

"I figured that; our building is brick so I didn't think it would be the original structure."

"It's not unusual for the owner of a property to re-build after a fire, so we can go back to the later maps and find out if the brick building was built later or by a different owner.

"I take it you come here often," Maude comment-ed as Abby navigated the obviously familiar rows of shelving that contained the oversized leather bound ledgers.

Abby chuckled. "Often enough, I suppose. The deed indexes are organized by date, so I have an approximate idea of where we need to look." She stopped in the very last row. "I don't often get a look at records this old, though." With an expert eye, she scanned the dates etched on the bindings and pulled out the one ranging from 1830-1840. "There's a table closer to the door," she said as she hoisted the oversized volume into a comfortable carrying position.

Setting the ledger on the wooded cradle meant to protect the binding, Abby flipped carefully to the year 1830. Knowing the year a building was constructed on the property didn't actually mean that the property had been purchased at that time, but it was a place to start. Trying to find the original owner of the parcel was a bit like finding a needle in a haystack without knowing the specific date of the land transfer. Running a finger down the page without actually touching it, Abby scanned each date looking for the parcel number. "Okay, the lot was purchased on March 1, 1830." She scribbled down the information listed in the index so that they could pull the document that would show the chain of ownership.

"Now what? Maude asked.

"Now we can pull the deed book." Abby closed the book and returned it to the shelf. "Wouldn't it be amazing if this building was once a boarding house and Sherman Carrington lived there?"

"Yeah, that would just be perfect!" Maude agreed, making a mental note to check the city directory for 1849 to see if there really was a Mrs. Cornish on Beak Street who owned a boarding house.

As they proceeded down the aisles in search of the correct volume, Maude took a moment to check her e-mail. She was expecting a message from Mrs. Lambert containing the pages of Maggie Fox's journal from the summer of 1849. Moving her fingers rapidly across the screen, she pointed and tapped until her e-mail account opened.

> Good morning Maude. Here are the pages from the journal you are interested in. Regarding the Carrington Family, I was able to locate them in the records. They joined the original camp community that began to settle permanently here in the late nineteenth century. Their story is rather fascinating and I'd rather tell you in person, so call me as soon as you get a chance.
>
> Charlotte

Maude's eyes got larger as she read Charlotte's e-mail. More fascinating details about the Carringtons… Maude could not wait to call and hear everything. That would have to wait, though, and she focused her attention instead on the pages from Maggie Fox's journal. The attached files were digital scans too large to open on her cheap smart phone. It was times like this that Maude regretted settling for the free upgrade instead of opting for an iPhone like Don had. "Stupid phone," she mumbled as she tapped on the "forward" icon.

"Did you say something?" Abby asked, looking up from the row of books she was examining.

"No, nothing." Maude typed in Christine's e-mail address and a brief message asking her to take a look at the pages to determine if the Fox Sisters were in Laona at any point during the summer of 1849. The young historian had offered help, and although Maude would take a look at the pages herself later, it would not be today or any time over the upcoming weekend, whereas Christine would have the time now to find the answer to this very important question. By the time she hit "send" they had reached the right shelf.

It took only a few more minutes to locate the book, but then it seemed like it took forever to flip through the pages to find the deed record.

The record consisted of two pages. The top of the first page described the boundaries of the parcel as determined by the Holland Land Company, the original Dutch investors who, in 1792, had purchased over three million acres of what is now Western New York. The first date of purchase was in July of 1825 by a man named Rufus Wescott. "I can't make that out," Maude remarked trying to look at the second date of purchase on March 1, 1830.

Abby pulled a magnifying glass from her purse and extended it in Maude's direction. "I brought this along figuring we might need it," she explained.

Maude took the tool and held it over the page, adjusting the height until she could see the name clearly. "You. Have. Got. To. Be. Kidding. Me!" She could do nothing to keep the surprise from her voice as the magnifying glass hovered over the name Daniel Nolan.

"Do you recognize a name?"

Maude ignored the question and looked at the name below Daniel's. In November of 1855 the building changed hands again. This time she did not need a magnifying glass to read the name. The third owner of parcel 17 was John Quinn. The floor felt like it was moving underneath her and Maude pressed her hand to the table to keep from falling over.

Abby became concerned as the silence stretched on and the color receded from Maude's face. "Is everything okay? You look like you might collapse."

"Um, yeah, I'm fine. I'm just surprised, that's all." She had to force herself to look up from the document as she continued speaking and Abby noticed the effort it took for her to do so. "I do recognize two names on this deed."

When the two names were not forthcoming, Abby gently took the magnifying glass from Maude and bent to look at the deed herself. "I recognize the name Rufus Wescott, too. He purchased a good chunk of the land in what is now the city of Buffalo from the Holland Land Company. Is there something I don't know about him?"

"What? No, I've never heard of Rufus Wescott. I recognized the name Daniel Nolan. He owned the Nolan Dry Goods Emporium." Maude was talking more to herself than to Abby and her eyes had drifted back to the deed. "I can't believe I am living above the Nolan Dry Goods Emporium. I can't believe I have worked in the same building as Daniel Nolan once did for 13 years. Johnny must have bought the business or maybe inherited it."

Abby was completely lost. "I'm sorry, but I don't know who Daniel Nolan is."

Maude looked at Abby as if she had just seen her for the first time today, but then quickly realized where they were and what they had been doing. "I'm sorry, Abby, but this is a bit of a shock. Last year I was working on the Erie County Poorhouse Cemetery Project at the university and I came across a journal, Ciara Nolan's journal. She was the first Keeper of the Buffalo Orphan Asylum. Daniel Nolan was her father-in-law. He owned one of the first dry goods stores in the city. Apparently I'm living in his house."

"Wow, that is a curious coincidence."

* * *

"I'm telling you, Don, the woman probably thought I had lost my mind. I was just about speechless when I read Daniel Nolan's name on that deed."

Don pressed a refilled tumbler of whiskey into his wife's hand and sat down next to her at the kitchen table. "Yeah, well, I can see where that would be quite a shock. I can't believe there was no mention of the location of his store in that journal."

"I was so drawn in by all the body snatching drama, I really didn't pay attention to where it was. Now that I think about it, I vaguely remember some reference to the shop being located on Main Street. I never would have put it together, though, because our store front is on Chippewa, not Main Street."

"I don't suppose I would have either. I guess somewhere along the line somebody subdivided the plot. Maybe our shop was built later."

"That's just it, Don. I think this is the original building. Wait, let me rephrase that. I know this is the original building. I can feel it." Maude took a sip of her whiskey before she continued. "I mean what are the odds that we would find Marcia Carrington's ring underneath the floor, and that I would have all of those dreams about her son and the cholera epidemic and the Nolan family, two of whom knew Sherman Carrington. On top of all that, it turns out that the man whose death I first dreamed about, then verified as historically accurate, owned the building where we live and work."

"Well, when you put it that way, it does sound convincing. Maybe the entrance to the shop was changed when the property was subdivided." Don looked at his wife, who seemed fixated on the contents of the tumbler in her hand. "How are you feeling about all of this? You don't sound as unnerved as I expected you'd be."

"I'm waiting for the host from one of those hidden camera shows to jump out from behind the stove!" Maude laughed at her own joke, but Don only smiled. "Frankly, I don't know what to believe. Mrs. Lambert told me this was a journey and that I seemed to be on the right track, so I guess today's revelation is all part of the adventure." Maude looked up from her glass, "That reminds me: I have to give her a call."

"I wonder what it all means?" Don mused. "More to the point, what have we really learned here that tells us why the ring ended up under the floorboards?"

Maude nodded, prepared to throw her concerns into the discussion. "We don't know if Marcia Carrington was ever in the Nolan's Dry Goods Emporium, or how her ring might have ended up there."

"Well, let's break it down. Sherman is Marcia's son. His friend and colleague is Martha Sloane, who is Daniel's adopted granddaughter. Am I right about the connections?"

"Yes. Are you suggesting that somehow the ring passed from Marcia to Sherman, then to Martha, then to Daniel?"

"I don't think it was that linear. It seems like the ring and the shop are connected through Martha Sloane and Sherman Carrington. I wonder if they ran off and got married or something?"

"No, I don't think so. I think Martha marries Johnny Quinn." Maude said the words with certainty, although she had no proof of the event. "She had talked about it as a child. Ciara Nolan had mentioned it in her journal. I dreamed about their courtship. Besides, if Martha and Sherman ran off and got married, how did the ring get left behind?"

Don thought for a moment. "So maybe the connection to the building is through John Quinn. Didn't you say he owned the building after the other guy died?" She nodded and he continued, "Maybe there was some kind of love triangle. Maybe Sherman wanted to marry Martha and ran off in a jealous fit when she married Johnny. You know, you can probably try and find some record of a marriage. Did they have marriage certificates back then?"

"No, but if Martha and Johnny got married in the church there might be a register of marriages."

"Do you think it would have been at St. Louis? Why don't you check it out?"

"I'll have to add it to the list." Maude looked at her watch, noting that it was nearly eight o'clock. "I think it's probably too late to give Mrs. Lambert a call to-night. Besides, I'm not sure I'll be able to take any more surprises."

Later on that evening, Maude lay in bed wondering if the room she and Don shared was the very room that Daniel and Katherine Nolan had shared, and Martha and Johnny after them. The room felt different now that she had some sense of the people who had lived in it before her, like it was somehow pleased she was finally in on the secret.

Just before dawn she woke with a start and sat bolt upright in bed. "What is it? What's wrong?" Don asked, disoriented at having been startled awake himself.

"Nothing. I'm fine, but I need to get to my computer!" Without another word, Maude flew out of bed and ran straight downstairs to her office so she could record every detail of the dream she'd just had.

Chapter Twenty-Three

October 3, 1849

Johnny held the back door as Martha entered the kitchen. He stood there for a moment watching as Ellie and Katherine fussed about clearing the dishes from their morning meal. Martha seemed to know what he was thinking and she smiled. This would be their home one day, a home they would share with Katherine for the remainder of her days, and with Ellie for as long as she wanted to stay with them. He took her hand, squeezed it gently and gave her a questioning look. Her smile grew wider, signaling that she, too, wanted to share their news.

"Ye're back already?" Katherine asked. "I didn't hear ye come in." She had put aside a few bolts of cloth to send along to Batavia with Felicity in addition to a few items for Megan and her family. Johnny could have easily packed them in the wagon, but Katherine insisted

Martha come give her opinion of the colors and fabrics she had chosen. Johnny was happy to go and fetch her, realizing that the old woman simply wanted to see Martha before they left town.

"Aye, we rushed right back, for we have important news to tell ye Gran." Pulling Martha closer, he continued. "Martha has finally agreed to be my wife."

Ellie put down the dish she was drying and came over to join them. "That is grand news, is it not, Gran?"

"Surely it is. I'm that happy for the both of ye. Have ye told Ciara and Michael, for all they've been expectin' an announcement for some time now. We all have."

"Aye, we did just this mornin'" Johnny told her. "I only just got an answer last night. It took her a while to succumb to my considerable charms." He grinned and pressed his lips to Martha's temple.

"Oh, Johnny, the two of ye have been a pair since the first day ye met, and no mistake." Katherine wrapped her arms around him and the next few minutes were filled with hugs, kisses and well wishes from Ellie and Katherine.

"When will you marry?" Ellie asked.

"Martha must finish her education first," Johnny told her.

Among the happiest days in Katherine's memory were when Michael had rescued Ciara, her sisters, Johnny, Bruns and Ellie from a deadly influenza outbreak at the poorhouse and had brought them to the Nolans to stay. The living space above the shop was just about bursting with six extra people, two of them infants, but Katherine and Daniel had loved every minute of it.

"It will be a blessing to have the house full again," Katherine mentioned, knowing that Martha would move in after the wedding. "I only wish yer Granda would be here to see it."

* * *

The morning had long since passed and Sherman lay in bed, his lean naked body wrapped around Millicent, feeling that his transformation was complete. The boy who would not think of defying his parents was gone and the man who had replaced him possessed the courage to do what must be done, with regard not only to his current situation but the rest of his life. He considered for just a moment how he could disentangle himself from his beloved without disturbing her, but then realized that it was important for her to know that he was leaving her bed and that he would be back to share it with her every night thereafter. The things they had done through the darkness and into the dawn had bonded them more than any marriage ceremony in a church could, and he wanted nothing more than to watch her while she slept and then to do them all over again when she woke. But he had an obligation to make sure that Agnes knew their engagement was really over.

He bent his head and pressed his lips just behind her ear. "My darling," he whispered, but she did not stir. Part of him wondered if sleeping with Millicent was the final push he needed to ensure his courage would not waver when he spoke to Agnes, and then to their parents, who by his reckoning should be arriving sometime today. No, he would never use her in that way. Neither of them had planned for it to happen. It just seemed a natural extension of their love for each other and neither of them had any reservations about expressing their feelings in that way, although they were not yet married. Still, there was no turning back now and he would have this unpleasantness over so that he could return to Millicent. He placed another lingering kiss behind her ear before continuing down the length of her neck to her shoulder. "My love, I must leave you for just a while." He was rewarded with the most radiant smile as she turned toward him and opened her eyes.

"Be kind to her, Sherman, for she loves ye as I do."

"No, she doesn't. Agnes does not know love like this." He kissed her lips long and slow to prove his point. "She thinks she is in love with me because she has been told her whole life that we are a good match. I know now that releasing her from our commitment will give her the opportunity to find someone who can make her truly happy."

"In time she will see that," Millicent assured him.

"I hope so."

After a long farewell filled with kisses and promises, Sherman set out for the American Hotel hoping he had timed his departure correctly. It was late afternoon and he would be needed at the hospital in a few hours. The plan was to have a discussion with Agnes privately, thereby leaving very little time to argue with his parents before he had to leave. With any luck they would be on a canal boat in the morning heading back to Albany before his shift was over. Millicent insisted that he should allow plenty of time to reconcile things with his parents and the Pollards, but Sherman knew that no reconciliation would be possible. His parents would have no more to do with him as a result of his defiance. That was a regrettable certainty. Thankfully the funds they had given him to complete his medical education were secure in an account bearing his name alone, so he would be able to maintain his frugal lifestyle until his education was complete. After that, he would earn his own way in the world.

Agnes had been watching the street from her window waiting for Sherman to arrive. He was later than usual, but she would not complain. She had used the time to consider all that had transpired over the last few days. Sherman had expressed a desire to stay in Buffalo. At first the idea seemed ridiculous, but the more Agnes thought about it, the more she began to see the advantages. During the days she had traveled the city unescorted, she had grown quite fond of keeping her own schedule, as well as saying and doing what she pleased. It might not be so bad settling here, away from the watchful eye of her mother.

Marrying Sherman became linked to her ability to maintain her independence, which Agnes would not part with willingly. After their meeting yesterday, she no longer considered Martha a threat to her plans. Surely Sherman would see the woman's true nature when Agnes told him of the deaf child Martha had taken in. If he did not give up the foolish notion of breaking off their engagement when she announced her willingness to come back to Buffalo after they were married (providing that the Fox sisters proclaimed it safe for them to return), he was sure to when she told him of Martha's scheme. Agnes saw his familiar grey mare coming up the street and ran down with her coat in hand to meet him in the lobby before he had even exited the carriage.

"Sherman, darling, we must talk. I have so much to tell you. Let's take a walk, shall we?" She handed him her coat so that he could help her into it.

He thought it odd that she was alone. "Have our parents arrived yet?"

"No. Were they due to arrive today?" Agnes had been so busy running about the city that she had completely forgotten her parents were traveling from Laona.

"Yes, they were supposed to arrive on the afternoon coach." He extended the coat in her direction and Agnes shrugged into it. "Let me check at the front desk before we leave."

Agnes followed him over to the desk and learned that the coach that was due to arrive in Buffalo earlier in the day still had not arrived. "Have you any idea what has delayed them?" He asked the hotel manager.

"No, sir. It could be that the coach broke down somewhere along the way."

Sherman thanked the man and left the hotel with Agnes on his arm. They walked down Main Street in the opposite direction of the Nolan Dry Goods Emporium. Sherman and Millicent would eventually make a life here and it wouldn't do for people he knew to see him with Agnes. Sherman had hoped for a few minutes of silence to gather his thoughts, but Agnes started chattering as soon as they had left the hotel.

"Sherman, I have something very important to tell you. I have reconsidered your idea about living in Buffalo and I am agreeable, after we have been married, to return here with you, provided it is safe for you to return."

Sherman's pressed his lips together in response, and shook his head. "Agnes, I meant what I said yesterday…"

"No, I do not believe that you do. That woman has been tricking you, Sherman. She is the danger the Fox sisters warned me about, I am certain of it."

"Agnes, leave Martha out of this. She has absolutely nothing to do with my decision."

Agnes held her hand up to silence him. "Now Sherman, before you finish let me just tell you that I paid a call to your friend Miss Sloane yesterday afternoon and found that she has taken in a child: a child that cannot hear, Sherman. Can you imagine such foolishness? I fear her only interest in you is as a father to the pitiful waif."

Sherman did not think it was possible for Agnes to shock him more than she already had. "You did what?"

"I had to find out what she was up to, my darling. Did you not hear what I have just told you? She intends to trick you into marrying her so that you can support that unfortunate wretch she has taken in."

Sherman took a deep breath and appealed to the heavens for some patience. Millicent had told him to be kind and he was determined to treat Agnes with dignity no matter how much she infuriated him. "Please tell me you did not go to Martha's home and insult her with these preposterous accusations."

"I did no such thing. I merely went out there to get to know her better. You speak highly of her and I thought she and I might be friends when we return. I met the child during the course of my visit, and I must say, Sherman, she is a peculiar child."

Agnes was a convincing liar, but Sherman had known her all of her life and did not believe a word of what she was saying about a desire to get to know Martha better. "Agnes, I have told you before: Martha is only a friend. As for the child, I understand that she has family in Batavia willing to take her in. She will be leaving any day now."

The relief that showed on Agnes' face was only fleeting. "She is deceiving you in an effort to divert your attention while she continues to gain your affection. Your only recourse is to leave Buffalo with me. When we return as man and wife she will see that you have made your choice."

Sherman managed another deep breath and another silent prayer. "Agnes, I want you to listen to what I need to tell you. Although we have been friends since we were children, and I do care about you, I do not love you and I cannot marry you."

"Please stop this nonsense. We have been betrothed since our childhood because we are a perfect match. Our parents saw it from the beginning. If only you would return to our life in Albany until we are married, you would see it too. I know you would."

"I want no part of my old life in Albany."

"How can you say that? We are the best of friends, Sherman, we always have been," she insisted.

"At one time, we were, but you and I have grown up to be very different than the children we once were. I can see the change in you even if you can't see it in yourself. I want to stay here and become a physician and you want to travel in search of more free thinkers like yourself. You would not be happy here and I would not be happy traveling with you."

Agnes was unaccustomed to Sherman disagreeing with her and she was growing frustrated. "Say these things to me if you must, but I doubt you will have such courage when you attempt to explain yourself to your parents."

Sherman pulled out his pocket watch, more to give him time to find the right words than to see what time it was. "Agnes, I will speak to both our parents and try to make them understand that it was never my intention to hurt you or them, but I will not allow them to change my mind on the matter. I'm sorry."

"You will change your mind, Sherman, because we belong together."

They had reached the lobby of the hotel and Sherman was hoping that he could send Agnes off to her rooms without drawing the attention of the entire hotel staff. "Please tell our parents that I will come directly to the hotel in the morning when my shift at the hospital is over." She nodded, certain that she would get what she wanted in the end. "Goodbye, Agnes."

Back once again in her rooms Agnes looked out her window as night began to fall over the city and wondered how it all had gone wrong. She was certain Sherman would come to his senses. Looking back on her visit to Martha Sloane the previous day, Agnes thought she should have simply told the woman outright to stay away from her fiancé. The truth was that she had lost her nerve — and who wouldn't have, with that odd little girl glaring at her. There wasn't much to be done about that now. She dared not leave the hotel with her parents due to arrive at any minute. She would be in trouble enough for running through the city of Buffalo unescorted and without any warning. It would be harder to draw on her parents' sympathies if she were not in her rooms when they arrived. Brooding at the window suited her fine for the time being. Between her parents and his, they would talk some sense into Sherman.

* * *

Sherman approached the hospital slowly, allowing himself plenty of time to think. It would be difficult to maintain a professional demeanor around Millicent, and not just because of the evening they had spent together. She would need to know how things had worked out with Agnes. It would take longer than a few minutes to explain what had happened when he had gone to the hotel earlier that evening, and he wondered how he could get Millicent alone long enough without arousing suspicion. There were just enough patients to keep the reduced staff busy, but the chores that would allow them to leave the building, like laundry and the scrubbing of buckets, were fewer and further between. It could be hours before they could sneak outside for a quiet word.

Sherman entered the hospital to find five of the cots occupied and Martha already at work reading the notes Dr. Grant had left about Mrs. Hodskin in the ledger. He peered over her shoulder from a respectable distance.

> *First symptom was a diffuse discharge of the bowels at 4 o'clock this morning. Since then discharges have almost been constant and involuntary and accompanied by cramping of the limbs and moderate vomiting. I saw her at 5 am , gave calomel and morphine- was repeated before 6 and at 9 -at 8 calomel alone was given. Collapsed at 10 am.*

"These last few cases all seem to be in the acute phase of the disease," Martha told Sherman as she got up so he could have a better look at the ledger.

"I thought Dr. Grant had agreed to reduce the morphine dosages after he had read the results of your notes on the subject of opiate overdose?"

"He must have thought her condition justified the increase," Martha suggested. "We'll need to pay close attention to Miss Butler." Martha pointed to the cot next to Mrs. Hodskin. "She keeps tryin' to leave the hospital, for all the poor woman can barely stand." Millicent had found Sheila Butler trying to crawl out the door screaming that she would surely die there if she stayed.

Sherman nodded as he looked at the woman's record. "Perhaps a dose of laudanum is also justified in this case so she can rest."

"Aye, Dr. Grant did just that this afternoon. He's left a note to give her another dose if she wakes and tries to leave again."

Surveying the room, Sherman was relieved to see that he, Martha, Erik and Millicent were the only medical staff present. Now that only a few patients were trickling in the physicians were keeping regular hours and leaving the students in charge of the night shift. Surely the opportunity to speak to Millicent alone would present itself before their shift was over. He dreaded telling her that his parents had not yet arrived and, instead of falling asleep in her arms when their shift was over, he would have to leave her again to deal with them. It would be such a relief when the whole unfortunate situation was over so they could marry and build a life together. His eyes wandered across the room and caught hers. She had been stealing glances in his direction since he walked in and blushed at having been noticed doing it again. He acknowledged her with a subtle nod, hoping she would receive all of the messages that simple gesture conveyed.

"Sherman?" Martha had to call his name three times to regain his attention.

"Oh, I beg your pardon. What did you say?"

Martha suppressed a smile, knowing very well who had his diverted attention. "I said there's not much to be done for the others."

"No, it appears not."

In fact, the patients stayed quiet for most of the night. On any other evening Sherman would have been grateful and found that he was ashamed to be disappointed there were no buckets to empty or bed clothes to carry out to the laundry. He took some time to consider what he needed to say to Millicent. Sitting at the desk, staring out the window he reviewed all of his options. When he had made up his mind, he stood and surveyed the room. Martha was busy folding smocks and Erik had disappeared into the supply room. "Things seem quiet here, Martha," he commented as he walked in her direction. "I'm going to step outside for a bit of fresh air if you don't mind."

"Not at all, away ye go. I'll call ye if I need ye."

Sherman managed to pass by Millicent on his way out the back door, glancing in her direction as he went and after a few minutes she made her way to the front of the hospital.

Erik came back into the main room and noticed Millicent leave through the front door. He took a quick look around and found that Sherman was nowhere to be seen and Martha was absorbed with her task. Without a word, he followed the nurse out.

* * *

Agnes pressed her cheek onto the cool window pane in an effort to keep from dozing off, thinking it would be in her best interest to greet her parents when they arrived. It was well into the night when she realized that they weren't coming, and if by some chance they did arrive in the hours before dawn, they would not expect her to be there to welcome them. She began, for the first time, to consider what might happen if she and Sherman did not marry. Returning to Buffalo after the wedding would ensure the independence she had grown to enjoy. If by some absence of fortune he was able to convince their parents he would not marry her, she would be forced to go back to Albany alone. Agnes did not see how she could go back to living under her mother's supervision after having such a glorious taste of freedom. Suddenly relying on their parents to explain to Sherman the error of his ways seemed a risk she was unwilling to take. Agnes rose from the window and went in search of her coat. There were a few hours yet before dawn, time enough to confront Martha once and for all if she hurried.

It was so late that even the saloons had closed for the night as Agnes made her way on foot down Main Street to Niagara in order to approach the hospital from the rear. She no longer felt compelled to pat at her coat pocket to remind herself of the pistol concealed within, as she had almost every night she had left the hotel. Agnes smiled to herself. For all she had been told of the dangers lurking on the city streets at night, she never had cause even to draw her weapon, let alone use it to bargain for her safety, but it was there if she needed it.

The sound of voices in the clearing behind the hospital caused her to proceed with caution to her usual spot among the saplings. Even if she hadn't recognized the tall silhouette of Sherman, she knew his voice. He was with someone, but Agnes couldn't tell who was standing directly in front of him. She took a careful step forward and when it did not draw their attention, moved around to get a better view. He was with that woman! Agnes could not see clearly in the darkness and leaned closer to eavesdrop.

Erik followed Millicent around to the back of the building. He was about to call out to her when her pace quickened and she ran directly into Sherman's waiting arms. "Well, I'll be damned," he whispered to himself. His mission thwarted by another man, Erik was about to turn and go back inside when he saw a woman step into the clearing. The couple continued their intimate conversation as if they had not seen her.

"Don't you see, my darling? It is the only way we can be together. I thought all of this would be over by now," Sherman explained.

"Ye know I will go wherever ye decide. I only hope that whatever misfortune that has delayed yer parents is not serious," she answered.

"My sweet love, I do not deserve the magnitude in which your kindness and understanding are so freely given."

"Sherman, ye are a good man and I know well this situation tears at yer heart. I would have it over with, only so that ye will once again enjoy peace of mind."

Agnes could not believe what she was seeing; Sherman in the embrace of Martha Sloane. She let out a gasp when he bent his head to kiss her and watched in horror as his hands traveled over her hips and down her thigh. Furious, Agnes tore the ring off of her finger and whipped it with all of her might right at his head. "Sherman Carrington, you are indeed a rogue!"

The ring bounced off of his temple and hit the ground, startling the couple apart. Sherman turned to see Agnes standing just in front of a small grove of saplings, pale with fury. Without a word she drew the gun and leveled it at the other woman. "Agnes, no!" Sherman threw himself in front of Millicent and pushed her aside, intercepting the bullet that would have surely killed her.

Chapter Twenty-Four

Martha heard a shriek followed by what sounded like a gunshot. Rushing to the window she saw three silhouettes. Seconds later one crumpled to the ground and she ran toward the door.

"Oh, dear God, what have I done?" Agnes screamed. Tossing the pistol to the ground, she turned and ran off into the woods.

Erik ran back towards the hospital, ripped the door opened and thrust his head inside. "Come quick," he shouted to Martha and then turned and was off again.

Martha's sides were heaving as she reached her friends. "He's been shot," Erik told her, looking down on the scene, where Millicent had the hem of her skirt pressed into Sherman's left shoulder to stanch the flow of blood.

"Let's get him inside," Martha said as she bent to help lift the man to his feet.

Sherman was in shock and it was a struggle for Erik and Martha to keep him on his feet as they made their way to the hospital. Once inside, Millicent removed his coat and shirt while Martha and Erik hastily assembled the supplies to dress his wound.

There were no surgical tools in this makeshift hospital and Millicent hoped they would not need them. She examined his shoulder and gently wiped the blood from around his upper arm. "'Tis a superficial wound," the nurse told Martha, clearly shaken.

Martha examined the wound and said a silent prayer of thanks that the bullet had only grazed the deltoid muscle. It had done significant damage to the tissue, but thankfully not to the underlying bone, nerves or blood supply. "What happened?" she asked Millicent.

"That woman shot him!" Millicent looked to be in shock herself and Martha decided an explanation could wait until Sherman's wound had been dressed and they had all calmed down. After gently ushering Millicent off to clean herself up, Martha worked in silent efficiency and had the injured arm cleaned and wrapped with little fuss. "He'll need stitches, but that should do for now," she said.

When he refused a dose of laudanum for the pain, Erik walked over to the window and retrieved the bottle of whiskey he knew was kept in the drawer of the desk. It had seen the medical staff through many a stressful night and was desperately needed now. Returning to Sherman's bedside with four cups, he poured a healthy dram into each of them. "Drink," he told them, and they did.

Turning to Millicent, Martha asked again, "What happened out there?"

Millicent was reluctant to offer any information, but Sherman reached out a shaky hand and took hers. "It's okay, my darling, Martha knows everything." Turning to Martha, he continued. "I went to see Agnes this evening to break off our engagement. She must have followed me here and overheard us talking outside. She had a gun and was about to shoot Millicent."

"But ye jumped in front and pushed me out of the way. Ye could have been killed." Millicent's voice cracked and she did her best to hold back her tears.

"No, my dearest, it was you that might have been killed, and I could not bear it if you had been."

Erik stared in disbelief, uncertain how he had remained ignorant of Sherman's interest in Millicent and, more surprisingly, of his engagement to another woman.

The look on Sherman's face nearly broke Martha's heart. She wanted to get up and give them a moment alone together, but Sherman stopped her as she rose to leave, motioning for Erik to remain as well. When they were both standing before him again he spoke in a voice made steady by whiskey. "We have made rather a mess of things and I am truly sorry to say that I must impose upon our friendship one last time."

Erik's brows rose with interest, but Martha sat back down, concerned by the note of finality in Sherman's voice. "What would ye ask of us?"

"Millicent and I were planning on leaving town this morning and given all that has occurred, it seems like the wisest plan. I would ask that you say nothing of what has transpired here and nothing of our plans."

Erik, still stunned by the most recent revelations, merely nodded, but Martha was not so easily convinced. "Sherman, how can ye just leave? The woman shot ye.

Surely ye must tell yer parents," Martha stared at him in disbelief.

Sherman took a deep breath and winced as he exhaled. "I am reasonably sure Agnes has run off again. She either thinks she has killed me or does not want to risk the consequences if I inform either our parents or the constable of her actions. If our parents have not arrived already, they will be here in Buffalo sometime today and I can think of no explanation of this situation that they will understand or accept. I am tired of all of this nonsense and I will have it over right now."

"Where will ye go? Surely ye must wait until yer arm is healed," Martha cautioned.

"We will leave today. I do not want to have to explain my injury to anyone, least of all my parents, and I will not risk Millicent getting dragged into this mess."

Martha turned to Millicent and tried to appeal to her common sense. "Do ye think this wise?"

"If Sherman wishes to leave, I'll go with him. I'll tell Dr. Grant that I'm going home to Springville to help my family."

"Sherman, won't yer parents try and find ye? Surely they will come here and ask questions." Martha couldn't see how he could just leave town with nobody the wiser.

"Yes, they will try and find me, especially if Agnes is gone, too. That is why Dr. Grant must see me here and think that all is well when we leave for the day. That way, he will have nothing to offer my parents but the truth, and so will the both of you. If Millicent explains that she is leaving to be with her family, Dr. Grant will have no reason to suspect that we are together."

"'Tis much we ask of ye, Martha, and if ye must tell the truth, I only ask that ye give us a chance to leave before ye do," Millicent asked her.

Martha considered their request. Sherman had been shot, but he would not pursue it to the authorities. They were not asking her to lie, only to stay silent. The patients had not been harmed in any way by all that had transpired, so she saw no reason for Dr. Grant to be informed of the incident. Also, if neither she nor Erik had knowledge of when they were leaving or where they were going, they would be able to say so with a clear conscience. The couple was only seeking a life together in peace. If holding her tongue would help them to find happiness, she would do it gladly. "I'll keep yer secret, too."

Sherman breathed a sigh of relief. "Thank you, both of you. You are good friends."

Erik noticed Mrs. Butler had managed again to crawl to the floor and went off to settle her to bed once more. Martha looked out the window. The sun was rising. Dr. Grant and the day staff would be arriving within the hour. "Millicent, please fetch a clean shirt and help Sherman into it; it won't do for Dr. Grant to know he's been shot." She rose and grabbed the bloodstained shirt and jacket. "I'll just bury these out back."

Outside, Martha saw the pistol on the ground and bent to retrieve it so she could bury it with Sherman's things. "What's this?" she asked out loud and picked up a ring that was just a few inches from the pistol. Martha remembered Agnes wearing it when she had come to the farm for tea and assumed it had been a gift from Sherman. Slipping the ring in the pocket of her skirt, she tossed the pistol and the soiled clothes into the pit where they emptied the buckets of excrement, shoveled in some quicklime as they did to keep the flies and the animals away, and covered them with dirt. If anyone came looking for the pistol, they certainly would not look there.

By the time Martha returned to the hospital Dr. Grant had arrived. Sherman and Erik were updating him on the status of the patients. Sherman's injured arm was well-wrapped and no blood had seeped from the bandage, yet. He was pale and Martha could tell he was in pain by his rigid posture. She approached and stood next to her friend, but slightly in front of him, essentially blocking his left arm from view. As they moved from one patient to the next, she retained that position in the hopes that the doctor would not notice anything was amiss.

The three medical students were all relieved when Dr. Grant gave his permission for them to leave. Millicent asked to speak with him so that she could tender her resignation, so he didn't even notice Sherman stumble as he made his way toward the door. Martha caught the nurse's eye, hoping to convey her good wishes with a small wave and a smile. Millicent offered back a barely perceptible nod as she led the doctor to the back of the hospital.

Outside Sherman said his goodbye to Erik and thanked him again for keeping their secret. The two men exchanged a handshake and Erik was on his way. Johnny's carriage could be seen making its way up the road to pick up Martha. Sherman turned toward her. "I guess we are both embarking on an adventure today," he remarked, smiling. "You have been a good friend to me Martha, and I will miss you. Thank you for keeping our secret."

"Be safe, Sherman, and be happy."

Sherman climbed slowly into his carriage and set out down the road to wait for Millicent to join him. Johnny waved as he trotted by and slowed the carriage as it approached the front of the hospital. "Are ye ready?" He asked.

"Aye, I'm all packed," said Martha. "I just need to change my clothes."

"Bruns stopped by the farm to pick up the wee lass. We've got yer things at the shop, so ye can change there." She nodded and they took off at a trot toward Main Street.

They entered the shop through the kitchen, where Katherine was bouncing wee Felicity on her knee.

Martha smiled and was glad Katherine could meet her before they left. "I'll just be a minute," she said as she headed toward the stairs.

"Yer things are in Ellie's room. Just ye leave yer dress on the hook behind the door and I'll add it to the washin' later."

"Thanks, Gran." Martha kissed Katherine on the cheek, tussled Felicity's hair and trotted up the stairs. Although she had worked all night and made it through the morning with nobody the wiser for the events that had transpired at the hospital, Martha was not the least bit tired. She was excited to be on her way and wasted no time slipping out of her hospital clothes and into a fresh dress. She picked up her soiled dress and moved to hang it on the back of the door when something fell out of the pocket. "Oh no, I completely forgot about that ring!" she said out loud as she bent to pick it up off the floor.

Martha stared at the ring wondering what to do with it. She had no way to return it to Sherman. He would certainly have left town by now, and he purposely had not told her where they were going. It was such a beautiful ring, and looked to have cost a fortune.

Martha briefly thought about trying to find his parents so that she could return the ring to them, but thought better of it. Sherman wanted nothing more to do with them and she certainly did not want to have to answer any questions about how such an expensive ring came into her possession. In the end she decided to hold on to it in the hopes that one day she would hear from him again and could return it.

After she hung the dress on the back of the door, Martha went over to the closet in the far corner of the room. She remembered that, when they had lived here briefly as children, this room had been Johnny's and that he had once shown her the secret place where he had hidden all of his treasures. She got down on her knees and used her fingers to pry loose the piece of floorboard in the back of the closet. The space was empty. Johnny had taken the arrowhead, the red tail hawk feather Daniel had given him and his collection of interesting pebbles with him when they moved to the farm on North Street. Martha smiled at the memory of that day when he had shared his special things with her and realized that she had probably fallen in love with him back then. She placed the ring in the place underneath the floor, returned the board and went downstairs.

Felicity's attention was immediately diverted from Katherine when Martha rejoined them in the kitchen. She crawled down from her lap and motioned for Martha to pick her up. The child began patting her about the hair and face like she had on the day of Agnes' visit to the farm. For the first time Martha was unnerved by her penetrating stare. It was almost as if she knew what had transpired at the hospital and she was checking to make sure that Martha was alright.

"Ready to go?" Johnny asked, oblivious to the exchange.

Martha kissed Felicity on her forehead, and smiled, hoping to reassure the child that all was well. "Aye, I think we are."

* * *

The instant Agnes pulled the trigger she realized that, in fact, it was her own actions that the Fox Sisters had warned her about. Something terrible had happened to Sherman and she was the perpetrator of the evil that had befallen him. Was he dead? Agnes knew not. She just dropped the pistol and ran into the darkness, heedless of direction, wanting to be as far away from the hospital as possible. She ran until she thought her lungs would explode, and then fell to the ground sobbing. It was well past dawn when she finally pulled herself together.

Looking up, she found that she was in the woods, but could see the road from the trees. It felt safe under the cover of the canopy and she saw no need to move on right away. The woods were quiet, offering a much needed opportunity to sit and think about what had just happened. The thought of Sherman in the arms of another women infuriated Agnes at first, but if she was being honest with herself, she could see very clearly they were deeply in love. Just a few minutes of observation revealed they shared feelings she had never felt for Sherman, nor he for her. Having known the man all of her life, Agnes considered him her dearest friend… her only friend, actually. She could not deny him the love of this other woman.

"Dear God, I actually tried to kill her," Agnes confessed to the tall trees that surrounded her, but could not bring herself to finish the thought with words, '*and I may likely have killed Sherman instead.*'

She forced herself to confront that which she was so afraid to lose that she was willing to take the life of another to keep it. If Sherman had married Martha, he would not have married Agnes, that much was obvious, but did she really want to be Sherman's wife? Up until recently, she would not have hesitated to say yes, she did. As a young woman, Agnes became infatuated with the relationship between her parents and the Carringtons, as well as the adventures they shared roaming the country in search of free thinkers like themselves. Agnes thought if she had married Sherman, they would have enjoyed that same life. What she had learned in the last few weeks was that *she* hadn't been free at all. Traveling with her parents, Agnes had been subject to the same restrictive rules that had governed her life in Albany. She hadn't been able to interact with most of the people they had met during their travels because her mother did not think it proper for a young, unmarried woman to engage in such pursuits. She had only been able to talk to Maggie and Katie Fox because the girls were close to her own age. Agnes began to wonder if her parents were really free thinkers at all, or if they were just enjoying the latest pastime that tickled the fancy of their wealthy peers.

The more Agnes thought about it, the more she realized that, from the beginning, the idea of marrying Sherman Carrington had more to do with her getting what she really wanted out of life than it did with building a life with him. At first she saw marriage as an opportunity to be able finally to explore the fascinating things that were happening among the mesmerists, but in the end it was her independence she really coveted. Sherman's desire to stay in Buffalo would have allowed her to live separately from her parents and given her the freedom to explore who she was.

"Was that important enough to trade for another person's life?" She presented the question to the forest and as she waited for it to reply she heard the sound of a wagon passing by on the road.

* * *

"I think the lass is in need of a piss," Bruns told Johnny as Felicity was wiggling on the bench between them.

Johnny looked in the bed of the wagon and found Martha bundled up under the blankets sound asleep. He didn't have the heart to wake her. "Aye, alright. We'll stop here and I'll run her into the woods." He pulled the wagon over to the side of the road and Felicity scrambled down, taking off like a shot into the woods. "Just ye wait for me," he called, feeling instantly foolish because he knew she could not hear him. From the edge of the forest, he could see her squat and decided he would wait for her there.

Agnes kept herself hidden as the wagon stopped on the roadside. She saw a young girl catapult herself over the man at the reins and run into the woods, stopping just in front of the tree behind which she stood. Agnes recognized her immediately and craned her neck to see if she could identify the man calling after her. Yes, she knew him, too. She had seen him come to pick up Martha Sloane from the hospital. Shifting her gaze to the wagon, Agnes gathered from the contents loaded into the back that they were traveling a fair distance.

Still watching the wagon, Agnes hadn't realized that she stepped away from the tree to get a closer look and gasped when she looked down to find that Felicity had finished her business and was staring at her. While

Agnes was startled to have been discovered, she found that she was not unnerved by the child's attention as she had been before. Felicity smiled and held her gaze, as if trying to tell her something. If Agnes hadn't been watching the girl so intently, she would have thought the words had been spoken aloud. She distinctly heard a child's voice tell her '*They are alright, they are happy,*' but she had not seen the child's lips move. In a flash Felicity was off and running back toward the wagon. Agnes started out after her, but thought better of it, and stayed within the safe confines of the forest.

Just then, a gentle breeze parted the leaves on the trees above her, allowing the morning sunshine through the forest canopy to warm her face. Agnes was relieved beyond measure that Sherman had not been seriously injured by her actions. She also realized that because Sherman had settled for nothing less than true love, he had also given her the gift of being able to search for the same herself, and for that she was grateful.

Chapter Twenty-Five

It was late on Saturday morning when Don walked into the office with two cups of coffee in his hands. "Oh, you are down here. I thought I might have dreamed your dramatic departure from our bedroom last night."

Maude smiled, gratefully accepting the coffee and the kiss on the cheek that came with it. "Yeah, sorry about that. I had to get down here and write it all down before I forgot the details."

"So, you had another dream?"

"Yes, and this one was a whopper. I found out how the ring got into the floorboards!"

Don took the seat closest to the door, propped his stocking feet on the antique desk and took another long sip of coffee. "Well, don't keep me waiting. I'm all ears."

Over the next hour Maude told him every detail of her dream, sometimes stopping to consult the laptop to be sure she had the particulars correct. "So, I was right. Martha did marry Johnny and ended up living right here. Can you believe it?"

Don raised his coffee mug to his mouth, noticed it was empty and put it down on the desk. "Well, it was a dream, after all. So the question is, do *you* believe it?" He was pretty sure he knew the answer to the question before he asked it.

"Well, there really aren't any new details I could verify historically. I'll never know if Agnes actually shot Sherman or if Martha hid the ring underneath the floor before she left for Batavia."

"But do you *understand* the dream? Maybe the better question is: did you find out what it all means?"

Maude considered the question, but didn't answer it directly. "I think what you are trying to get me to understand is that this is not over, right?" Don nodded and she continued speaking. "The real question isn't how did the ring get under the floor. The real question is why am I so attracted to the Erie County Poorhouse, particularly the Nolan family and all their connections."

"Exactly! What it looks like to me is that, from the time you started graduate school, you have been led in a particular direction, learning what you needed to know to keep you on the path, but not things you weren't ready to accept. The question is: why?"

Maude thought about it for a minute and realized he was right. "I wonder if that's why we ended up working in this building, to stay connected to the Nolans after I left academia. Remember? At first you didn't want a shop. You wanted to run the business off the internet. It took a while to convince you that we needed a retail location in the older part of the city."

Don smiled, remembering that Maude had liked the building on Chippewa the best out of the three they had considered, even though it was the smallest. "I remember exactly what you said. You told me 'This is our place, Don, I can feel it!' So, yeah, you're probably right about that." It would take more than one cup of coffee to figure all of this out, so Don picked up the empty mugs to go back up and refill them. "What's next?" he asked as he headed for the door.

"Well, regardless of what it all means, my dream makes a great ending for my book. I am pretty sure I got all of the details, so I guess I'll still try and track down the leads I was working on before…which reminds me I owe both Christine and Mrs. Lambert phone calls."

"I'll leave you to it, then." Don got to the stairs and then stopped and turned around. Poking his head back into the office, he asked, "So, what are you going to do about the ring?"

When Maude looked puzzled, he continued, "Well, it seems as though the mystery of the ring has been solved, so what are you planning on doing with it? Will you keep it or sell it?"

Maude considered the question for a moment before she answered. "I could never sell that ring. I guess I'll just hold on to it, like Martha did."

Don nodded in agreement and proceeded upstairs without another word. It seemed only fitting that Maude take her turn as the guardian of the ring. He smiled as he considered putting it back underneath the floor boards along with a copy of Maude's book for the next owners of the building to discover.

Maude looked at her watch and determined it was a bit early on a Saturday to disturb Mrs. Lambert, but that Christine likely spent the night reading the journal pages and would certainly be up by now. Maude smiled when her friend picked up on the first ring.

"Would you mind telling me what the Hydesville Rappers have to do with your cholera epidemic or the mysterious ring?" Christine usually dispensed with the formalities when she was in interrogation mode.

Maude panicked for a minute, not sure how to explain the Lily Dale connection. "Actually, smarty pants, the Carrington family was among the earliest Spiritualists of the time. They were called free thinkers, I think."

Christine didn't sound convinced. "That still doesn't tell me what the Fox Sisters have to do with your mystery."

"Well, now, I was hoping you would be able to tell me. We know the ring belonged to Sherman's mother, and I found out from my contact at Lily Dale that the Carringtons were fascinated by the ability to talk to spirits. The Fox sisters were gaining notoriety around that time and I was wondering if they had gone to Laona to see the girls, then maybe found their way to Buffalo to visit their son." The idea sounded plausible as Maude suggested it and she crossed her fingers that Christine would accept her explanation.

"That's a stretch, but you were right: the sisters were supposed to be in Laona in June, but were delayed by the cholera epidemic and didn't arrive until the end of August."

"Well then maybe it's not such a stretch after all. The ring had to get to Buffalo somehow."

"I guess you're right. By the way, what were you looking for during the middle of November?"

"What are you talking about? I only requested the journal entries through the first week in September."

"Well, you have a page from November fourteenth. Do you want me to read it to you? I can pull it up on my laptop."

"No, don't worry about it. I was planning to read them eventually. I was just working on another part of the puzzle when the files came in and I knew I wouldn't get a chance to really study the journal pages until next week. I really appreciate you reading them for me."

"What other piece of the puzzle? Have you found out something new?"

Maude gave herself a smack in the head for letting that slip. She was not ready to share the newly discovered details about their shop with anyone. Now, in light of her most recent dream, she really needed a chance to think about what it all meant. She would have to divulge a few half-truths for now and hope Christine bought it. "I was at the history museum looking up my building in the property map atlases."

"I've never had a reason to take a look at those. What did you find out?"

"We found that there was a building on the property in 1830, but we could not determine if it was *this* building, or who had built it. The original parcel record in County Hall would allow us to pull the deed and identify the property owners prior through the earliest date on my current title." All of that was true, she just didn't mention that they had already pulled the actual deed.

"Hmm…let me know what you find out."

Maude looked up to the heavens and gave a silent prayer of thanks. "I will, and thanks again for your help. Take care, Christine." She clicked the end button before the conversation could continue any further.

Thinking it might be useful to take a look at the November entry in Maggie Fox's journal before she called Mrs. Lambert, Maude opened up the e-mail and downloaded the scanned pages. There were only a handful of entries during the summer months and most of them were brief paragraphs, so she was able to read through all of them in chronological order before reaching the page dated November 14th. The entries were few and far between during those months because the girls had gotten stuck in their older sister's house in Rochester, New York. Finally, on the seventeenth of August, they continued their journey to Laona. It seemed reasonable that the travel bans would have been lifted earlier in Rochester because cholera would have struck there before it hit Buffalo and run its course sooner. The next few entries chronicled their journey and the interesting people they had met in Laona. When Maude reached the entry dated November 14, she could hardly believe her eyes.

> *November 14, 1849*
>
> *Sister and I were once again asked to demonstrate our unique abilities to Communicate with the spirits in Corinthian Hall in Rochester. We were delighted to find among the interested parties our friend Agnes Pollard*

> *from Albany whom we had met in Laona. Agnes has offered to travel with us as a sort of chaperone in exchange for the opportunity to study our techniques and learn the art of communicating with the spirits. Katie thinks it a splendid plan, but mother insists that Agnes write to inform her parents. Agnes has agreed to do so and will soon become our constant companion.*

Maude read the journal entry over three times to make sure that she wasn't seeing things. Somehow Agnes had found her way back to the Fox Sisters. She shook her head in disbelief. "This just keeps getting more interesting," she said out loud as her phone started to ring. She glanced quickly at the caller ID before she answered.

"Hi, Mrs. Lambert. I was just about to call you."

"Hello, dear. I thought I might try and catch you before the day got away from the both of us."

"It sounds like you have a lot to tell me, and I can't wait to hear every detail."

"I do have quite a bit to tell you, more now than when I sent you that e-mail. I was hoping that you might be able to come out and see me again. I think you need to hear what I have to tell you in person."

Maude felt that familiar chill coming from behind and couldn't decide whether she was excited or scared to death. "Well, I don't have any plans for today, but I'd rather not drive alone. Let me check with my husband and I'll call you right back."

Thirty minutes later Maude and Don were on their way to Lily Dale. Unlike their last trip, both the roads and the sky were clear and they made the journey in just over an hour. Unsure what she might learn in her discussion with Mrs. Lambert, Maude thought it wise to bring Don into the museum with her for a bit of moral support. "I hope you don't mind my husband joining us this time."

"Not at all." Turning to Don, she extended her hand. "Welcome, Mr. Travers."

Don gently shook her fragile hand. "Thank you, and please call me Don."

Leading the couple to the counter at the far end of the room, Mrs. Lambert pointed to the old ledgers she had placed on it. "I did some digging around and found that Ashton and Marcia Carrington were among the original families to have purchased stock in the Cassadaga Free Lake Association in 1879. That was the name of the corporation established to purchase the land for the camp. Back then there were campgrounds where meetings were held each year. Over time they evolved into year-round communities like Lily Dale."

Opening up a file folder, she drew their attention to a fragile piece of paper. "I also found their name on one of the earliest leases granted. You see, it was the same then as it is now. The property on which a cottage is built was owned by the corporation and leased to tenants. The tenant owned the house, but signed a ninety nine year lease for the property. Back then leaseholders paid three dollars a year. Cottages are still bought and sold, but the land stays in the hands of the corporation to maintain the religious integrity of the settlement and to protect it from developers. Even today a person seeking to purchase a cottage in the Dale must be a member of a Spiritualist church."

"That was a smart move," Don said. "These days lakeside property would be worth a fortune. There are more than a few developers who would love to get their hands on Lily Dale."

Mrs. Lambert only smiled. "Since the Carringtons were year-round residents, I looked in a few of the early papers to see if I could find out anything else. One of the earliest papers was called *The Sunflower* and it had a section called *The Lily Dale News*, which was sort of a gossip column." Charlotte Lambert paused before she continued. "Perhaps the rest of this conversation is best had over tea. Why don't we move upstairs where we can be more comfortable?" Collecting the ledgers, she said, "We can bring these things upstairs with us."

Maude and Don looked puzzled, but agreed and they all shuffled upstairs. While Mrs. Lambert plugged in the electric kettle, Maude looked at the volume that recorded the individuals who had purchased stock in the Cassadaga Lake Free Association and was really not surprised to notice that the Pollards had also purchased stock a year later.

Mrs. Lambert came in with a tray and the next few minutes were filled with the sounds of clinking cups and spoons as they prepared their tea. "Maude, do you remember my friend Mrs. Westner?"

Maude smiled. Only in Lily Dale would someone refer to the ghost of the first school teacher as a friend. "Yes, I do. Is she here now?" She nodded to Don, who also remembered the name and they both looked around but could see nothing. It had felt chilly from the time they entered the building, but Maude had thought nothing of it on such a cold day.

"Oh, yes, she's been pestering me since you walked in the door. Well, really since you left the last time." Charlotte looked to her left and addressed the empty space. "Yes, yes, I'm getting to that. Patience, Agnes."

Maude froze, teacup in midair, when she heard the school teacher's first name. "Her name is Agnes?"

Charlotte nodded, knowing that Maude had already put together what she was about to reveal. "Yes, and she is who you think she is, but let me tell you from the beginning."

Don looked thoroughly confused but decided to just listen and see what clarification could be obtained from Mrs. Lambert's story.

The old woman took a sip of her tea and then placed the cup down on the saucer. The clink of china meeting china was the only sound to be heard in the room. "When I was putting the pages of Maggie Fox's journal together to send to you, Mrs. Westner kept insisting I include the entry dated November 14th. I told her repeatedly that you had not requested it, but she insisted. She kept telling me *'Martha needs to know!'*

Well, I had no idea who she was talking about and finally I just included the page to quiet her down. It can be difficult to focus on what is happening in this world when someone is pestering you from the other side."

"I read that entry and I couldn't believe that Agnes Pollard had actually reunited with the Fox Sisters," Maude told her.

"Yes, well, she stayed with them for a while, but in 1855 she went back to join the Religious Society of Free Thinkers in Laona. That is where she met and married Horace Westner." She looked at the empty space again and smiled. "They were both free thinkers and were very much in love. Horace loved Agnes for who she really was and supported her interest in the spirit world. She's calling him her soul mate."

Charlotte redirected her attention toward Maude and Don and continued her story. "The Westners were also among the earliest stock holders in the Cassadaga Lake Free Association. Anyway, after I sent you the journal entries, Mrs. Westner kept giving me the image of a sunflower. I'm embarrassed to say it took a while before I figured out she was talking about the old newspaper. It is odd, really, sometimes she is very specific and sometimes she is not. I don't know why." Mrs. Lambert looked off toward the window as if to ponder the issue, but then remembered her guests and continued speaking. "Anyway, luckily the old papers are available online and can be searched. I was quite surprised to find this story printed in the gossip section in the fall of 1880." She handed the printed version to Maude.

Mrs. Pollard was delightfully reunited with her daughter after over thirty years when she and Mrs. Carrington met her during a tour of the Children's Lyceum. Having been married to Mr. Horace Westner these 22 years and looking much different from the girl she was, neither Mrs. Pollard nor Mrs. Carrington, who had known her since birth, recognized Mrs. Westner, who has been committed to the children's education since her arrival in August. Mrs. Westner knew Mrs. Pollard and her companion immediately and the three enjoyed a blissful reunion.

Maude was speechless. She read the blurb under the section heading *Lily Dale News* over again and then handed it to Don, who had been trying to read it over her shoulder. "Well, I'll be damned," he said, handing the printed page back to Charlotte.

"That's exactly what I said," the old woman agreed. "I had only learned of the first school teacher as Mrs. Westner. She had been long since married when she came here. What I don't know is why she needed you to know this information."

Maude had come to think of Mrs. Westner as a living person and so asked what she thought was a normal question. "Didn't she tell you?"

Charlotte gave her an indulgent smile. "I told you, dear, it doesn't always work that way. Those on the other side aren't able to have long and detailed conversations. That is why it can be difficult to understand what they are trying to tell us. It's also why I thought you needed to be here when I gave you this information." Charlotte turned to address the unseen person next to her. She stared in that direction as if trying to understand the message she was being given. "She is mentioning Martha again. She wants Martha to know she is sorry. She knows the truth now."

Maude looked completely confused. "She can't want me to tell her. Martha is long dead. I would think she could deliver that message easier than I could."

Charlotte looked annoyed at both the person who was physically in the room and the person who wasn't. "My dear, the other side isn't a big beach party where everyone knows everyone else. I mean, do you know everybody here on Earth?"

"Well, no, of course not, but I don't know how I would get a message to Martha Sloane."

"Oh, so you know who she is talking about?" Charlotte asked.

"Yes, I do." Maude took a few minutes to relay the pertinent points of her recent dreams to Mrs. Lambert so that she would know who Martha Sloane was and where Agnes Pollard Westner fit into the scheme of things. She added in the information about their building on Chippewa. The old woman listened with rapt attention, eyes widening as Maude recounted her dream from last night.

"She actually tried to shoot the woman? I must say, I am surprised. That doesn't fit at all with what we know of the school teacher I have read about. By all accounts she was a kind and gentle soul, the very essence of graciousness and generosity. Small wonder she wants to apologize to the woman."

"My sense of Agnes from my last dream was that before she left Buffalo she had undergone a transformation similar to the one Sherman was undergoing throughout the summer. She was no longer the same overindulged and selfish child who had traveled from Albany to Laona with her parents."

Mrs. Lambert smiled. "She is telling me she is glad that Martha understands."

"Is Martha here, too?" Don asked, having trouble trying to keep track of the number of women in the room.

Charlotte stared again into the empty space next to her, concentrating. After a few frustrating moments of silence she turned back to Maude. "My dear, I believe she thinks you are Martha Sloane."

Maude was not aware that she was leaning forward in her chair until the force of those words made her muscles go slack and she started to fall forward.

Don reached forward and pushed Maude back into the chair, making sure she was secure in her seat before he took his own again. "Excuse me, Mrs. Lambert, but are you telling me that Maude was Martha Sloane in a past life?"

"No, dear. Mrs. Westner is telling you." Charlotte closed her eyes for a moment. "I'm feeling a deep sense of regret, maybe over the shooting, or for suspecting that Martha was trying to steal her fiancé, or maybe even because she was trying to force Sherman into honoring his commitment to her when he was honestly and truly in love with someone else. A bit of each, I expect."

"Wait a minute. Martha never tried to steal Sherman," Maude corrected her. "Martha always loved Johnny. It was Millicent who fell in love with Sherman, and she didn't know about Agnes until Sherman told her."

"Agnes didn't know any of that until just now. She thought it was you, or Martha rather, that she tried to shoot," Mrs. Lambert told her.

Don listened while the two women discussed dreams as if they had really happened and dead people as if they had known them well. He waited for a pause in the conversation to ask some questions. "Excuse me, but I just want to make sure that we are all on the same page here." When he had their attention he continued. "Okay, so Mrs. Westner is Agnes Pollard, and she believes that Maude was at one time Martha Sloane?" Mrs. Lambert nodded and Don went on. "Well, is it reasonable to assume that all of these experiences thus far have been leading up to this?" When the old woman looked confused, he rephrased the question. "Did Mrs. Westner, Agnes, in some way orchestrate all of this?"

Charlotte thought for a moment, and maybe even consulted the school teacher. Don couldn't tell. "No." She paused again, clearly trying to choose her words carefully. "Truthfully, I can't say for sure how or why all of this is happening to you. I can tell you what I think, though."

Maude nodded and reached casually for her husband's hand. "Yes, please do."

Charlotte took a sip of her tea, which had gone quite cold, before she continued. "It appears to me that Spirit has been keeping you close to the Erie County Poorhouse for quite a while now, and I think it was no mistake that you ended up living in the same building that Martha Sloane lived in during different periods in her life." Maude nodded, remembering Don had suggested the same this morning. "However, I believe that both Mrs. Westner and Mrs. Kaiser were, for lack of a better explanation, two side streets that lead back to the main road."

"I don't understand," Maude interjected.

"Well, I think that they both had unfinished business and you just happened across their cosmic path and helped them to complete it. Mrs. Kaiser needed to have the Nolan family acknowledged for all the help they had given her at the end of her life and Mrs. Westner needed to confess remorse over her actions at the cholera hospital…even though it turned out that it wasn't Martha she tried to shoot."

"So what about this business of a past life?" Don asked.

"Well, Agnes may not have realized that it wasn't Martha that night at the hospital, but she seems very certain that it *is* Martha sitting here in the room today," Charlotte said, gesturing to indicate that she meant Maude.

"So are you telling me that if it weren't for a case of mistaken identity, I would not have known about this whole past life thing?" Maude asked.

"Spirit tells you only what you are ready to know. I think that the messages you have received from these two departed souls were meant to return you to the path you have been on for some time. Why you are on this path remains to be seen."

Maude leaned forward in her chair so that she could look directly into the old woman's eyes. "Do you believe that I was Martha Sloane in a past life?"

"You are probably not going to like my answer to that question. The truth is it doesn't matter whether or not I believe it. Honestly, it doesn't matter if you *really* believe it either. You have been presented with information. If it makes you think about your life differently, or makes sense in the context of your life, or provides an answer to an important question you have been pondering, or changes your behavior, that is what really matters."

Don looked as if he accepted the answer, but Maude was skeptical. "What if I were looking for a more definitive confirmation?"

"Remember I mentioned before that you could go through a meditation exercise or past life regression hypnosis. However, people who are unwilling for whatever reason to believe that what they have experienced was genuine will dismiss what they learn from hypnosis or meditation as confused or implanted memories." She paused but maintained eye contact. "Really it comes down to how *you* receive the messages that you are given."

* * *

Mrs. Lambert and Mrs. Westner stood side by side as they watched the Travers drive away, although only one of them was visible to the average passerby. "You are right, dear, they have no idea, and we were wise not to say anything. They are not ready," Charlotte told her friend in spirit.

The old woman moved away from the window, but the school teacher remained. There was still more on her mind. Charlotte listened carefully to the unspoken message. "No, she does not see how much of Johnny's character has returned with him in this life." She thought about it for a moment and then continued. "He is more accepting of the true nature of things, I think, so perhaps he will understand that they have always been on this path together before she does," Agnes nodded, content to wait and see what happened next, for she knew the couple would be back to see them again.

Chapter Twenty-Six

The ride home from Lily Dale was a quiet one. Finally when they reached the city Don asked her the usual question. "So, what's next?"

"I don't know. I think Charlotte is right. Until I decide what I think of all of this, any attempt to reveal more information through meditation or hypnosis will only create more questions than answers." What she really meant was, she had to decide if she was going to actually believe the answers she received.

Don nodded in agreement, understanding both what Maude said and what she didn't say. "I know you already have a lot on your mind, but can I offer you some advice?"

Maude smiled, knowing Don would have distilled the experience down to what was most important. "I would love some."

"If this were happening to me, I would ask myself only one question."

"Well, don't keep me waiting!"

Don chuckled. "Well, it might not be the same question you would ask. I think you would ask if you really were Martha Sloane in a past life."

"Well, yeah," Maude rolled her eyes, indicating that the "duh" was implied. "Are you telling me that you wouldn't want to know for sure?"

"Actually, yes, I am. I would wonder *if* I were Martha in a past life, then *why* do I need to know that in this life. In other words, what is to be gained from confirming it one way or the other?"

That was worth pondering, and Maude told him so. "As usual, you are right." She allowed him a smug smile before she continued. "If I have been on this journey to ultimately learn that I was Martha Sloane in a past life, the question becomes: why? What am I supposed to learn from that?" Don was silent but she could see he was processing her comments. "What?" she asked, knowing he had an alternative point of view.

"Well, what if Martha Sloane is just another side street?"

"I'm not sure what you are getting at here."

"Yeah, I'm not either. I guess I am drawn in by Mrs. Lambert's notion of side streets leading back to the main path. Frederika Kaiser was a side street. Without that experience you might not have decided to write your book." Maude nodded and he continued. "It gets a bit jumbled when you think about Sherman, Martha, Agnes and the ring. Maybe the ring, rather than Agnes, was the side street. If we hadn't found it, you would still be struggling to write your original story. Instead, you have nearly finished the first draft of a different story in record time."

"Okay, I'm following you so far. What about Sherman, Martha and Agnes?"

"Yeah, I'm the least certain about all of that. All those years ago Agnes wrongfully assumed that Martha was trying to trap Sherman into marriage and went so far as to shoot at her, or the person she thought was her."

Maude took up where he left off. "Right, and if we believe Mrs. Lambert's interpretation, Agnes came upon me by chance when I first visited Lily Dale. She knew me to be Martha Sloane and wanted to apologize for her actions, only learning after the fact that it was not Martha whom she had shot."

Don shook his head. "See, the thing is, I think Martha Sloane was a side street. I think you were supposed to find out that you were Martha in a past life so that you would continue the journey."

Maude wasn't sure. "Maybe."

"Consider what you would have done if you hadn't received that piece of information today. You told me this morning that your dream provided a perfect ending to the book. You would have finished it and considered the mystery solved. Finding out that you were Martha in a past life will keep you digging for more answers."

"You seem to have no trouble believing in the whole past life thing."

Don gave her a questioning look. "Does that bother you? I just think Mrs. Lambert's explanation makes sense. You are given pieces of information to keep you on the right path. From where I am sitting, that path leads to the Erie County Poorhouse. All of your experiences, in one way or another, involve that institution. Mrs. Lambert said so as well."

"Okay, then why? What am I supposed to learn from all of this?"

"I don't know. Maybe it's not over."

Maude snorted. "Some help you are!"

The remainder of the day was spent in silent contemplation. Maude only participated marginally in the dinner conversation, and paid no attention to the movie they watched after supper. When she went to bed later that night Don had his nose buried in a book, so she kissed him on the cheek and attempted to settle her mind for sleep. It came as no surprise twenty minutes later that she was still wide awake. Maude knew herself well enough to realize that this would be the first of many sleepless nights if she didn't find an explanation for her experiences with which she could abide. After fifteen more minutes of mental abuse for her inability to clear her mind (during which Don had set his book down and instantly nodded off), it occurred to her that it wouldn't do any harm to try the meditation exercise Charlotte had described. If nothing else, it might quiet her mind enough to get some rest.

She closed her eyes and took a deep breath and then another. Charlotte had told her to think about a long hallway full of doors. She conjured up the image of a well-worn oak floor with doors of the same wood on one side and wall sconces on the other. Not electric fixtures, these held thick white candles at shoulder height and were distributed down the hall. The doors were all rectangular, without adornments or carvings, only each had a different knob. Some were brass, some porcelain or crystal. The first few looked very new, like something purchased in a modern hardware store, but they got older looking as she continued down the hall. Between each candle was a heavily draped window. The window coverings were plum damask, fringed with a darker shade of the same color. Maude wasn't sure why, but she felt compelled to touch them and ran her hand gently over the textured surface. They felt cool, like they were keeping out the cold. She also noticed that the silk wall coverings were a lighter shade of plum. When she turned to continue down the hall, Maude noticed that a door on the opposite side of the hall was different from the rest in that it had a forged iron rim latch instead of a knob, and a beautiful wreath of flowers and foliage hanging on it. Maude glanced further down the hallway at the remaining six doors, but did not feel the need to continue towards them.

This was her door. She was certain of it. Maude remembered it was important to comprehend the reasons she knew it was her door, because Charlotte had told her that they would also help her to understand the journey she was on. The wreath was made of many different plants, vines and shrubs, with rocks, shells and branches tucked in. It did not look like a carefully manicured arrangement; rather more like the various elements had grown there naturally. Maude understood that the wreath represented her connection and respect for the natural world. The door latch was made of forged iron. She examined it carefully, trying to understand its significance. Iron is old and will stand the test of time. It is also strong and does not yield easily. The design of the latch was simple and would serve its purpose as long as it was needed. She committed those facts to memory so that she could recall them later.

Placing her hand on the latch, Maude was not at all surprised that it fit perfectly in her grasp or that the heavy oak door opened easily. She invited her spirit guide to join her inside, as Charlotte had told her to do. She thought, rather than spoke the request, feeling that the sound of her voice would disturb the energy in the room. The room was not a room at all, but a cave, and the woman tending the open fire in the middle of it did not look like a modern human. Her skin was dark and she had long, bushy black hair, unbound around her shoulders. Her brow was heavy, but her broad nose was the dominant feature of her face. She wore a tunic made of some sort of animal skin, and Maude recognized her as belonging to the group *Homo erectus*, an ancestor of modern humans dating back nearly two million years.

Maude briefly flashed back to middle school where she had watched a movie about human evolution in social studies class. It was then that she decided that she wanted to be an anthropologist. The woman smiled, nodding her head ever so slightly, and Maude understood the gestures to be an answer to her unspoken question. '*Yes, anthropology.*' It became clear to Maude that her interest in the human condition was an important part of who she had been in each life and would continue to be so in future lives.

The woman stood and moved away from the fire such that it was now between them. She turned around to face Maude and smiled again. *'Storyteller.'* Maude wasn't sure whether the woman had spoken the words or not, but there was no opportunity to ask. The woman turned and receded into the cave.

"Wait!" Maude called out to her, but she was gone. "Come back. What does that mean?"

"Maudie, wake up." She felt someone nudging her shoulder and then heard the words again. "Wake up! It's just a dream."

Startled, Maude sat upright and Don recoiled to the edge of the bed. "Where am I?" she asked.

Don turned on the light and closed the small distance between them cautiously, waiting for her breathing to settle before he touched her. "You're here, in our bed. You had a nightmare, I think." Carefully, he put an arm around her shoulders. "You okay?"

Maude took a deep breath and slowly exhaled. She rubbed her hands over her face and pushed the hair away from her eyes. "Yeah, I'm fine. That wasn't a nightmare, though. It was my spirit guide."

"What?"

"I couldn't sleep, so I tried the meditation Charlotte told me about and I met my spirit guide. Would you believe she was a *Homo erectus* woman?"

Don smiled, "Well, that sounds about right. Do you want to talk about it?"

Maude reached for the notebook and pen she kept by the bed to record the details of her dreams and handed it to her husband. "Yes. Would you mind taking notes?"

Don listened carefully, dutifully recording everything and stopping her for clarification when needed. Maude continued to sit bolt upright as she spoke, obviously rattled by the experience. When she was done, he repeated her last words back to her. "Storyteller?"

"Yup, that's all she said… or thought… I'm not sure which. I tried to get her to come back. I guess that was when you woke me up."

"Okay, so to summarize, the door had a wreath and an iron latch. The wreath connects you to nature, I can see that. Iron is old, strong, and durable. Am I right so far?"

"Yes, but I feel like the simplicity of the latch was important too."

"Okay, old, strong, simple, durable or maybe resilient. Beyond that we have anthropology, and storyteller. Is that everything?"

"Yes."

Don looked at the list and crossed out the word anthropology. "I think we can agree that you understand that part." Maude nodded. "Okay, the wreath makes sense too. You have always preferred a camp site to a fancy hotel room." Maude smiled in agreement and wondered out loud if her need to seek out the natural world wasn't somehow related to her connection to human origins. "Well, that would make sense," Don mused. "Now, that brings us to the iron latch. I think I get it."

"Do tell."

"Well, each of those words relates to you in some way." When she started to protest, he laughed. "I mean that you are an old soul, not that you are old. You are also unyielding about things that are important to you. You are, without a doubt, the strongest person I know." He could see she was finally beginning to relax.

"The idea of simplicity is a little complicated. Although you value simplicity, you over think everything instead of accepting the simple explanation. I think the idea that a simple design will be able to serve its purpose for a long time is a lesson you still need to learn. If you receive the messages that are given to you with a clear mind, maybe you will better understand the path you are on." Don smiled, obviously pleased with himself.

"Okay, genius. What about 'storyteller'?"

"That is really the easiest one. I'm surprised you don't see it yourself."

Maude rolled her eyes. "Perhaps I would have if I hadn't been distracted by the cave woman who told me!"

"Fair enough, Maudie. I think you are connected to these people because you were meant to tell their story. I mean, who really knew anything about that part of Buffalo's history before you finished your dissertation? I think your scholarly career allowed you to publish some articles, but writing novels will be where your contribution will have the most impact."

"How so?"

"Haven't you always said that if the scholarly literature were accessible to the general public, there would be considerably fewer problems with the world?" She nodded. "Well, a great many more people read novels than journal articles. By writing novels, you have the opportunity to share this story with the world."

It sounded so dramatic, but yet so simple, and he was right, sort of. "I get what you're saying, but this is only one book. I doubt very much it will change the world, even if it does become popular."

"You still don't get it, do you? The book is your *latest* work. You have continued to be involved in the poor house project and there will be scholarly publications as the result of that as well. I also have no doubt that you will manage to come up with an idea for another novel."

"Another novel about what? My body of work, as you think of it, already includes the poorhouse, the orphan asylum and the hospital. What's left?"

"Stay on the path and I'm sure you'll find out."

Maude blew out a sigh of frustration. "Stay on the path? Seriously? After all of the revelations of the last few days, your best advice is to stay on the path?

Spoken like someone who didn't recently find out he was someone else in a past life *and* that he has a freakin' cave man as a spirit guide!"

Although it was the wrong thing to do, Don laughed out loud. Before she could beat him with her pillow, he pulled her into his arms and planted a kiss on the top of her head. "Okay, okay, I get it. I guess it is a bit much to process all at once."

"Ya think?" Maude leaned back so she could see his face.

"Look, I know it's ridiculous to suggest that you get some sleep, although you should try to, but I think this will all look different in the light of day," Don told her. "Better yet, if you can, leave it alone for a few days. Just leave it all - the book, the dream, the past life - for a while. Maybe in a few days things will make more sense."

"How long have you known me?"

Don smiled. "Long enough to insist you at least try to put everything aside for a day or two." He reached to turn off the light, indicating that he was willing to follow his own advice even if she wasn't. "C'mon, let's get some sleep."

Maude settled back against her pillow and began making a list in her mind of the revelations she understood and/or could live with and the ones that would require further effort, be it emotional or cognitive. The door in her dream - it was a dream, wasn't it? Putting that question aside, she got back to the door. It was meant to represent her true self and the latch indicated both the strengths and weaknesses in her character. Reluctantly, Maude admitted that she had a tendency to overthink things and that it was something to work on. She wondered briefly what Don's door looked like and if it would be the knob that would reveal similar characteristics about him or some other aspects of it. '*Stay focused or you'll never get to sleep!*' she silently, but firmly, reminded herself.

This business about past lives was not so easy to accept. Maude would have to decide whether there was anything to be gained by seeking to verify the claim that she was Martha Sloane in a former life. Perhaps another visit to Charlotte in Lily Dale would help her to understand all these side streets of which she and Don were so certain. That trip would be easier in the spring, when the weather was better and Maude wasn't so busy. She assured herself that she wasn't putting off something she didn't feel comfortable dealing with, it was just that she had commitments. The remaining weeks of winter would be spent tweaking her book and ironing out the details of the poorhouse memorial museum at the university. Yes, the notion of past lives could wait until other more important matters had been settled.

In the quiet of the night with Don sleeping peacefully next to her, it wasn't as hard for Maude to admit that she felt connected to role of storyteller. The advent of urban poverty in human civilization was a topic that had fascinated Maude as a scholar, and the chance to reach a larger audience by creating works of historical fiction based on her scholarly research was enticing. She began to relax as topics for the next book floated through her mind. Just as she drifted off to sleep the thin, dark skinned, bushy haired woman appeared in her thoughts and uttered two words: *insane asylum.*

Epilogue

Buffalo Daily Courier

Tuesday Morning, December 7, 1849

Office-Main and Lloyd Streets, upstairs

Medical Student Gone Missing

Family distraught

Mr. and Mrs. Ashton Carrington of Albany are greatly distressed over the unknown whereabouts of their son, Sherman Carrington, a student in the Medical Department of the University of Buffalo. Carrington was last seen at the conclusion of his shift at the cholera hospital on the beach the morning of October third. Anybody with knowledge of his activities or transactions on or after that date are urged to contact Mr. Barnard Hallbreck, Esquire, in Albany. The Carringtons will pay handsomely for information leading to the discovery of their beloved son.

Martha sat at her grandmother's kitchen table and re-read the article, feeling guilty for keeping Sherman's secret from his parents. Reading about the anguish they felt over his disappearance caused her to rethink the decision to stay silent. She put the newspaper down and looked out the window seeking distraction, watching as Bruns and Johnny unloaded the wagon from their trip. She had been relieved to see Felicity settled with kin who respected the child's special gifts and would protect her from those who didn't. To deny the Carringtons the peace of mind that would come from knowing that Sherman was safe and happy seemed wrong.

Taking the newspaper once again, Martha considered the implications of divulging what she knew. There was no mention of Agnes Pollard in the article, but if she revealed Sherman's plans to marry another woman, surely there would be questions about the young woman. After another few moments thought, it seemed evident that she could not provide the Carringtons with any information that would not also reveal what had happened at the hospital. That would mean trouble for all those who were present at the time.

Before she could change her mind, Martha carefully ripped out the article and climbed the stairs to the bedroom in which Sherman's ring was still safely hidden. Convincing herself that she needed more time to consider all of the possible implications before making a decision one way or the other, Martha folded the newspaper clipping around the ring and placed them back underneath the floorboard, knowing they would be safe until her decision was made.

Acknowledgements

To my husband, Bob, and my son, Charlie, I thank you for taking care of yourselves, the dogs, the house and the business when I needed you to.

My profound thanks also go to Julia, Claire, Ashley, Wendy, and Lucy for holding down the fort at work when I needed them.

My novels are inspired by my scholarly work and so I thank Drs. Joyce E. Sirianni and Douglas Perrelli for inviting me to join the Erie County Poorhouse Cemetery Project. It has been such a pleasure to work on this project. I have learned so much from the both of them and their friendship has inspired each of my books.

There were several historians who were incredibly generous in giving me both their time and their detailed knowledge of various aspects of Buffalo's history. Jennifer Liber Raines from the Western New York Genealogical Society is without a doubt the most gifted researcher I know. She provided me with countless municipal reports and period newspaper articles that helped me to understand where the Erie County Poorhouse existed in the public stream of consciousness. She also tracked down much of the secondary source data for the cholera epidemics in Buffalo and helped me to understand how to track down the deed information for historic buildings.

Cynthia Van Ness and her staff from the Buffalo History Museum provided me with the records that helped me to understand the cholera epidemics, the City of Buffalo Directories from the period that allowed me to incorporate real locations into the story, and Erie County Board of Supervisors Reports for 1849.

Charles Alaimo from the Buffalo and Erie County Public Library helped me navigate period maps of the city so that my characters could move about on foot, horseback or by carriage as they would have in Buffalo during 1849.

Douglas Platt from the Museum of disABILITY History in Buffalo, New York, helped me to understand education for the deaf in the early nineteenth century. I am also grateful to the Museum of disABILITY History for their general support and their commitment to preserving institutional cemeteries in New York State.

Ron Nagy from the Lily Dale Museum and Amanda Shepp from the Marion H. Skidmore Library, in Lily Dale, New York, provided me with period newspaper articles and other primary and secondary source material on the history of Lily Dale and Modern Spiritualism.

There is a real antique lamp shop located on Hertel Avenue in Buffalo, New York, called the Antique Lamp Company and Gift Emporium. John and Sue Tobin, the owners of this wonderful establishment, were very gracious and accommodating in answering all of my questions about their business and about the retail items mentioned in this book. I am also grateful for their support of both *Orphans and Inmates* and *A Whisper of Bones.*

Thanks to my readers, Bob Higgins, Casilda G. Lucas, Jennifer Liber Raines, Jacqueline Lunger, Kathy Harlock, Patty Higgins and Christine Hicks for helping me with everything from inner senses and local history to spelling and grammar.

About the Author

Rosanne Higgins was born in Enfield, Connecticut, however spent her youth in Buffalo, New York. She studied the Asylum Movement in the nineteenth century and its impact on disease specific mortality. This research focused on the Erie, Niagara, and Monroe County Poorhouses in Western New York. That research earned her a Ph.D. in Anthropology in 1998 and lead to the publication of her research. Her desire to tell another side of 'The Poorhouse Story' that would be accessible to more than just the scholarly community resulted in the *Orphans and Inmates* series, which chronicles fictional accounts of poorhouse residents based on historical data.

www.rosannehiggins.com/blog.html

www.facebook.com/pages/Orphans-and-Inmates/516800631758088